In Loving Memory

Emma Page first began writing as a hobby, and after a number of her poems had been accepted by the BBC and her short stories began appearing in weekly magazines, she took to writing radio plays and crime novels. She was first published in the Crime Club, which later became Collins Crime.

An English graduate from Oxford, Emma Page taught in every kind of educational establishment both in the UK and abroad before she started writing full-time.

T0312495

By Emma Page

Kelsey and Lambert series

Say it with Murder
Intent to Kill
Hard Evidence
Murder Comes Calling
In the Event of My Death
Mortal Remains
Deadlock
A Violent End
Final Moments
Scent of Death
Cold Light of Day
Last Walk Home
Every Second Thursday
Missing Woman

Standalone novels

A Fortnight by the Sea (also known as
Add a Pinch of Cyanide)
Element of Chance
In Loving Memory
Family and Friends

In Loving Memory

Emma Page

HARPER

Harper
An imprint of HarperCollins*Publishers*
1 London Bridge Street
London SE1 9GF

www.harpercollins.co.uk

This paperback edition 2016
1

First published in Great Britain in 1970 by Collins Crime

A catalogue record for this book is
available from the British Library

ISBN: 978-0-00-817596-2

CHAPTER I

TWO O'CLOCK in the morning. A silent hour, the time of darkness, of the first deep sleep. A stirring in the tall thick branches of the great trees standing sentinel at the rear of Whitegates, the sudden melancholy screech of a night-owl, a rustling of fieldmice in the thick carpet of old leaves.

In the bedroom next door to old Mr. Mallinson's room, Mrs. Parkes woke with a start, coming at once to full consciousness from long years of training and habit. She put out a hand and pressed the switch at the base of the bedside lamp, glanced at the little clock, screwing her eyes up against the light.

She turned her head in the direction of Mr. Mallinson's room, remaining rigid, listening.

The sound of confused movement, Mr. Mallinson's voice calling her name . . . "Mrs. Parkes! Mrs. Parkes!" A window being flung open.

"It's all right! I'm coming!" She snatched at a dressing-gown, shrugged it on and drew the cord tightly round her waist.

"It's all right," she said again with professional reassurance, opening the connecting door and going through into the old man's room. "I'm here, don't worry." He was standing in his pyjamas, leaning out of the window, drawing great gasping breaths of air.

"What is it?" She put a hand on his shoulder. He remained where he was, struggling for breath, unable to speak.

A whisper of footsteps in the corridor, a low double knock at the door. The handle turned and Gina Thorson put her face round the door. She looked anxiously at Mrs. Parkes.

"I heard you get up. Is there anything I can do?" Her young, pretty face looked frightened, her eyes asked a question of Mrs. Parkes . . . What's the matter? Is he having some kind of attack? Is he very ill?

"Run down and ring Doctor Burnett." Mrs. Parkes took a dressing-gown from behind the door and draped it round the old man's shoulders. He seemed unaware of her action. He was clutching at his chest now, breathing as deeply as he could, striving to conserve strength, to fight, to hang on. "Tell him I think it's Mr. Mallinson's heart. Ask him to come over right away. I'll stay here."

Gina closed the door and ran silently and swiftly along the corridor, down the long curving flight of stairs into the hall, switching on lights as she went. She dialled the number rapidly, stood listening to the brr . . . brr . . . willing Doctor Burnett to wake up, to pick up the receiver beside his bed.

At the fourth ring the phone was lifted from its hook.

"Rockley 47, Doctor Knight speaking." Richard's half-awake tones. In spite of her anxiety Gina gave a little involuntary smile.

"Oh, Richard, Gina here——"

"Gina!" His voice sounded suddenly alert, sharply concerned. "What's the matter? Are you——"

"It's not me, I'm all right, it's old Mr. Mallinson. Mrs. Parkes thinks he's having a heart attack of some kind. He's standing by the window, gasping for breath. You'd better come over at once." She paused for a moment. "Though Mrs. Parkes said to get Doctor Burnett. Do you think you'd better wake him? Mr. Mallinson might prefer——" A difficult man, Mr. Mallinson, a friend of Dr. Burnett's since they were boys together in Rockley; he might not be at all pleased to be fobbed off with Dr. Burnett's young partner, scarcely more than a lad in Mr. Mallinson's eyes, competent enough no doubt, but a lad all the same, no experience, no maturity, no judgment.

"Burnett's only just got to bed," Richard said. "Out on a case till midnight. Maternity." The partnership served a number of far-flung villages, a good sound practice, nothing showy but prosperous enough, well thought of in the countryside. "I'll come over myself. I'll be with you in five

minutes. Keep him absolutely quiet, don't give him anything, anything at all." He replaced the receiver and sprang
out of bed, knocking over the small upright chair that held
his suit neatly folded for the night.

"Damn!" He picked up the chair and began to struggle
into his clothes, listening for a sound from Burnett's room
farther along the passage.

He heard the door open, Burnett's measured tread coming
towards him. He flung open his own door and stuck his head
out.

"Terribly sorry to wake you, I knocked over a chair. I'm
off to Whitegates, Henry Mallinson's having a heart attack,
the nurse thinks. I can cope. You can get back to bed."

"Nonsense!" Dr. Burnett's tone disposed of argument.
"He's my patient, I'll go. You can go down and get the car
out for me. I'll be dressed by the time you get her started.
Then *you* can go back to bed, you can take my surgery in
the morning for me. I daresay I'll be some time up at
Whitegates."

He went back to his room and without apparent haste but
yet with swift, effectively-controlled movements he was
dressed, and neatly dressed at that, in three minutes flat.

Before he left the room he paused for a moment with his
fingers on the handle and glanced back at a photograph on
the mantelpiece. A heavy old-fashioned silver frame. A
young woman smiling out at the camera, a tall young man
standing beside her with one arm round her waist.

He switched off the light, went quietly downstairs and
out into the driveway where Richard Knight had the car
drawn up with the engine running.

Thirty minutes later Dr. Burnett drew the bedclothes over
Henry Mallinson's chest.

"You'll be all right now," he said. "You'll be asleep in
a few minutes. I'll look in again around lunch-time." He
suppressed a small unprofessional yawn. Before the lunch
hour raced to meet him there was the surgery in a neigh-
bouring village, the round of visits to be got through, the

never-ending paperwork to be tackled—and it was already almost three o'clock. He sighed and picked up his bag. With luck he might manage four or five hours' sleep. Retirement beckoned him once again with a smiling siren face . . . but in retirement a man might rust, might grow old, might die from nothing more deadly than simple boredom, from the unnatural emptiness that might descend like a lethal mist on a life suddenly released from the pressures of crowded days.

Henry Mallinson opened his eyes. His face looked peaceful now, pale and weary but free from distress.

"Thank you, Edgar." He gave a fragmentary smile. "I'm glad you didn't send young Knight. Old friends are best when you're ill. It's a comfort to have you near me." His eyes contemplated for an instant the possibility of death, of the vital forces within him being extinguished silently, without his knowledge, in the dreaming hours of some approaching dawn.

"I'd like to see Kenneth," he said, raising his eyes to Dr. Burnett. "Fix it for me, will you, Edgar?"

"Yes, I'll see to that. Where is he? Do you know his address?" Kenneth Mallinson had quarrelled with his father years ago over the running of the family business, the chain of garages and motor-sales establishments Henry Mallinson had built up single-handed, starting out as a lad of fourteen tinkering with bicycles.

"He's up north. Gina will give you the address, it's in the files." Mallinson's voice broke suddenly. "Get him to come, Edgar. I'd like to . . ." The voice tailed away. He can't say, I'd like to make my peace with him, Edgar Burnett thought. Even now, with the notion of death scarring his consciousness, pride and obstinacy clip off the end of the sentence.

"I'll speak to him myself, I'll phone him first thing in the morning. Don't worry, Henry, leave it to me." Would Kenneth come? Every inch his father's son, as proud and obstinate as the old man—and as gifted too? Had he made a success of the long years on his own? Dr. Burnett didn't know, Kenneth's name hadn't been mentioned between the two old friends since the day Mallinson's elder son had flung a few clothes into a suitcase and banged the door of Whitegates behind him.

"He's done well for himself, from what I hear," Mallinson said, answering the unspoken question. He would have his sources of information of course, he would have kept track of what his son was doing over the long hostile years. Perhaps he loved his first-born in his own stiff-necked way.

Mallinson's lids began to droop, the injection was taking effect. With an effort he jerked his eyes open again.

"Have a glass of whisky before you go," he said haltingly. His lips turned up in a weary smile. "It'll get you off to sleep again. Can't be an easy life, a doctor's." His face relaxed into a kind of peace. "I wouldn't offer the whisky to everyone. My own special brand."

Dr. Burnett glanced at the decanter and the glasses standing beside it on a silver tray set on top of a chest of drawers against the wall.

"Thank you," he said. "I think I will." There was no sound from the bed. He stood looking down at Henry Mallinson for a long moment. The old man's breathing was deeper now, more regular, he would sleep till well into the morning.

Burnett crossed to the chest and poured himself a tot of whisky, savouring the fine amber spirit with the relish of a connoisseur.

When he let himself quietly out into the passage he saw the nurse, Mrs. Parkes, standing a few yards away, talking in whispered tones to Gina Thorson, Mallinson's secretary. They were both in their dressing-gowns. They stopped talking when they caught sight of him, they looked towards him with their faces full of questioning. He gave them a reassuring nod and smile.

"He'll be all right now," he said in a low voice, gesturing them farther along the corridor, out of earshot of Mallinson's drugged slumbers. "I've given him an injection, he'll sleep for several hours. It was only a mild attack, no need to get him into hospital, he'll be all right if he's sensible, if he takes care. He may complain of a little indigestion when he wakes up, but it's of no consequence."

"Was it a coronary?" Gina ventured, stumbling over the frightening word.

He gave her a shrewd glance. "A kind of coronary. A 'silent' coronary, we call it. No pain, you see, just the extreme shortness of breath."

He spent a few minutes giving nursing instructions to Mrs. Parkes. A sensible woman, Mrs. Parkes, able to cope with emergencies. Dr. Burnett had recommended her to Henry Mallinson himself several months earlier when a severe bout of influenza had confined the old man to bed for some weeks. Mallinson had developed an unemotional attachment to the nurse, had come to depend on her more than he cared to admit, had resisted the notion of her going when he had finally recovered his strength after the influenza.

There were many little tasks she could perform about the great old house, he'd convinced himself, she was useful to the housekeeper, useful to Gina Thorson, his secretary, he was well able to afford her salary, there was no reason why he should deprive himself of the comfort of a trained nurse about the establishment, at his age one never knew . . . And so she had stayed on, glad enough of the comfortable post, the handsome salary. A widow with one son, a steady young fellow living down south, married with a couple of small children.

"How's the family?" Dr. Burnett asked Mrs. Parkes when she had indicated that she understood his instructions about his patient. "All well, I hope?"

He didn't miss the little flicker of unhappiness that moved across her face.

"Very well, thank you." She allowed the conversation to rest there, not inviting further questions. Burnett turned to the secretary.

"I shall need the address and phone number of Mr.

Mallinson's elder son, Kenneth," he said. "Could you look it up for me now, while I'm here? I promised Mr. Mallinson I'd get in touch with Kenneth first thing in the morning and I won't be looking in here again till lunch-time."

"Certainly, Dr. Burnett." Pleasant and efficient as always, Gina Thorson smiled at the doctor and gestured along the passage towards the ground floor. "If you'd like to come down into the office, I'll look it up in the files. I know we've got the address there. I'll write it down for you."

Mrs. Parkes stood for a few moments watching the two of them walking away towards the flight of stairs, then she tiptoed along the corridor and stood listening outside Mr. Mallinson's door. No sound from within. She turned the handle with great gentleness and put her head round the door. The bedside lamp was still on, it shed a mellow glow over the peaceful features of the old man, deeply asleep now, breathing easily and naturally. Satisfied, she closed the door and went back to her own room.

It was no good, she knew she wouldn't be able to go to sleep now for an hour or more. She switched on the electric fire and took a letter from her little bureau. She gave a deep sigh, opening the letter and reading it yet again, knowing by heart what it said . . . "We've talked it over a great deal recently," her son had written, "and we've finally decided our best opportunity lies in Australia. Without any capital the most I could hope for in this country is a position as a farm manager or a bailiff. It'll be a terrible wrench of course. If there was any possibility of getting a farm of our own here we'd much prefer to stay, even if it was only a small-holding to start with, but even that takes more capital nowadays than we'd ever be likely to raise. I've written off for the emigration forms. It will all take some time but we hope to be on our way next year. Once you've made up your mind about a thing, there isn't much point in hanging about. . . ."

Mrs. Parkes sighed again, staring down at the glowing bars of the fire. Just a few thousand pounds, that was all that was needed to keep her son and his family within reach, a few thousand pounds between herself and the long years of loneliness, the gap bridged by air-letters, a solitary trip scrimped and saved for, a reunion with grandchildren grown into suntanned strangers. A few thousand pounds, so little when you said the words aloud, so impossibly large a sum to a widowed nurse with only her monthly pay-cheque . . . only the expectation of what a grateful patient might see fit to leave her.

Mrs. Parkes sat up suddenly and pulled her dressing-gown more tightly around her. She turned her head in the direction of old Mr. Mallinson's room, held herself rigid while a multitude of thoughts ran through her brain. 'Stay with me,' the old man had said a few months ago. 'I won't forget you.' She had paid little attention at the time. It had suited her to stay on, not to have to bother about looking for a new post, not to have to begin all over again the weary business of adapting herself to the ways of a strange household. In a few weeks, she'd thought, in a couple of months at most, Mr. Mallinson will be himself again, he won't need me any more, he'll summon me one morning and say, 'You've been very kind, Mrs. Parkes, I'm very grateful, but I don't really feel I can detain you here any longer. . . .' In the meantime she'd been pleased to be able to take things easily for a while.

'You look after me and I'll look after you,' Mr. Mallinson had said. She'd thought little of it, they were all grateful when pain and misery swept over them, they didn't always find it convenient to remember when health and strength flowed back.

And now Mr. Mallinson was ill again. Just how serious was it? 'Only a mild attack,' Dr. Burnett had said. 'We must see he takes things easily from now on.' But Mr. Mallinson was an old man. Health and strength might flow back but never again with the strong spate of youth, never again in the full surge of virile manhood.

Perhaps he *had* meant what he'd said, perhaps he'd added

a codicil to his will. She stood up and began to pace about the room.

She could easily find out. A methodical man, Mr. Mallinson, there'd be a copy of his will downstairs in the office safe. Gina Thorson could be spoken to, a word at the right time and she could study the contents of the will.

Mrs. Parkes paused in her progress and bit her lip in fierce thought. It might be best though to say nothing to Gina, it might be best to consult the will without Gina's knowledge. She wasn't all that fond of the girl, it might be better not to be under any kind of obligation to her. She resumed her silent pacing. Yes, she must think of some way of getting hold of the keys of the safe. Not much difficulty there. Next time Gina was out on one of her dates with young Dr. Knight, Mrs. Parkes could take the keys and open the safe at her leisure. Late in the evening, perhaps, when the rest of the household was at rest, when Gina and young Dr. Knight were holding hands in some secluded moonlit spot, that would be the time.

She sat down abruptly by the fire and looked at the letter again. 'On our way next year,' her son had written. Just suppose old Mr. Mallinson *had* added a codicil to his will, just suppose gratitude had prompted him to translate promise into reality, exactly how long might he be expected to last? Several years? Or only a year or two? . . . Or was it only a matter of months? . . . Of weeks? . . . Or even days? . . .

'I'll look after you.' In terms of hard cash how much might that mean? Five hundred pounds? She shook her head sharply, dismissing the idea of such skinflint generosity. A wealthy man, Mr. Mallinson, a self-made wealthy man who'd come up the hard way. Not one of your soup-and-red-flannel-for-the-poor aristocrats, imagining a few hundred pounds spelled unimaginable luxury to an employee. He was a man who knew the value of money and what it might represent in terms of ease of mind and security. A few thousand at least. She stood up again. Her face wore a brighter, less anxious air. Yes, a few thousand at the very least, that was what he'd meant, surely, that was what he *must* have meant. And Mr. Mallinson was a man of his word. Even after only a few months she was aware of that. A man who said a thing and meant it, a man who would carry out a promise.

Dr. Burnett let himself into his house with the efficient noiselessness born of years of taking night calls. He stood in the dimly-lit hall for a moment, listening. No sound from any of the rooms. Richard Knight had gone back to bed again then, was in all probability by now sound asleep. And it took a lot to wake the housekeeper.

Upstairs in his bedroom Dr. Burnett sat wearily down on a chair and bent to unlace his shoes. Then he took from his pocket the sheet of paper on which Gina Thorson had written the address. He yawned widely. As soon as he woke in the morning he must ring Kenneth Mallinson and explain matters. He propped the paper against the alarm clock to remind him.

He stood up and removed his jacket. The other son, David—and David's wife, Carole—I suppose Mrs. Parkes will get on to them in the morning, he thought. David Mallinson lived on the outskirts of Rockley village in a fine old Georgian house. He had run the family business—under the close supervision of his father—ever since his elder brother had walked out. Not a man to quarrel with his father, David Mallinson, not a man in the least likely ever to quarrel with his bread and butter. Dr. Burnett hung his neatly-folded clothes over the back of a chair. David and Carole would be up at Whitegates as soon as they heard the news, bearing bunches of flowers, wearing suitably agitated faces. 'Such a pleasant, uncomplicated, refreshing girl,' old Mallinson had said a year ago when David had brought home the girl he wanted to marry.

Dr. Burnett gave a little worldly-wise smile. Carole Mallinson had proved herself a most attentive daughter-in-law

to the old man. Simple and refreshing she might appear to
the casual eye, Dr. Burnett thought, winding his watch, but
she had her head screwed on the right way. Just the wife for
David Mallinson, two of a kind.

He went over to the mantelpiece and stood looking at the
framed photograph, the young woman smiling out from
the circle of the young man's arm. He stooped and touched
the glass with a finger, then he crossed over to the bed,
took a pair of pyjamas from behind a pillow, yawning again.
With any luck he'd be sound asleep inside ten minutes, like
young Knight a couple of doors away. But unlike young
Knight, he wouldn't be dreaming about Gina Thorson.

In her room at Whitegates, a few yards along the corridor
from Mrs. Parkes, Gina Thorson lay on her bed with her
hands linked behind her head. Mr. Mallinson was going to
be all right, Dr. Burnett had said so. She frowned into the
darkness. It was very awkward, the old man's illness coming
just at this moment. She had planned to ask him for a rise
in salary in the morning, she had worked it all out in her
mind, intending to ask him as soon as she'd finished the daily
letters. He was always in a good mood at that time of day,
feeling alert, in control of the many facets of his life.

But it was out of the question now to ask for a rise. She
would probably be allowed to see him only about the most
urgent letters concerning the firm—and she might be told
to refer those to David Mallinson, not to bother the old man
for the present. She could scarcely go barging into the sick-
room to demand more money for her services, skilled as they
were.

And I need the money, she thought, I need quite a lot of
money right away. Richard Knight had asked her to go
down to Hampshire to meet his parents. Well-to-do people,
Richard's parents, she must make a good impression on
them. When she left their house at the end of her visit there
was a very good chance that she would be wearing Richard's
engagement ring.

Gina sat up in bed and switched on the bedside lamp. I simply *must* have some new clothes, she thought, swinging her feet over the edge of the bed. Expensive, well-cut country clothes.

She crossed over to the wardrobe and flung open the door, reviewing the contents for the umpteenth time, shaking her head at them in rejection. Pretty enough clothes, smart enough, but cheap, all she'd been able to afford so far, a girl on her own, without parents, without a family, without background. They'd passed muster up till now. With a slim young figure like Gina's you could get away with cheaply fashionable clothes for a time, but they wouldn't deceive the practised, assessing eyes of Richard's parents.

She closed the wardrobe door and climbed back into bed, sitting upright with her knees hunched under the blankets. A suède coat, three-quarter length, a skirt in fine tweed, a cashmere sweater—she knew exactly what she would buy if she had the money, she'd searched the windows of the more exclusive stores in Hallborough until she'd found what she wanted.

Mr. Mallinson will be all right, Dr. Burnett had said. But how soon would he be well again? A week? Two weeks? What was the earliest possible moment at which she could reasonably broach the subject of a rise?

She drew a long breath and flung herself back on the pillows. Was there any other way she could get hold of the money? Borrow it perhaps? From whom? Mrs. Parkes? Even as she formed the notion she shook her head, dismissing it. Mrs. Parkes would have nothing to lend and if she had there was her own family to play fairy godmother to. She was hardly likely to part with her hard-earned savings to help her employer's secretary to lash out on expensive new clothes. And it wasn't even as if Mrs. Parkes liked her very much . . . her manner was always polite, but nothing more. . . .

A hundred and seventy-five pounds, Mrs. Parkes calculated yet again, drifting drowsily towards sleep. That's all

I've got to show for the best part of a lifetime of hard work, one hundred and seventy-five pounds, not counting the change in my bag. That wouldn't go very far in setting her son up in a little farm of his own. She smiled grimly behind her closed lids; her thoughts began to swirl and dissolve, her muscles began to slacken. I must be up early in the morning, she told herself, I must see to the old man . . . something nice to eat . . . something easy to digest . . . he won't be awake for breakfast . . . but he might take a little lunch . . . I'll go down to the gardener's cottage and see if there are any tender young vegetables . . . any tempting fruit . . . Mrs. Parkes slipped into a dream where she was walking up the path to the gardener's cottage, raising her hand, lifting the brass knocker . . .

CHAPTER II

AT SIX-THIRTY the alarm clock pealed its shrill summons in the front bedroom of the gardener's cottage. Ada Foster came awake with a start, blinking at the new day without much expectation that it would differ very greatly from all the days that had preceded it. She sat up and rubbed her eyes.

"Half-six, George! Time to get up!" She gave a ritual thrust at her husband's shoulder.

"What's that? Time to get up?" George Foster rose protesting from the trough of sleep, "Make us a cup of tea, there's a good lass." His fingers reached out, scrabbling for the packet of cigarettes on the little table.

Ada was already thrusting her feet into ancient felt slippers.

"All right then. But don't go dropping off again. I'll put the sausages on." She jerked an old fawn dressing-gown from behind the door and went along the passage, calling, "Norman! Half-past six! Do you hear me, Norman? Time to get up!"

B

There was a muffled groan from the second bedroom.

"O.K., Mum, I'm awake."

"Mind you stay awake, then. Don't want to be late for work." Ada went slop-footed down to the kitchen and filled the kettle at the sink.

Norman Foster sat up in bed without any very marked enthusiasm. His first thought, as always these days, was for his pride and treasure, the darling of his heart, his motorbike, standing slim and powerful, silent and waiting, in the shed outside the back door. The thought brought with it a wash of anxiety that clouded his face now whenever the vision of his darling rose before his eyes—how long before she was snatched away from him for ever by the implacable forces of hire-purchase regulations?

'Three days late with your instalment,' the boss had said to him only yesterday. 'You've only had the bike four months and already you're falling behind. Won't do, Norman, my lad. Either pay up or hand the bike back.'

'I'll have the money by the end of the week, honest I will.' It was Norman's birthday in three days' time and on the evening of his birthday his godfather, old Mr. Mallinson up at the big house, unfailingly summoned Norman to receive his present. Between the ages of five and twelve the present had been a pound note, from his thirteenth birthday it had been two pound notes. In three days Norman would be eighteen. Surely, he thought with fierce expectation, surely this time he'll make it three—or even—exhilarating notion! five! At the idea Norman closed his eyes for a second in ecstasy. Five whole pound notes, crisp and new! Or one single imposing fiver perhaps, virgin from the bank!

He opened his eyes and sprang out of bed with renewed hope. Even with three pounds he could pay the instalment, with five he could put some aside for next month's inexorable deadline.

Melancholy clutched at him again. Even five pounds wouldn't last very long. There would be the month after next, the month after that, the whole inescapable procession stretching out for another year and a half, till the day when he could burnish his darling with polish and chrome cleaner in the blissful knowledge that she was his for ever.

He fumbled about on the floor, looking for his shoes and socks. Eighteen months! How on earth was he going to manage the instalments all that time? On an apprentice's wages in a Hallborough garage he couldn't put much by.

'A motor-bike?' his father had said, frowning. 'You'll never be able to pay for it!'

'I will, Dad! Honest, I will!' he'd cried. 'I'll save every penny. And if I don't have a bike, how am I going to get to work? They're stopping the seven o'clock bus.'

'You could ride a push-bike,' his father had said. 'Like I did at your age.'

But Norman had produced a scrap of paper covered with figures. 'Look, Dad, this is what I earn and this is what I have to pay out. Go on, read it, you'll see I've worked it all out. I can manage the instalments, it's all down there.'

'Go on, George,' his mother had said, seeing the look of pleading in the eyes of her only child. 'Let him have the bike. It'll be handy for getting to work.'

'Don't go coming to me for help, then, if you fall behind with the payments.' His father had shot him a keen look. 'If you can't pay for it it goes back and no arguments. Is that clear?' It had been clear all right, it was clear now, crystal clear. Pay up or else, the harsh law of the adult world. He threw a fleeting backward glance at the gentler world of childhood, at the cowboy outfit and the toy train that were handed over once and for all, all yours, nothing more to pay. He went along to the bathroom with a sigh for those easy, irresponsible, bountiful days.

And then the smell of frying sausages floated up to his nostrils. He smiled. A world that contained sizzling brown pork sausages wasn't after all such a dismal world. The high spirits of youth rose up inside him. He snatched at his toothbrush and anointed the bristles with a ribbon of white paste. Just suppose old Mallinson regarded eighteen as a landmark, suppose he made it not three, not five, but ten pounds! It was possible. Eighteen was really quite an important birthday when you came to think about it. Yes, it was more than possible, it was actually quite probable. By the time he was scrubbing at his face with a flannel foaming with soap he was quite certain the old man would make it a tenner. He splashed vigorously at his glowing cheeks with cold water, reached blindly for the towel and began to whistle.

Ada Foster speared the glistening sausages on to the expectant plates held out before her.

"Get those inside you!" she commanded. Footsteps ground along the gravel path. "Who's that? At this hour?" She thumped the frying-pan back on to the stove and flung open the kitchen door a couple of seconds after the double rat-tat assaulted her ears.

One of the young maids from the big house faced her in the doorway. "Sorry to be the bearer of bad news," the girl said importantly, delaying the moment of revelation, savouring her position as messenger. "It's the old gentleman——"

"Mr. Mallinson?" Ada cried, flinging the door wide, gesturing the girl inside. "He's never dead!"

"Well, no, not exactly." The girl looked a little put out, her tidings now appearing diminished, less weighty in their impact. Ada Foster might have the manners to wait without interrupting till a person had had their say. "But he was took bad in the night. Heart it was, Mrs. Parkes said. She had to call old Doctor Burnett out, two o'clock in the morning." The lateness of the hour lent a certain impressiveness to her tale. "Thought I'd pop in and let you know." She glanced about the kitchen, registering the pork sausages, the brown teapot, with practised eyes. "Thought you'd like to know."

"Just how bad is he?" George Foster pushed away his plate and stood up. "Does Doctor Burnett think he'll get over it?" A flood of anxious thoughts whirled through his brain. If the old man died Whitegates might be sold. Hardly likely young Master David and his wife would want to live in that great mansion of a place, not when they'd got their own house so nicely furnished and all. George saw himself all in a matter of weeks, days even, thrown out of work, given notice to quit the cottage.

"A mild attack," the girl said, a little grudgingly, cheated of high drama. "Got to take things easy, Mrs. Parkes said. Doctor's looking in again at lunch-time." Not that she wished the old man any harm, far from it. A good employer, Mr. Mallinson, strict mind you, but he paid a good wage and provided a good home and what more could a girl ask?

But it would have been interesting all the same to have knocked at the cottage door with a tear-swollen face, to bring news that would have shattered the easy peace of the sausage-savoury kitchen. It would have been nice just for once to have been able to say something that the listeners would remember for ever.

"A cup of tea," Mrs. Foster offered, picking up the earthenware pot. The maid shook her head.

"No thanks, I have to be getting back." She nodded in the direction of the big house, indicating vague and onerous duties awaiting her. "There'll be a lot to do to-day." She turned and stepped out on to the gravel path.

Norman sat at the table picking at his sausages now with a merely mechanical show of appetite, not listening to the animated interchange taking place between his parents. Just my luck, he was thinking, just my rotten luck! There would be no summons now on Thursday evening, no present would be formally handed over, there would be no tenner, no fiver, not even a single pound note. Disaster loomed before him, utter and total disaster, not a single ray of hope anywhere in the universe.

He lifted his head and threw a swift glance at his parents. Neither of them paid him the slightest attention.

"Not easy to get another job at my age," his father said heavily.

"I'll be off now," Norman mumbled.

"Don't you go starting to worry about it now, George," Ada Foster said, her voice habitually soothing in times of crisis, although her eyes were anxious.

Norman pushed his chair back quietly and let himself out into the fresh morning. He went over to the shed and unlocked the door. For a long moment he stood gazing down at his beloved gleaming dully in the light shining from the kitchen window. Then he moved over and gave her a pat, rubbing his fingers over the silk-smooth metal. His eyes were full of tears.

Gina Thorson stood at the foot of the staircase with a small sheaf of papers in her hand. The sound of a door opening and closing in the first-floor corridor—Dr. Burnett's visit must be over then. She could hear voices now, low voices, Dr. Burnett talking to Mrs. Parkes. Then the doctor's footsteps, brisk but quiet, moving along the corridor.

He came into view. Gina smiled at him.

"Good morning, Dr. Burnett. How is Mr. Mallinson?"

"Very much better this morning. Really surprisingly well." He gave a little astonished shake of his head. "Of course there's to be no work or excitement for the present, but I wouldn't be at all surprised if he isn't up and about again in a week or two."

Gina glanced down at the papers in her hand. "There are some letters here he ought to deal with. I can see to most of the mail myself, a lot of it is pretty well routine, but these—would it be all right if I slipped into his room for a couple of minutes? I'd make it as brief as possible."

Dr. Burnett shook his head. "Surely David Mallinson can deal with these queries?"

Gina looked faintly disconcerted. "Yes, I suppose he could." She raised her eyes to the doctor. "Though old Mr. Mallinson does like to keep the reins in his own hands."

Burnett smiled. "I'm afraid he's going to have to learn to

let go of the reins. It happens to us all in the end. You take your queries to David, my dear, he's very efficient, there won't be much he can't handle."

Gina sighed. "Very well." She detached one letter from the sheaf. "There is this one, though. It's a little more—personal—than the others. I don't mean that it's a private letter, but it is really for the attention of Mr. Mallinson and not his son." She held it out. "Perhaps you'd better read it. I'm sure you know all about what's in it. It seems everybody does, it was in all the papers, I believe, though of course it happened long before I came here."

Burnett frowned and took the letter. He ran his eyes over the closely-written sheet, turned it over to glance at the signature, then turned it back again and read it with care.

"I see," he said as he took it in. "From the widow of that man." He clicked his tongue against his teeth, recalling the case. Not a very savoury affair. Victor Stallard, employed in the Accounts department at Mallinson's, accused of embezzlement—quite a sizeable sum involved, several thousands of pounds. A tall, quiet, bespectacled man with a wife and a baby son, he'd protested his innocence throughout his trial but the evidence had been there. Seven years he'd got and lucky to get off so lightly, old Mallinson had said loudly at the time. Stallard couldn't have altogether shared this view of his sentence, six weeks later he'd hanged himself in his cell.

All this had happened some years ago, the widow and the baby son had dropped away out of sight. No provision had been made for them by Mallinson's, for after all why should they? "Stallard must have put the money away somewhere safe," Henry Mallinson had said. "She'll have plenty of cash, *my* cash. I wish her joy of it."

And then a couple of weeks ago a senior accountant at Mallinson's, struck down in the road as he was coming out of a pub after his usual late-evening drink, a jovial, well-liked man, highly-respected in the firm, had opened his eyes in the hospital ward where he lay dying from appalling injuries, had asked for Matron to be summoned, had made a statement, cleared his conscience before his eyes closed again for ever. He'd taken the money and let Stallard carry the blame. Stallard had known nothing whatever about the embezzlement, he had been completely innocent.

The papers had got hold of it of course. Reporters had come hanging round Whitegates, trying to get old Mallinson to talk, there had been persistent phone calls but he would answer none of them, would say nothing, wouldn't even discuss the matter with Dr. Burnett when he'd tried to raise it. And now—this letter from Stallard's widow.

"She intends to see him then." Burnett raised his eyes from the letter. "Hardly surprising." He glanced down at the address, some village on the East Coast. "She must have had a hard time of it, with a child to rear." There hadn't been any money hidden away of course, there had been no pension, nothing. How had she managed? He shook his head. "A nasty business all round." He didn't like the tone of the letter. It made no specific demands, only the fierce, long-pent-up outpourings of a woman who had suffered a very great deal, who had forgotten nothing and was prepared to forgive nothing.

"I imagine she wants money," Gina Thorson said. "I don't know what the legal position is but I would think she'd be entitled to a good deal of money."

"She never once mentions compensation," Burnett said. Could the woman conceivably want something else? The restoration of the good name of her dead husband, that of course. But what besides? Revenge?

He handed the letter back to Gina. "I fancy some provision could be made out of court, for her and the child. But Mr. Mallinson must not on any account be bothered by this just now. David must see to it, he must answer the letter, explain that his father is ill. He can make an appointment to see the woman, he can get on to the lawyers, he can settle everything. If it *is* necessary for his father to sign any papers, they can wait over for a week or two. After all these years another week or two isn't going to make all that difference to Mrs. Stallard."

"David Mallinson and his wife came round first thing this morning," Gina said. "As soon as Mrs. Parkes phoned them. They were very anxious to see old Mr. Mallinson, but she wouldn't allow it, said you told her he had to be kept very quiet."

Dr. Burnett nodded. "Yes, she told me about it. She was quite right. In any case he was sound asleep this morning, they couldn't have spoken to him. I shall be looking in again this evening, they can see him for a minute or two after my visit, if everything continues to go smoothly."

Gina gave a little smile. "Mrs. Mallinson brought a huge bunch of flowers. At seven o'clock in the morning."

A trace of answering amusement looked out from the doctor's eyes. "I fancy Carole Mallinson would always be able to lay her hand on a suitable bunch of flowers whenever the occasion demanded."

His manner changed abruptly. "Was there anything else you wanted to see Mr. Mallinson about?" He had the notion that there *was* something else, something personal perhaps.

Gina slid him a little considering glance. Then she made a small movement of dismissal with her hand. "There was something, but it isn't very important. It can wait."

"I'll look in again this evening." Burnett moved towards the front door. He turned his head and gave her a quizzical smile. "Shall I give Richard Knight your love?"

Gina felt a blush rise to her cheeks. "No need for that," she said lightly. "I'll be seeing him myself this afternoon. He said he'd look in for a cup of tea."

A damp misty evening in London, a thin depressing drizzle filming over the tall windows of the studio flat right at the top of the house. Not at all a gay evening, no help from the weather to raise despondent spirits.

Tim Jefford gathered up the unpaid bills into an untidy

pile and dropped them on top of a battered desk against the wall. He crossed to the window and stood looking out at the dismal evening, rubbing his unshaven chin, wondering just what he was going to do with himself.

He drew the long curtains together with a savage gesture, shutting out the evening. He turned to face the appalling clutter of the room. Painting materials everywhere, brushes thrust into jars, squeezed-out tubes of paint, a couple of half-finished canvases propped up on easels, other canvases stacked against the walls, dozens of them, unsold, unwanted. Paint-stained cushions tumbled in a heap along an ancient divan, one end supported on a pile of broken-backed books, pieces of brilliant-hued material thrown in a jumble on the floor. He ran his fingers through his hair.

"Not much to show for eight years' work," he said aloud, wryly.

In the corner of the room a Siamese cat uncurled itself from a nest of rags, stood up, arched its back, yawned widely and picked its way towards him. He thrust his hands into the pockets of his old jacket, searching for cigarettes, finding only an empty packet and another containing a squashed-out stub. He flung them away in disgust, stooped and picked up the cat which was rubbing itself against his leg. He stroked the silky fur.

"Do you want something to eat, Princess? So do I. I'd better go out and see what I can find." He deposited the cat without ceremony on the heap of cushions, snatched an old fawn raincoat from behind the door and slammed out without bothering to switch off the lights.

Twenty minutes later he came banging into the house again. On the first floor Hilda Browning jerked her hands from the typewriter, waiting for the rush of feet going up the stairs, the studio door being flung open, being crashed to again. She shrugged her shoulders and smiled. One day middle age would descend on Tim Jefford, one day he might actually walk up a flight of stairs, might enter and leave a room without making the walls shudder. . . . But not for a good many years yet. She smiled again, gathered together her wandering thoughts and returned to the long hard slog of her novel.

"Food, Princess!" Tim ripped apart the sides of the brown-paper bag and spilled the contents out on to the table. First, the tin of catfood. Princess had already begun her low anticipatory growl. Tim rummaged about in a drawer, found the tin-opener and carved the top of the tin into ragged edges. He thrust a spoon into the tin and scooped out the meat on to a plate.

"Here you are, Princess, get stuck into that! Feast on the nourishing liver and gravy!" Princess crouched on the floor like a devotee at prayer and began to wolf the food, managing at the same time to keep up an ecstatic purr.

Tim opened a new packet of cigarettes and surveyed the rest of his purchases. A greaseproof packet of sliced ham, a waxed carton of potato salad, a crusty French loaf, a packet of butter, a squashy bag of ripe foreign cheese and a small jar of instant coffee.

"A feast, Princess," he said, jangling the few coins left in his pocket. He looked down at the cat single-mindedly disposing of the chunks of liver. "Make the most of it," he said on a wry note. "It may be the last you'll get for some time."

He went slowly over to the sink and ran water into the battered kettle, set it on the stove and lit the gas. He sighed and glanced at the top of the bureau, at the pile of bills. He plunged his hand into his pocket and drew out the meagre handful of coins, running his eye over them, calculating. Nine shillings and fourpence-ha'penny.

He crossed to the desk, unlocked the bottom drawer, thrust his hand under the jumble of papers, books, tubes of paint, and pulled out a metal cashbox. He lifted the lid and stared down at the folded notes. No need to count them, he knew how much there was. His last reserve, absolutely his last-ditch reserve. Twenty-five pounds, folded away two years ago during a brief surge of prosperity when he had actually sold three canvases in the same month. He lifted his eyes to the wall and grinned. He'd thought then that things had really begun to move his way, he'd thought hard times would never return. It was only the memory of months and years of near-starvation that had made him press the notes into the box, a permanent insurance, never needing to be touched, a gesture of remembrance towards the chaotic, rumbustious past, a salute to old times that would never come again.

But the wave of good fortune had subsided into a ripple, had died away at last. He was lucky now if he sold three canvases in a year, let alone in a month.

"I'm at the watershed, Princess," he said. The cat gave her entire attention to cleaning the tin plate of all traces of gravy. Her tongue made a tiny rasping sound against the metal.

"Do I start on my last-ditch reserve?" Tim asked the cat. "Or do I stop now? Make a bonfire of the lot of it?" He threw a look of fond contempt at the paintings, the easels, the heaps of brilliant rags. "Spend the money on some clothes? Go out and get a job?" He saw himself serving in a shop, clattering a luggage trolley along a railway platform, washing up in the cavernous kitchens of some vast hotel.

"I'm not getting any younger, Princess," he said sadly. "And that's an indisputable fact." Princess gave the plate one last appreciative dab with her tongue and then retired to the cushions to deal with her fur.

The kettle spouted steam towards the ceiling. Tim laid the cash-box tenderly down on the desk and went over to the stove. Hunger stirred sharply inside him again. He made the coffee, sat down at the table and tore open the packet of ham. Half-way through his meal he remembered the evening paper thrust into the pocket of his raincoat. He glanced idly at the headlines. Student unrest, somebody robbed, a controversial speech by a junior Minister.

He scooped up the odorous cheese on to a hunk of bread,

turned the page and sat up suddenly, letting the piece of bread drop from his fingers on to the brown paper bag.

Carole! By all that was holy! Carole Stewart, staring out at him from a wedding group! Men in morning dress, tall broad imposing-looking men with an air of solid wealth. Slender women in silk suits and airy hats of puffed organza, fragile girls in drifting high-waisted dresses. The bridegroom no longer in the first gay flush of youth—thirty, thirty-five perhaps—a good-looking man with a figure already bidding good-bye to slimness, an air of well-founded prosperity, of mellow country houses, a London flat with a good address.

"Carole Stewart," he said aloud with a note of brooding. So this was what had become of her! He'd often wondered. There had been a good many girls in the last eight years. Tall and short, plump and slender, dark and fair, never any shortage of companions to share the sardines and the rough red wine. He could hardly remember their names, their faces, their taste in cigarettes.

But he remembered Carole. Oh yes, he remembered Carole Stewart all right. When she had swept up her belongings into a fibre suitcase, tired of hand-to-mouth living, the unruly disorder of the studio, when she'd grabbed her coat and stormed down the stairs after their final and most spectacular row, he'd wandered the streets for days, looking for her in coffee-bars, in lodging-houses, among the open-air stalls of the street markets. But he'd looked without success.

'I'm getting out!' she'd cried. 'I'm going to make something of my life, I'm going to know where next week's rent and to-morrow's meals are coming from! You can stay here and rot, Tim Jefford, but I'm pulling out while there's still time!'

He jerked his thoughts back from that tempestuous evening two years ago and began to read the paragraphs under the wedding-group. Some old man, Henry Mallinson, some well-heeled tycoon with a string of garages defacing the broad acres of England, had suffered some kind of heart attack. There he was, on the left of the group, at the wedding twelve months ago of his younger son, David, to Miss Carole Stewart.

Tim raised his head. So she'd embarked on a new life after all, a good life, the life of country houses unshakeably reared on a foundation of petrol pumps and motor-sales. He dropped his eyes again, seeking the address.

Whitegates, a good name for a house, a reassuring name with its implications of rolling parklands, of sinewy sons of the soil bedding out plants in the herbaceous borders.

He drank the last of his cooling coffee at a single gulp and stood up. He paced about the cluttered studio, assessing the information and its possibilities.

"You've done well for yourself, Carole old girl," he said with affectionate admiration. Might there not be a little to spare for an old and intimate friend, might there not be a little handout—or not such a little handout—a good fat handout, in memory of old times?

He flung himself down on the sofa and screwed up his eyes in concentrated thought. Mallinson—he'd heard of the old man, he'd seen bits about him in the paper now and then. Gave money to charities, didn't he? Fulminated sometimes about the decline in moral standards, loudly and publicly regretted the disappearance of the old virtues. Tim examined the photograph again with care, searching the lines of Henry Mallinson's face for clues to his character.

A hard face, the face of a man with strong and rigid views, a man who would stand no nonsense, a man who liked his own way and was accustomed to getting it. A man who would lend his presence to the wedding of his younger son only if that son had seen fit to marry a girl his father approved of, a girl who would do credit to the family name.

A heart attack. Mild enough, apparently, but Mallinson was an old man, the attack might be the first of many, death might be raising the first beckoning finger. There was a large fortune to be disposed of, there would be a will, there would be the sharing out of property, of huge and glittering assets.

Tim stood up again, feeling excitement, exhilaration beginning to flow through his limbs. This was precisely the moment to pay a visit to dear Carole, exactly the moment at which she would most earnestly desire the long shadows of the past to dissolve and vanish for ever, so beautifully and rightly the moment at which she would be prepared to dip her pale and pretty hand into her well-padded wallet and pay tribute to an old and well-loved friend.

He pulled open the bottom drawer of the bureau and took out a bunch of letters secured with an elastic band. Carole's letters, written during one of their stormy separations, kept out of sentiment. He slipped off the elastic band and drew a letter from its envelope, running his eyes over the pages with satisfaction. She'd let herself go in the letters, hadn't minced matters. Not at all the kind of letters a tycoon's daughter-in-law would care to see produced in her elegant drawing-room.

He began to hum a little tune. All he needed now was a cover-story, a good excuse for a visit to Rockley.

The final lines of the newspaper story gave him his cue. Among his many and varied interests Mallinson apparently numbered a passion for old coins. His collection was among the finest in the country, he had made a particular speciality of Roman coins. Tim grinned with pleasure at his own ingenuity.

One good rarity, surely he could lay hold of one decent Roman coin with twenty-five pounds? One flawless specimen and he was in business as a dealer. He frowned suddenly, biting his lip in agitated thought.

He'd need money for the train-fare, money to stay somewhere near Whitegates for a day or two—the village pub perhaps? Money for some presentable clothes. How much would be left when he'd bought that coin? He hadn't the faintest idea how much it would cost, whether anything at all would be left, whether in fact the whole twenty-five pounds might not even be enough to buy the coin, let alone leave anything over for the other expenses.

He banged his palms together. He could dispense with the notion of buying a train ticket, he could thumb a lift as he'd done countless times before. He could borrow a respectable suit from one of his cronies, beg a suitcase from another. That left only the money for the pub. How long would he need to stay in the village—what was the name? Rockley, that was it. They wouldn't be likely to charge much in a place like that. Bed and breakfast, he could get by on that. He'd made do with one meal a day before now, with no meals a day often enough. You could stoke yourself up on a good pub breakfast with enough calories to keep you going all day.

He looked round the room, his eyes searching for saleable goods, for anything that might fetch a few shillings. The transistor radio—he could do without that. If his gamble came off he could buy himself a dozen radios. The easels, they'd fetch a bob or two. And of course the coin might only cost a few pounds, he might not have to sell anything at all.

Too late to do anything to-night. Frustration stabbed at him but he brushed it aside. First thing in the morning he'd be down at the shops looking for his coin, then he'd have to make a round of his mates to collect the clothes and the suitcase. The afternoon should see him on the way to Rockley. But no—why spend to-morrow evening in the Rockley pub, paying out good money when the day would be already nearly over, useless to him? Sleep the night here in the studio, start out the following day at the crack of dawn, thumbing a lift from the early lorries, get to Rockley before the morning was well advanced, that would leave him the rest of the day to pay his calls. With any luck he might finish his business before the day was out, might not need to spend a single penny on a night's lodging.

The Siamese cat sprang down from the sofa and rubbed

herself against his leg. He glanced down at her, stooped and picked her up, burying his cheek in the soft fur.

"Can't let you starve while I'm gone, Princess," he said. "When I get back there may be salmon and cream for you, but in the meantime——"

In the meantime there was Hilda Browning, tap-tapping at her hopeless novel on the floor below.

"Come on, Princess!" He went rapidly from the room, down to Hilda Browning's door and rapped loudly.

"Open up, Hilda! It's me, Tim!"

The typewriter keys rattled to a halt. Footsteps inside the room, the door flung open and Hilda Browning smiling at him with sudden renewed hope.

"Tim! It's been ages——" Ages since he'd banged on her door, ages since their brief flare of affection had fizzled out into darkness. "Come in!" She threw the door wide open.

"I have to go away for a day or two," he said, stepping inside. "On a matter of business. Would you do me a favour?" He threw her his most winning smile with the charm turned full on. "Look after Princess for me while I'm gone? I'm leaving the day after to-morrow, very early. I'll make it up to you when I get back." He kept his smile going at full beam. But Hilda didn't even pause to consider the matter.

"Of course I will!" she cried. "I'd be glad to, you know that! Bring Princess down to-morrow evening. She'll be quite at home here." She ought to be, Hilda thought with a fleeting thrust of nostalgia, she spent most of her time down here a few months ago. She stretched out a hand and stroked the cat's fur. "I'll take very good care of her."

Tim began to edge his way back towards the open door.

"I knew I could rely on you," he said, allowing his face to glow with gratitude. "Thanks, Hilda, I won't forget." He let his eyes send out a beam of promise. "I think I'll have something to celebrate when I get back. You can help me to celebrate."

Another minute or two of rather fatiguing encouragement and radiant goodwill and he was able to make his escape back to the studio. He dropped Princess on the sofa, picked up the newspaper and with great care tore out the half-page to be folded away safely in his pocket. He dropped a kiss on the demurely smiling features of Carole Stewart, now Carole Mallinson of happy memory.

"Get out the champagne, Carole, my love!" he said. "Old Tim's riding into town!"

CHAPTER III

BREAKFAST-TIME at Tall Trees. Fragrant coffee in a silver pot, hot rolls in a napkin-lined basket, delicate whorls of creamy butter in a crystal dish. The uniformed maid lifted the cover from the platter of bacon and kidneys. She left the room, closing the door behind her with well-trained noiselessness.

"I don't want any of that." David Mallinson frowned at the succulent kidneys. "I'm not very hungry." He took a roll and broke it in two. "I didn't sleep very well."

"I slept like a log." Carole Mallinson had acquired that knack in the grim days, when she'd been Carole Stewart, she'd learned that sleeplessness didn't help. Whatever disasters the morning might see fit to bring, it was better to meet them rested and refreshed. It was just a trick, really, you closed your eyes and switched off—pouf! like a bright light being extinguished, you sank down, down into the pit of unconsciousness where there was no yesterday and no tomorrow, no ambitions, no memories, no hopes, no fears.

"I thought Father looked surprisingly well yesterday evening," she said. "I think he'll start getting up for a little while in a day or two. He can't bear staying in bed." She had started calling Henry Mallinson *Father* as soon as the wedding-ring was safely on her finger. No father of her own, it gave her a feeling of security, of background, to use the name. And the old man liked it, she knew that. Such a pleasant, unspoiled girl, his son's wife—she was aware of the regard in which he held her—so refreshingly unsophisticated and uncalculating in this day and age.

David glanced at the small French clock on the mantelshelf.

"Kenneth will be arriving some time this morning." It wasn't anxiety for his father's health that creased David's brow into deep lines. The old man had the constitution of an ox, it would take more than a heart spasm to finish him off or even keep him out of action for more than a day or two. It was the thought of his elder brother walking up the curving staircase at Whitegates that took away his appetite, the prodigal son come home again—to what? To the fatted calf, reconciliation, the old man's will changed, his fortune sliced in two instead of being delivered whole into the hands of his younger son, the one who had faithfully stayed at home, who had run the business, had taken care in the whole of thirty-eight years of living, never once to cross swords with his father, knowing even in childhood on which side of his bread the butter lay?

Carole ate her bacon and kidneys with relish. "I would have expected Kenneth to drive down immediately, as soon as Doctor Burnett phoned," she said. "He's certainly taking his time."

David shrugged. "Some business matter, some meeting he couldn't postpone, apparently." Kenneth was doing well by all accounts. A busy man couldn't just drop everything and jump into his car, however urgent the summons.

"Then I don't imagine he'll be staying very long," Carole said soothingly. "If he's as busy as all that."

"No, perhaps not." David crumbled his roll moodily. Long enough though, Kenneth would spare a day or two all right as soon as he got wind of the solicitor being sent for, a new will being drawn up. He pushed his cup forward. "More coffee, please."

Carole lifted the silver pot. "I take it he'll be staying at Whitegates?"

David jerked his head round. "Why yes, of course. Where else would he stay? Not here, surely?" The two brothers had never got on well together, not even as small boys. There had always been the twin swords of jealousy and resentment between them.

"Well, no, not here." It hadn't even crossed her mind that Kenneth would think of staying at Tall Trees. It would have been too difficult, the atmosphere too charged with tensions, with all the long hostilities of boyhood and youth that might explode into the fierce quarrels of grown men. "But I thought perhaps one of the Hallborough hotels. It might be awkward up at Whitegates, a visitor, with illness in the house."

David set down his cup with a tiny clatter. "Kenneth is hardly a visitor. And they can cope at Whitegates, there's staff enough up there to cope with a dozen visitors." He picked up a fragment of his bread roll and smeared it with butter.

"Mother always liked Kenneth best," he said abruptly, taking Carole by surprise. David hardly ever mentioned his mother to her. Dead these ten years or more, closing her eyes and letting herself drift out of life after a minor illness, her painted likeness still hanging in its great gilt frame over the fireplace in the entrance hall at Whitegates, the calm, disciplined, beautiful, unhappy face turned a little to one side, the wide thoughtful eyes looking back into the past, at the memory of pain.

"Does it matter now?" Carole asked softly. "You're both grown men." Almost middle-aged, she added in her mind. Surely swept by the maturing years to some point beyond childish jostlings for position?

"Of course it matters," he said, astonished at her lack of perception. It would always matter, now when they were middle-aged, in thirty years' time when they were old. The passage of time might erase many things but not that, never that. His mother's eyes going first to Kenneth when the two boys came together into the room where she sat by the window, the tiny habitual difference in her tone when she spoke to her elder son, her first-born.

"I've thought once or twice lately," Carole said, playing with a spoon, "that your father's developed—I don't know—some little oddnesses. He seems to be growing old quite suddenly." She raised her eyes to her husband. "I imagine he'll get over this attack—and pretty quickly—but I wonder . . ." She didn't finish the sentence, but it finished itself in both their minds. I wonder just how long he will last? Will there be a second attack? A third and perhaps a final one? And before too long?

"Oddnesses?" David said sharply. "Exactly what kind of oddnesses?"

"He's got rather strange about money, for one thing."

"He was always careful about money." Not mean, but careful, everything accounted for, no waste, no pretentious lavishness. Solid comfort, good value in return for cash laid out—but never stingy.

"I don't mean that, I mean the way he's taken to keeping a little hoard of money in his bedroom. He never used to."

"I didn't know he was doing it now."

Carole pleated a fold in the crisp damask of the table cloth, looking down idly at her fingers in their meaningless task.

"Quite a lot of money, in notes." She smiled. "He has an old-fashioned cash-box. I saw it a few weeks ago, I called in to see him one morning, he was rather tired, he was having breakfast in bed." The first signs of advancing age, that. He'd have been appalled at the notion of breakfast in bed only a couple of years ago. "He was counting the money, fivers mostly." She looked up and smiled again. "Just like a miser in a storybook. He snapped the box shut as soon as I came in. He pushed it into the drawer of the bedside table, but I saw it all right." She stood up. "And the housekeeper was complaining to me that he'd taken to querying the domestic accounts in a way he never used to. Saying they were ordering too much milk. Silly little things like that."

David got to his feet. "I shouldn't think it's of much consequence. An old man's fancy. People do have funny notions when they get old. It's only to be expected."

"Hardly a good idea, though," she said. "All that cash. With servants in and out of the room. And that secretary, Gina Thorson . . ." She let the little implication lie there. A hundred pounds, forty pounds, even twenty or ten, might represent temptation to a girl like Gina Thorson.

Carole's practised eye had assessed Gina and her possessions when the girl had first arrived at Whitegates, recognising from harsh experience the signs of skimped means, the striving after an appearance of well-kept respectability, the cheap smart clothes, shoes and handbags designed to imitate leather.

David raised his eyebrows. "Gina's all right. She wouldn't take anything she wasn't entitled to." He lost interest in Gina Thorson and what she might or might not feel herself entitled to. He let his mind slip back to its major preoccupation. "Do you think we should ask Kenneth to dinner this evening?"

She pondered the delicate question. Would Kenneth wish to dine with them? Would he prefer the quiet of a Hall-borough hotel? Or to take a meal in solitary state at the long polished table in that great shadowy room at Whitegates? Or not a solitary meal perhaps, Gina Thorson might be there, smiling at him above the gleaming glasses and the glittering silver, leaving Dr. Richard Knight to his own devices for once.

"I don't know. Perhaps we'd better leave the first move to Kenneth. See if he calls here to see us, if he's willing to be friendly." She'd never met Kenneth. He hadn't come to their wedding, although a formal invitation had been sent to him. He'd despatched a present with a printed card enclosed in the wrappings, a present that could be displayed with all the others, an expensive, carefully-chosen present, a set of handsome Venetian goblets. Family enmities need not be made plain to the prying eyes of outsiders.

"If *he's* willing to be friendly?" David echoed. "I'm not sure *I'm* willing to be friendly with him." Packing his bags and slamming out like that, leaving David to cope with the family business as best he could. One didn't forget things like that in a hurry. Nor the long hostilities of childhood, the twisted tangles of emotions. They weren't to be dissolved all in a moment by a knock on the door, an impersonal smile, a ritual meal eaten together.

"See how it goes," Carole said, willing as always to bend to the exigencies of the moment, ready to trim her sails as expediency demanded.

David glanced at his watch. "I must be going. I'll just call in at Whitegates, see what kind of a night Father had. I don't suppose he'll want to see me at this hour. Then I'll go on to the office." Rather a grand building in Hallborough these days, the main offices of Mallinson's, a far cry from the single room in a back street fifty years ago. "I don't know what time I'll be home this evening, I'll try not to be too late." Old men might weaken and grow ill but the business had to be kept running smoothly, Henry Mallinson would have been the first to acknowledge that.

"Suppose Kenneth calls here before you get back?"

"You'll just have to play it by ear." He could trust Carole to do that. She would handle the situation as well as he could himself, better actually, if he were to be honest. She had an instinctive knack of saying the right thing at the right time.

"I'm leaving in five minutes," Kenneth Mallinson said into the phone. "I spent a couple of hours last night going into the figures." Up till four o'clock in the morning, staring at the wretched figures, if the truth were told, but one didn't need to tell one's junior partner everything. "And I've decided to hang on for a little while longer, I think I may be able to raise some more capital."

"Just how long is a little while?" The junior partner knew better than to ask Kenneth Mallinson exactly where he proposed trying to raise twenty thousand pounds. If the information weren't volunteered in that first moment, a direct question wasn't going to elicit it.

"Two or three weeks, less perhaps. I can let you know in a day or two."

When he gets back from Rockley, the junior partner thought, after he sees his ailing father. Was he proposing to approach the old man for a loan? Hoping for a death-bed reconciliation? Something of that kind? He might pull it off of course. One never knew with families. It might be possible.

"About that job I've been offered," he said. "They'll want an answer in a few days." All things being equal, the junior partner would much prefer to stay on in business with Kenneth Mallinson. But if the firm was on the verge of bankruptcy he'd be glad of the job. Quite a good opening really.

"I'll let you know," Kenneth said. "You can stall them for a day or two."

"What do you want me to do while you're away?" the junior partner asked. "Go round to the bank and try to talk the manager into giving us more time?"

"Yes." Quite good at that, the junior partner, better than Kenneth Mallinson, who found it hard to go cap in hand to any man. "Tell him I'll be in touch with him in a day or two."

"Right you are. I hope you find your father on the road to recovery." Though was that what his senior partner wanted? Would it not in many ways be more convenient if he found his father on the point of death? With just enough remaining strength to put his signature to a cheque, to summon his solicitor to draw up a new will?

"I don't think he's all that ill," Kenneth said. "From what Doctor Burnett told me. You can phone me at the local pub, Rockley village that is, the Swan, if you need to get in touch with me urgently."

"You're not staying at the house then?" Surprise in the junior partner's tone.

"No, they won't want to be bothered with extra work just now. It'll be more convenient for them if I get a room at the pub."

And more convenient for you as well, the other man thought, smiling wryly to himself. No-one to overhear your phone calls, no-one to realise just how rocky our finances are at this moment.

"Have a good journey," he said, and replaced the receiver.

A few minutes later Kenneth Mallinson picked up his overnight bag and let himself out of the flat. No wife to smile a farewell on the threshold. He had never felt the impulse to marry. The deep channels of his emotions had always been directed towards his mother, the youthful energies of his affections had spent themselves in trying to ease the silent unhappiness of her existence, to make up to her in some tiny measure for the huge error of her marriage to Henry Mallinson, a man whose cold strong nature could not even begin to comprehend how a woman with a warm and loving nature might shrivel and wither from simple lack of the caressing hand of love.

It had taken Kenneth years to recover from his mother's death—if he had ever truly recovered. He had come in the end to accept the fact that she was gone, that things hadn't after all come right for her, that she had died at last from nothing more complicated than a broken heart. By the time he had contrived to construct a shield of armour around his inner turmoils, he was approaching forty and as far as marriage was concerned it was already too late.

He eased the car out on to the main road and pointed it towards the south, towards Rockley and Whitegates. I suppose I'll have to see David, he thought, staring out through the windscreen. And that wife of his, Carole.

He had seen the photographs in the newspapers, the pretty, fair-haired girl standing demurely smiling beside her new husband. Father would like a daughter-in-law like that, he thought, a quiet, compliant girl, one who would fall in with his wishes, play her part in the Mallinson scheme of things, provide him in due course with grandchildren to carry on the family business long after he was dead and gone.

The early-morning traffic began to thicken. As he drove through the outskirts of a town he saw the first sleepy shopkeepers beginning to raise the blinds, to attack the windows with wash-leathers and buckets of water.

"Thirty pounds!" Tim Jefford stared at the proprietor of the tiny shop with horrified disbelief. "Thirty pounds for one miserable coin!"

"Guineas," said the proprietor smoothly. "Thirty guineas. You won't do better elsewhere. Fine condition and a rarity of course. You'd be hard put to it to find another like it in the whole of London." He didn't waste time addressing the wild-looking young man as Sir. Hardly likely that a fellow like that, greasy jeans and a shirt very little acquainted with the wash, would spend thirty guineas on a Roman coin. He yawned delicately into his hand.

"Twenty-five pounds," Tim said desperately. "Not a penny more." No use in buying anything cheaper, the coin had to be a rarity if it was to serve any purpose at all.

The shop-keeper flicked up his eyes with new interest.

"Twenty-seven pounds ten," he said briskly.

"Twenty-five," Tim repeated, regretting now that he hadn't started bidding at twenty. "I've only got twenty-five."

"Twenty-five it is," the shop-keeper said at once, recognising the truth when he heard it. The fellow thrust his hand into the pocket of his jeans and drew out a fistful of notes, a scattering of coins. When he had counted out the money there were only the coins left on the counter, a few shillings at most. Paint-stains on the long fingers with their grimy nails. A sudden access of sentimentality took the shop-keeper by surprise, carrying him back all at once to the far-off days of his own youth, to his stall in the street market, his poverty-stricken cronies for ever dabbing at canvases with oils, for ever tapping out their immortal novels on ancient typewriters, hacking in unquenchable optimism at great lumps of stone.

"You can have it for twenty-two pounds ten," he said abruptly, astounded at his own folly. The fellow looked as if he hadn't eaten three good meals a day since he'd left home, whenever that might have been.

Tim snatched back the two pounds ten before the shop-keeper could change his mind.

"Thanks," he said with a grin. "You've saved my life. Could you put the coin in a box? Something impressive-looking?"

The man nodded and groped on the shelf behind him, restraining himself with difficulty from enquiring why his customer should be willing to spend every pound he had on a coin of a long-dead empire.

And now for the public library, Tim thought, standing on the pavement again. A book about coins, two or three books perhaps. He'd have to study them on the way to Rockley, pore over them in his room at the pub, if he was going to be able to make any kind of showing with old Mallinson.

He walked along the busy street, whistling. A dark grey suit—he knew a lad who still had a dark grey suit, hadn't yet parted with it for a few pounds to a second-hand shop. And he knew where he could borrow a couple of near-white shirts. And a decent suitcase. Pyjamas, he remembered suddenly. Better have a pair of pyjamas. He frowned and ceased his whistling. He'd better try and lay hands on a dressing-gown too.

He glanced down at his shabby shoes. A dead give-away those shoes. He let out a long breath of dismay. Things were getting a trifle more complicated than he'd bargained for. Who on earth did he know with a newish pair of shoes? And a second pair to wear while he lent Tim the newish ones? One of his friends might know some college kid, some lad still with the remnants of his parent-bestowed wardrobe. He couldn't afford to be too fussy about the size.

His face took on a grim expression as he turned into the

public library, envisaging the long agony of the next few days with his tortured feet squeezed into size seven or slopping awkwardly around in number tens.

Life isn't merely a battlefield, he thought, going up to the crowded shelves. It's a ruddy massacre.

CHAPTER IV

"I HAVE TIME for a quick cup of coffee," Richard Knight said, smiling at Gina. He would never do more than smile at her in front of the maid who had answered his ring at the door and who was still hovering in the hall, giving the secretary an enquiring glance. The servants at Whitegates were by now all quite certain that romance was brewing between Miss Thorson and Dr. Burnett's young partner. They viewed the developing situation without envy, with interest and pleasure. A pleasant young woman, Gina Thorson, one who had seen hard times somewhere, not a girl to give herself airs with the domestic staff—not like Mr. David's wife up at Tall Trees, who fancied herself more than somewhat in spite of the fact that she had apparently sprung from nowhere at exactly the right moment to catch Mr. David and marry him.

"Could we have some coffee, please?" Gina smiled at the maid, making an ally of her, as was her way. "Dr. Knight hasn't much time."

"Certainly, Miss. Right away." The girl disappeared in the direction of the kitchen quarters.

"I'm just off on my rounds," Richard said. He slid an arm round Gina's waist and dropped a light kiss on her cheek. She was aware as always of a slight distance between them. Until his ring was actually on her finger he would always treat her with a trace of reserve and formality. "How's the old man?" he asked, walking up to the great fireplace and looking down at the logs burning in the grate.

Gina followed him. "He seems to be doing very well.

He's getting restless, I suppose that's a good sign." Richard gave a little nod. "Doctor Burnett was in earlier this morning, Mr. Mallinson was pestering him to let him get up."

Richard raised his head. "And is he going to let him?"

"Yes, for a very short time this afternoon, Mrs. Parkes said. Just to sit in a chair in his room. I don't suppose that will satisfy him for long, though."

The maid came in with the tray of coffee. Gina began to pour it out. "Kenneth Mallinson is here," she said. "Did you know?"

"I knew he'd been sent for, I didn't know whether or not he'd arrived."

Gina handed him a cup. "He got here about ten minutes ago. I didn't see him, Mrs. Parkes told me he was here." She inclined her head towards the curving stairs. "He's up there now, with his father. Doctor Burnett said he could have visitors, provided they didn't stay too long or excite him in any way."

Richard stirred his coffee thoughtfully. "I should have thought seeing his elder son again, after all these years, might be rather distressing. I don't know that I would have allowed it at such an early stage."

"Oh but you see, Mr. Mallinson particularly wanted to see him, he asked Doctor Burnett to send for him as soon as he was taken ill. It would have upset him far more if the visit hadn't been allowed."

Richard began to drink his coffee. "Yes, I suppose so. In any case Burnett knows what he's doing. He's a very sound man and of course he knows everyone here for miles around, knows all the family ins and outs, the feuds and alliances. It all helps when you're trying to do what's best for a patient."

"Has he always practised here?" Gina asked. "I would have imagined a clever doctor like that would have been tempted away to a city, or a big hospital somewhere." She knew that Richard himself was only putting in a year or two with Dr. Burnett, his sights were set on broader horizons, Rockley would not hold him for ever.

"He was born here," Richard said. "He's a man who sends down deep roots, a man with strong loyalties. But he did leave Rockley, he spent the greater part of his working life up north, in an industrial area of Yorkshire, I thought you knew that."

Gina laid down her cup and stared at him in surprise. "No, I had no idea. I thought he'd always practised here. I had the impression—from the servants, I suppose—that he'd been here for years and years. Mr. Mallinson always treats him as if they've known each other all their lives."

"They have, in a way. They were boys together in Rockley. Poor boys, both of them. Whitegates was owned by a county family then. Henry Mallinson's father was a groom and Dr. Burnett's father was the gardener here at Whitegates. He was born in that cottage where the Fosters live now. They were bright lads, both of them. Mallinson came up the hard way, using his brains and hands to build up the business, Burnett read books and won scholarships. He came back here to practise after he qualified. Then, when he was about thirty or thirty-five, he went off to Yorkshire and didn't come back till about ten years ago. I suppose he found he was growing old, thought he'd like to end his days where he was born. Not an uncommon wish."

"Did he never marry?" Gina spoke the words with a trace of hesitation, hoping that Richard wouldn't think she was sending out a feeler of any kind. Marriage had never been mentioned between them, but she knew that he had considered it, that during their visit to his home he would make up his mind.

Richard shook his head. "No, not so far as I know. He certainly never mentions a wife and I've never heard that he married. Rather surprising really, when I come to think about it. A wife is very useful to a doctor, most doctors marry. And Burnett, in particular, I would have thought he was the type to fall in love deeply and permanently." He laid down his cup. "By the way, Gina, I haven't pressed you, but *are* you coming with me? Next month, when I go home?

I'd like you to meet my parents, I'd like it very much." He gave her a level, direct, unsmiling look. "It's important to me."

She felt her heart give a sharp leap. "I'd like to, Richard, I'd be very pleased to. It's only——" She broke off and bit her lip.

"Only what? What silly notion have you got into your head?"

It was utterly impossible for her to open her mouth and mention such a ridiculous trifle as her clothes. A man would never understand, and particularly a man like Richard. He would brush the words aside with impatience. But it *does* matter, Gina thought, it matters a lot to make the right impression. With the right clothes, I'd feel at ease, adequate, able to hold my own, however grand his parents are.

"They mightn't like me," she heard herself say, and was instantly depressed at the stupidity, the childishness of the remark. "I'm no-one," she said, plunging even deeper into foolishness. She abandoned all pretence and let the words come out in a rush. "I've no family, no background. Your parents are well-to-do, they live in a big house, they'd wonder why on earth you bothered to bring home a girl like me." It was out, she'd said it. She closed her eyes for an instant in despair.

A moment later she was astounded to hear Richard laugh. A deep amused laugh, echoing round the hall. She jerked her eyes open.

"You silly child!" He bent down and put his arms round her, kissed her lightly and firmly on the mouth.

"You're someone very special, to me," he said, suddenly serious again, looking down into her eyes. "Don't ever let me hear you talk such nonsense again. My parents will love you—as I do."

"Oh, Richard——" Upstairs she heard a door open and close. She pulled back from his arms and glanced nervously towards the stairs.

"It's all right," he said in a low voice. "There's no need

to act like a startled fawn." But his manner resumed its customary trace of formality. "I take it you'll be coming with me, then? If your objections are nothing more serious than that?"

She drew a deep breath. "All right, I'll come."

He patted her hand. "Good girl, I knew you'd see sense." He glanced at his watch. "Now I really must be off or my patients' relatives will all be ringing the surgery to find out where I've got to."

She went with him to the door. "I'll phone you," he said. "This evening or to-morrow, it depends how I'm fixed. We'll go out and have a meal together as soon as I can manage a couple of hours off." He brushed her cheek with his lips and was gone.

Gina closed the door and stood with her back to it, her hands clasped together. I *will* go, she thought, and I'll be a credit to him. I'll get the suède coat and the skirt and the sweater. Shoes, bag and gloves. I'll get them all. Somehow. I'll look poised, elegant, suitable. I won't let Richard down. She unclasped her hands, stood up very straight and looked up at the stairs towards the corridor beyond, towards the room behind whose door old Mr. Mallinson lay.

"Doing very well indeed," Kenneth Mallinson said. "Still plenty of room for expansion of course." He gave a little smile. "We're not in the same class as you, not by a long chalk, but our balance sheet is pretty healthy."

Henry Mallinson put the tips of his fingers together. "No, I don't suppose you are in the same class as me. Took me fifty years to build the firm up. And things were different then. More opportunity for a young man with vision. Not so many rules and regulations, taxation wasn't so crippling." He looked back into the past for an instant with pleasure, remembering the old days, the struggles, the triumphs, the near-disasters. He gave a little smiling sigh, wishing it was all to do again, that he could turn back the clock and start the whole long battle all over again.

"There isn't a thing I'd do differently," he said suddenly, following his own train of thought. "Not a thing." He'd enjoyed every moment of it, the difficulties and conflicts, perhaps those most of all.

"Nothing?" Kenneth asked in an altered tone. He wasn't thinking of the business, he was thinking of his mother, of her spirit bruised and crushed over the long years of marriage to a man whose first and only thought was for the firm he had reared with so much toil and sweat. He was thinking of his own quarrel with his father and the years of silence. "Nothing at all?"

Henry Mallinson raised his eyes. "Not a thing," he said. "I'd do it all again exactly as before."

Kenneth stood up and walked over to the window. He stood looking down at the sweep of lawn, at Foster kneeling by a bed, patting the earth around a plant. One learns nothing from the past, he thought, one learns nothing from one's mistakes, we are all bounded inexorably by the limitations of our own natures. Myself as well as other men. He felt suddenly and acutely depressed.

"You're quite settled up north, then?" his father's voice asked. He didn't add, 'Not thinking of getting married one of these days?' It wouldn't have occurred to him to ask. A confirmed bachelor, his elder son, he would retreat year by year further into his shell, growing more solitary, more self-sufficient. Any grandchildren Henry Mallinson might hope for must be looked for elsewhere. The firm would not be carried on, nurtured and served by any descendants of Kenneth's. "You've given up all notion of coming back here?" He didn't say, 'Of coming home.' Whitegates was no longer home to Kenneth, hadn't been home to him since the day he'd followed his mother to Rockley churchyard where she lay at last in peace, beyond unhappiness, beyond the possibility of pain.

Kenneth turned from the window. "I don't know," he said with an air of lightness. "I haven't totally ceased to consider it." His own business concern might go bust in a

D

matter of days. He had to keep the door open, he might be very glad indeed to creep back to Rockley and make a niche for himself in the family business. But what kind of a niche would it be? Would David even contemplate relinquishing command? He gave a fractional shake of his head at the notion. No, David would not contemplate it. He would take very great pleasure in assigning his elder brother to some inferior position, in issuing orders and waiting for them to be carried out.

I couldn't do it, Kenneth thought. But reality stared back at him implacably. He might have to do it, there might be no other conceivable course.

"There's always room for a little more capital in a growing concern," he said, smiling at his father. "I don't have to tell you that. Do you fancy a sound investment? I could offer you very good terms." He smiled again, a shade less cheerfully. "Seeing it's one of the family."

His father gave him a long shrewd look. What was it about his elder son that had always irritated him? Why had he been content to turn his affairs over to David, without resentment, without perpetual fault-finding and interference, when he had been totally unable to leave Kenneth alone for one single day to run the firm as he thought best? He didn't know, and he would never know now, it was by many a long year too late to find out.

"I wasn't altogether fair to you in the past," he said slowly. He saw Kenneth's eyes jerk open at such an acknowledgment.

That's how he sees me, Henry thought, a man who could never admit to a mistake. But we change when death looks us in the face, not by very much perhaps, but we change all the same.

"There was never enough time," Henry said without regret. "Never enough time to look at every aspect of living." An apology of sorts. As much as he could ever bring himself to utter. It would have to do.

Kenneth looked down at his father. It crossed his mind

for an instant that he could reach down and touch his father's hand, pale and oddly fragile-looking, the fingers extended against the coverlet. But he remembered his mother lying there in Rockley churchyard and the impulse passed.

"I'd like to put a little money into your business," his father said. He gave a brief smile. "I'd like to diversify my interests. What figure did you have in mind?"

Kenneth drew a deep breath. "Twenty-five thousand," he said without emotion. Might as well allow a margin. "Thirty if you prefer. It can all be gone into."

"I'll speak to my solicitor. He can look into it. How long will you be staying?"

Kenneth took a pace or two about the room. Impossible to stand still now when relief flowed violently through his limbs.

"As long as you wish. My junior partner is a very sound man, he can carry on till I get back." I'll phone him the moment I get to the pub, he thought. I'll tell him it's all right about the loan, he can turn that job down now. With immense difficulty he restrained himself from laughing aloud, so great was his sense of release.

"A few days then," his father said. "I know what business is, you can't stay here for ever." He flung him a glance that held a trace of appeal. "You'll be down again, I imagine. Before very long."

"Oh yes, I'll be down again. It isn't all that long a run in the car." Strange to contemplate the notion of being on visiting terms at Whitegates. He'd have to put things on to some kind of acceptable footing with David and his wife. Matters would have to be handled very delicately there.

"My solicitor can draw up a new will while he's about it," Henry Mallinson said, almost off-hand. "The present one cuts you out, I imagine you realised that?"

Kenneth inclined his head. "Yes, I realised that."

"You're my elder son," his father said. "No getting away from that." At the end of life the ties of blood assumed im-

mense importance, a significance he hadn't altogether bargained for. "No getting away from that," he said again,
heavily, and closed his eyes. "I'm tired now, I think I'd
better rest. I'm old, Kenneth, really old." He opened his
eyes, wearily. "I never thought it would happen to me. The
years go by. You know it happens to other people. But you
never imagine it will happen to you."

Even now Kenneth couldn't bring himself to take his
father's hand. Later perhaps, in a day or two, before he
left Rockley. But not just yet. He couldn't stretch out a
hand and destroy the past all in a moment. Not just yet.

"I'll go then," he said, moving towards the door. "Is there
anything you want?"

Henry closed his eyes. His face looked peaceful, infinitely
weary. "Send Mrs. Parkes along. I'll get her to see about the
solicitor. Later on to-day perhaps. Might as well strike
while the iron's hot." While there's still time, he added in
his mind, time to put things right, in some measure at least.
"You'll be staying here?" His eyes came open again, slowly.
"In the house?"

Kenneth shook his head. "No, I'll get a room at the pub.
It'll be less bother for the servants."

"Just as you wish." So he isn't ready to forgive yet,
Henry thought, not altogether with surprise. The Mallinson
blood ran in Kenneth's veins and no Mallinson forgave
easily, at the first sign of an outstretched hand. He heard
the door close quietly. He raised a hand to his face and
found to his astonishment that his lids were moist with
tears.

Kenneth walked slowly towards the stairs with his mind
in a tumult of conflicting thoughts and emotions. The wave
of relief which had washed over him in the bedroom was
subsiding now. It isn't going to be as simple as it seemed
in that first moment, he thought. Father is no fool about
money and the solicitor is even less of a fool—if that is possible. Twenty, twenty-five, thirty thousand pounds, that kind
of money wasn't going to be invested without searching en-

quiries and the most casual enquiry would elicit the fact
that Kenneth's business was standing on the very edge of
bankruptcy. Oh yes, with a good lump sum of capital he
was absolutely confident that he could set the firm on its
feet again, that it would go forward soundly and smoothly.
But to convince his father of that—and his father's solicitor?
Another matter altogether.

He put a hand on the banister, staring down at his feet
moving one after the other, a single step at a time, re-
luctant now to carry him towards that phone. Just what
was he going to tell his partner?

There is the new will, some insistent part of his mind
said clearly. Drawn up to-day, signed to-morrow, in all
probability. The whole family fortune split down the
middle between himself and David. Father looked tired and
old, he thought, striving to suppress pity, he looked like a
man who could not last many months, many weeks—or
even many days.

His fingers gripped the rail tightly. If his father were to
die quite soon, inside a week, say, there need be no investigation about a loan. He could either shore up the firm with
another loan from the bank till his father's estate was paid
out, or he could simply let the firm go bust, sit back and
wait for probate, secure in the knowledge that he need never
again lift a finger unless he wanted to. And his father had
looked so weary, so ill . . .

Nonsense! said another part of his mind, loud and distinct, he isn't very ill at all. He suffered only a mild spasm
of some kind, he has an iron constitution, he isn't all that
old as age goes nowadays, he'll be up and about in a day
or two, quite capable of poring over accounts, of recognising rocky finances when he studies a balance sheet.

Kenneth raised his shoulders in perplexity. I'm really no
better off now than when I spoke to my partner this morning, he thought with a stab of hopelessness. He felt all at
once acutely angry, obscurely cheated. A way out had
seemed to open up before his feet and then to close again,

vanishing into the mist. There is no way, he told himself and then paused for a moment, feeling the banister smooth and slippery beneath his hand. There is one way, he thought . . . if I dared to take it . . .

Downstairs at the front door, a sudden sharp ring at the bell. Kenneth jerked himself out of his calculations, allowed his face to resume its normal expression and walked quickly down the remaining stairs.

A maid crossed the hall and opened the front door. A few moments later she admitted a man in a dark overcoat, a white-haired man carrying a bag in one hand, his hat in the other.

"Doctor Burnett! How are you? It's been a long time——" Kenneth walked swiftly across the wide spaces of the parquet floor with his hand held out.

"You got here then," Burnett said, giving him a rapid, assessing look. "Have you seen your father?"

"Yes, I've just left him. He seems to be coming along very nicely. He's a little tired at the moment—we had a rather long talk, but he wasn't distressed in any way. I don't think he's expecting you."

"No, but I was passing on my way home for lunch. I've some new tablets, I'd like him to try them, I think they might be useful."

They had moved together into the centre of the spacious hall. A chilly room, in spite of the logs burning in the grate. Always a chilly room, Kenneth remembered, even when I was a lad it struck cold into my bones, even in the height of summer. He glanced at Burnett and saw that his eyes were resting on the gilt-framed portrait over the fireplace. Kenneth looked up at his mother, at her calm, sad, disciplined face turned a little to one side, her hands folded together in resignation on the dark blue silk of her skirt.

He had a sudden impulse to speak of her to someone, to this doctor perhaps, standing beside him. He wanted to pluck her back for a moment from that shadowy land in which, impossibly, she could no longer experience sadness or resignation, pain or heartbreak.

"You never knew her, did you?" he said in a low voice. Dr. Burnett had left Rockley for some teeming grimy city in the north before Henry Mallinson brought home his bride. "You came back to Rockley after she——" He found himself totally unable to utter the bleak finality of that word, *died*.

"A beautiful face," Burnett said in a voice with over-tones that Kenneth couldn't quite identify. "In spite of the unhappiness, a face of great beauty."

So you see it too, Kenneth thought, it isn't just to my eyes, the eyes of love and knowledge, that her unhappiness still speaks from the careful oils. It is clear after all these years to a stranger who never knew her, never saw her.

"You didn't come to the wedding?" he asked suddenly, surprisingly. They had been boyhood friends, the doctor and his father, one would have expected him to leave that grimy city and take a train south to stand beside his old friend on that special day.

Burnett shook his head. "I couldn't get away, I was single-handed at the time." His voice remembered the driving work of those days, the brief hours of sleep, the endless, appalling fatigue. "It was a hard life." He gave a little sigh and returned to the present with a movement of his shoulders.

"You'll be staying here?" he asked. "For a few days, I imagine?"

"For a few days at least. But not in the house. I'm going along to the Swan now to get a room. I don't imagine there'll be any difficulty." Never more than two or three guests at a time in the Swan, for what was there to attract a horde of visitors to a little village like this? "I thought I'd spare the servants here the trouble——"

"I could give you lunch," Burnett said. "If you'd care to wait till I've seen your father. It won't be anything very fancy but it might be better than the Swan." Hardly noted for its fine cuisine, the village pub. He was surprised at Kenneth wanting to stay there. Plenty of servants at Whitegates. What else were they paid for but to look after the family? All those bedrooms, half of them never used from one year's end to another nowadays.

"It's very kind of you, but I think I'll go along right away and see about booking a room. And I've some business matters to attend to." Kenneth smiled a little. "You know how it is. I've left my junior partner in charge, he isn't quite as experienced as I am. One has to keep in touch."

Burnett turned towards the stairs. "I'll be seeing you again, of course. We'll both be in and out of Whitegates. Perhaps we can take a meal together another time."

"Father is all right?" Kenneth asked suddenly. "I mean he is going to——"

"To recover?" The doctor gave him a shrewd look. "I see no reason why not. He isn't all that old." He smiled. "That is to say, he's exactly the same age as I am. I suppose to you that seems a very great age indeed but here in the country——" he spread the fingers of one hand—"it's no very great age as they reckon things here. I think you can set your mind at rest."

At rest, Kenneth thought, letting himself out of the front door a few moments later. A strange word to express the present state of his mind. Behind him the door opened and the maid came running out.

"Oh—Mr. Kenneth—aren't you going to stay for lunch? Cook is expecting you—and your room, it's all ready for you!"

Kenneth turned. "No, I'm not staying in the house. I'm sorry, I didn't realise you thought I was. I'm staying at the Swan." The girl looked disappointed. They would welcome a visitor or two, he saw suddenly. It must be dull for the staff in the half-empty house. He gestured towards his car drawn up a few yards away. "I'm taking my things along there now. I'll be back, of course." He gave her a cheerful smile. "I'll be popping in and out all the time."

As he headed the car towards the tall iron gates he saw a girl walking along the little path leading through the shrubbery. She raised a hand to part the overhanging branches and stepped fully into view. He slowed the car for a moment and their eyes met. He inclined his head briefly in acknowledgment and let the car glide forward again.

A pretty girl, an extremely pretty girl, pale shining hair and wide blue eyes. A slender figure, a diffident, vulnerable-looking face. His mind flicked rapidly through a catalogue of the residents and neighbours of Whitegates, striving to place her. A face too delicate and sensitive to belong to a servant, the clothes a little too tailored for a village girl.

As he drove out through the gates he remembered all at once that his father had said something about a secretary. That would be it, his father's secretary. He considered the notion with a trace of surprise. There had been secretaries before, middle-aged women or older, lean and sinewy women, thickset, comfortable-looking women, but never one like this, never one with graceful limbs and palely-gleaming hair.

The pub came into sight. He put up a hand to his mouth and yawned, all at once extremely tired. It had been a long morning, full of surprises.

"Very well then," Dr. Burnett said. "Lunch now, a light lunch of course. Light meals only for the present. There must be no strain on the digestion. Then a nap. Afterwards, if you still feel like it, and only if you feel like it, you can sit up for half an hour this afternoon. Put on a dressing-gown and sit in that chair——" He indicated a large upholstered chair near the window. "See that you're warm, it's most important to keep warm. Then back to bed again. And no further attempts to get up till I've seen you again, seen how you are. If everything goes well, we'll think about letting you take a walk along the corridor to-morrow."

"Get along with you, you old fraud," Henry Mallinson

said, grinning at him. "Who do you think you're impressing
with all this professional mumbo-jumbo? I'm as fit now as
I was before this happened, just a little tired, that's all. I'll
be as right as rain in a few days. I'll see you into your grave
before me. I'll be the one who buys the wreath, not you,
and well you know it."

"You can't brush old age away by refusing to acknowledge it," Burnett said, unwilling to return the grin. "You're
not one of your own cars, you know, you can't have a rebore,
a new carburettor, a new engine. There's to be no more
driving on the brake and the accelerator for you from now
on, you've got to get down to a slow steady speed."

Henry acknowledged temporary defeat. "Oh, all right.
Have it your own way. I'll sit in my dressing-gown like a
sick child in a nursery. Am I allowed comics? Or would the
excitement prove too much for me?"

"I have some new tablets here," Burnett said, ignoring
the tedious humour. "I'd like you to try them. Some quite
promising reports of them." He dug into his bag and produced a white cardboard drum. He removed the lid and tilted
the drum forward under Henry's gaze. "Tiny, as you see, no
difficulty about swallowing them. One with a drink of water
three times a day."

"What are they?" Henry asked suspiciously. Didn't like
tablets, didn't hold with any kind of drugs, pumping alien
chemicals into perfectly good blood, unnatural, potentially
dangerous.

"You wouldn't understand the name if I told you, you
wouldn't even be able to pronounce it. Just do as you're
told for once and take them for a few days. We'll see how
you get on with them, then we'll think about continuing
them or changing over to something else."

"I'm not a guinea-pig," Henry said without much hope.
"You can carry out your experiments elsewhere, somewhere
where they'll be appreciated."

Burnett opened the bedroom door and thrust his head
out into the corridor.

"Mrs. Parkes! Could you come here, please?"

The nurse came out at once from her own room next door where she had been awaiting just such a summons. She came briskly into the room in her clean crisp uniform.

"Yes, Dr. Burnett?" She slid a glance at the old man propped up against the pillows. He looked less tired now, stimulated by his exchange with the doctor.

"Mr. Mallinson may sit up for a short time when he has had an afternoon nap." The doctor repeated his instructions about care and warmth, about the dosage of the tablets.

"And you are to remember particularly, both of you, that the tablets are on no account to be taken with alcohol."

"Alcohol?" Henry frowned. "Do you mean I can't have a glass of whisky?" One of the few pleasures left to me, his aggrieved tone implied, I am to be robbed of that as well. Is there no limit to these infernal restrictions?

"I didn't say that." Burnett's voice grew a trifle impatient. "I said the tablets were on no account to be taken with alcohol. If you *must* have a glass of whisky——" and his tone conceded that in all probability Henry must—"then you must dispense with the tablet. That is, if you insist, for instance, on a glass of whisky before you go to sleep, then you are on no account to take a tablet later than, say, four o'clock in the afternoon. The effect on the system will have ceased by the time you drink your whisky."

"Is he still to take the three tablets a day?" Mrs. Parkes was a little puzzled.

"Yes." Dr. Burnett sighed. He strove to make his meaning clear, as if to inattentive children. "One tablet on waking in the morning, one at noon, and the last at four o'clock. If by any chance either of you forgets and the last tablet is administered later, say at five or six, then there is to be no whisky on that evening. Do I make myself clear?"

"Perfectly, thank you." Mrs. Parkes was just the tiniest bit put out, not altogether caring for the doctor's tone. After all, he *had* been rather confusing at first. "I'll see Mr. Mallinson takes the tablets at the correct time, in the correct dosage, and never with alcohol. I'll make myself responsible for remembering."

Nice going, Henry thought, allowing himself to fling a cheerfully defiant grin at old Burnett. Getting to be a bit of a dictator in his old age, ordering patients about as if they were babies, wouldn't do him any harm at all to be put in his place for once. And by a nurse at that.

Burnett's old cheeks showed a faint trace of heightened colour. He stooped to close his bag. "I'll be looking in again," he said. "I can't say exactly when. I don't imagine it makes a great deal of difference to you."

"No difference at all," Henry said airily. "I feel a great deal better for your visit, I must admit. By the way," he added, slipping in the information with an air of casualness, "I'm having my solicitor call in later this afternoon. One or two things to discuss." He flicked his eyes upwards at Burnett. "A change of will among them." Mrs. Parkes's head came sharply round.

"Is that all right, Doctor Burnett?" she asked with a touch of anxiety. The first she'd heard of any summons to the solicitor, any change of will.

Dr. Burnett considered the matter. "I suppose so," he said reluctantly. Henry was clearly going to see the solicitor whether it was all right with his doctor or not, not much use in uttering an ineffectual veto. "Don't overdo it, though. Make it as short as possible." Of course, the reconciliation with Kenneth—and now a change of will, Kenneth being put back into the will. For how much? The lot? Or half? Mm, might be stirring up a nest of trouble there with his brother David.

"I rely on you not to let the visit drag on too long," Burnett said to Mrs. Parkes. But he knew that a sick man would rest more easily after his will was made, when his mind was at peace.

And it was only right that Kenneth should have his share. Cutting him out like that, the elder son, most unjust. Wouldn't do to take a chance, delay matters, might end up with old Henry dying without the will being changed, Kenneth deprived of his inheritance. A tricky thing, the heart, one could never tell. Mallinson's heart might be good for another ten years, might flicker out all in an instant. That's the thing to remember about the heart, Burnett repeated in his mind, no-one can ever be sure, no-one can ever tell.

Mrs. Parkes walked with the doctor to the head of the stairs. "You can safely leave Mr. Mallinson to me," she said with firm confidence. "I won't allow him to do too much."

She watched Burnett walk away down the stairs and through the hall. She stood where she was for a minute or two. No-one about, the hall and corridor deserted. She put a hand into the pocket of her uniform dress and drew out a much-creased envelope, pulled out her son's letter and glanced at it yet again, not needing to, knowing the contents by heart, but unable to restrain herself.

"If there was any possibility of getting a farm of our own here——" She raised her eyes from the letter and stared at the wall. Kenneth Mallinson come home, the will to be changed. What of her own legacy now? Might it be swept away in the general redistribution of the estate? Might her claim on Mr. Mallinson's generosity be forgotten? And she had convinced herself by now that the legacy actually existed, that it was a very good sum indeed. She dropped her eyes to the letter.

"Once you've made up your mind about a thing," her son had written, "there isn't much point in hanging about. . . ."

"Mrs. Parkes!" The old man's voice calling from his room.

"Coming!" She thrust the letter and the envelope together into her pocket, cleared her face of the traces of emotion and went briskly back to the bedroom.

"I want my lunch, Mrs. Parkes! Have you forgotten my lunch?"

"No, of course not!" She smiled at him. "I'll bring it up right away. I was just seeing Dr. Burnett off."

"And tell Gina to bring up a couple of trays of my coins after lunch." He grinned like a mischievous boy. "Burnett didn't say anything about not looking at my coins. The two trays from the first drawer of the left-hand cabinet, tell Gina. Have you got that?"

"Yes, I'll tell her." She went quietly from the room.

Henry lay back against his pillows with a contented air. He hoped there was something a trifle more substantial for lunch than the miserable couple of spoonfuls he'd been allowed for breakfast. Still, there were the coins to handle afterwards. Quite some time since he'd run his fingers over the carefully-cleaned surfaces. There were one or two little compensations to be enjoyed from illness after all.

CHAPTER V

"HALLBOROUGH?" the lorry driver said.

"A village near Hallborough, actually. It's called Rockley. I don't suppose you've ever heard of it. I hadn't myself till a couple of days ago."

"No, I can't say I have. But I know Hallborough, been through there a couple of times. Not going through it this trip though, but I could set you down about fifty miles away. You could easily thumb another lift from there."

"Right, thanks, that'd do me fine."

"Hop in then and we'll be on our way."

It was damp and chilly in the pale light of early morning. Tim Jefford was glad enough to hop in out of the cold and settle down as best he might on the uncomfortable seat beside the driver. Very high up in the world, and very cramped. Very warm as well, the driver had the heater going full blast. He pulled out a crumpled packet of cigarettes and thrust them under Tim's nose.

"Smoke?"

"Thanks." Tim fished out a box of matches. With a roar

and a growl the vehicle got under way again. With some difficulty Tim managed to extract a book from his pocket. He gave a deep sigh. He'd sat up till two o'clock perusing the information-packed pages, peering at the photographs, the illustrations, trying to memorise dates and names. He flipped open the pages till he came to Chapter Seven, held the book towards the window, striving to read the small print in the difficult light.

"Student, are you?" the driver said sympathetically, sorry for students with all that bookwork, all those years of drudgery. Small wonder the poor devils let fly with a riot or two from time to time, he didn't blame them, wonder they didn't go round the bend altogether, all that studying couldn't be good for the brain, it stood to reason.

"In a way," Tim said. "I have to learn this book more or less off by heart. And I've got a couple more in my bag I'll have to look through as well."

"Exams coming up then?"

"You could call it that."

The lorry driver abandoned his questioning out of regard for his passenger's need to concentrate. He started to whistle through his teeth in a tuneless, halting kind of way that before very long began to play on Tim's nerves with peculiar acuteness. He made a strong effort to shut out the sound, to force his attention on a hoard of Roman coins dug up five years before on Salisbury Plain, some of them among the rarest ever found.

The miles flashed by, the pages turned, mercifully the driver lapsed after a time into a silence punctuated only by occasional discordant bursts of song. Tim fell into a half-hypnotic state, lulled by the motion, the print, the trees going past on the edge of his vision.

Suddenly he was jerked into full consciousness by the lorry stopping abruptly.

"Tea!" the driver said cheerfully. "And a good fry-up."

Tim yawned, glancing out of the window. They were in an open space in front of a grim-looking café with a board outside bearing chalked intimations of the delicacies within. Bacon sandwiches, fried-egg sandwiches, sausage sandwiches. Egg and chips, fish and chips, beans and chips. Bacon and egg and chips, sausages and chips, bacon and sausages and chips. Bacon and egg and sausages and chips. Tim's head began to reel.

"Come on then," the driver said, climbing stiffly down from the cab. "We haven't got all day."

Tim put away his book and followed him. His stomach was hollow with hunger. He'd eaten the last few crumbs of the stale French loaf in the black dawn, there had been plenty of coffee, the only thing there was plenty of. And he couldn't afford to go throwing his money around now on bacon, egg, sausages, and chips, however permutated or combined.

"What are you going to have?" the driver asked, pushing his way among the tables.

"Just tea, thank you," Tim said, averting his eyes from a fragrant plate of beans and chips being carried past by a cheeky-looking young girl.

"Tea!" the driver echoed with disbelief. "You on a diet or something?"

"That's right," Tim said, too hastily. "I'm allowed to eat only once a day, in the evening. After the sun goes down," he added with some vague recollection of tropical planters and their rules for drinking.

"Go on!" The driver laughed aloud, showing teeth badly in need of restoration. "You're skint, aren't you?"

Tim felt depression descend on him. In spite of the dark suit handed over by one of his mates after a preliminary show of force, in spite of the near-white shirt forced with oaths and imprecations from another, in spite of the fiendish toe-pinching shoes and the socks with holes only in the toes, his appearance didn't apparently deceive even the most casual observer for so much as a minute. Skint, the man had said. And skint he was, skint he looked.

"I know what you students are," the driver said knowingly. "Go on, have what you fancy, I'll stand treat. You might be rich one day when you've passed your exams, you can do the same for some other poor devil."

"Thanks, I won't say no," Tim said, restraining a wild impulse to fall upon the fellow and clasp him like General de Gaulle.

"Bacon and sausage and egg and chips," he said clearly, in case there was any question of one of the items being overlooked. "And tea, and bread and butter." There might be nothing more to eat till breakfast at the Rockley pub to-morrow morning.

"That's the spirit," the driver said. "That's what made Britain great." He winked at Tim for some obscure reason.

I'll get his name and address, Tim thought in an excess of gratitude. If he pulled off the Rockley coup he'd send the man a fiver. No name, no letter, just a fiver in an envelope.

The driver exchanged a few ritual pleasantries with the cheeky-faced girl, eventually getting down to the serious business of ordering. Then he gave Tim a shove in the dir-ection of an empty table, calling out a few words of greeting here and there to other drivers. He sat down and took out a tube of white lozenges, thrust a couple into his mouth and sucked them loudly.

"Want any?" He flipped the packet across the table. Tim picked it up and looked at the label.

"Trouble with your digestion?" he asked.

"I'll say. Got an ulcer, I fancy. Most drivers end up with an ulcer."

Tim pushed the packet back. "Then why on earth do you eat all this fried stuff? It's the worst thing for ulcers."

"What else is there to eat?" The driver was astounded. "Use your eyes, mate. Take a dekko at the ruddy board. What else is there to eat? You tell me that."

Three hours later Tim followed the odd-job boy upstairs to a first-floor room in the Swan at Rockley. A decent enough room, clean, comfortable-looking bed. Stage One completed, he thought, dropping the borrowed suitcase on the floor. A

E

good wash and brush-up, and then to work. He became aware of the odd-job boy lingering in the doorway with one hand extended in a deeply significant manner.

Oh well, Tim thought, shrugging his shoulders, no point in economising on the ha'porth of tar. Might as well establish myself here and now as a citizen of ample means.

"There'll be nothing further at the moment, my lad," he said in a lordly fashion, plunging his hand into his pocket and drawing out some coins. He selected a sixpence, pondered for a brief moment, rejected it and picked up a shilling. "Here you are."

The boy looked at the coin with contempt, raised his eyebrows and departed, banging the door behind him with unnecessary force.

"Cheeky devil," Tim said aloud. "Spoiled, like all the younger generation." He flung himself down full-length on the bed, tired from his studying, from the jolting, the cramped mode of travel. As he closed his eyes for a quick nap he remembered all of a sudden that he had completely forgotten to make a note of the name and address of the driver, the fellow with the ulcers.

"Yes, this morning, if at all possible." The solicitor's voice sounded urgent in Gina Thorson's ear.

"Is it about the new will?" she asked.

"No, not exactly. I've had a draft will typed, I'll be bringing it out with me for Mr. Mallinson's approval, but it's something else I want to discuss with him. Tell him it's the other matter he raised yesterday afternoon, he'll know what it is, tell him it's important."

"Dr. Burnett hasn't called in yet this morning," Gina said with a note of anxiety. "I really ought to ask his permission——"

"I won't keep Mr. Mallinson long." The solicitor swept objection determinedly aside. "I'm in court at eleven, and I'll probably be there all afternoon as well. I'm afraid it will have to be this morning."

"Just a moment then. I'll ask Mrs. Parkes." She laid down the receiver and ran upstairs to find the nurse.

"I don't know that I can allow it." Mrs. Parkes shook her head, looking rather grim. "Not without Doctor's permission. There'd be the witnesses to get together, people tramping in and out of the bedroom——"

"Oh, it isn't to get the new will signed, that isn't why he wants to come."

"It isn't? Are you sure?" Mrs. Parkes put up a hand and touched her top lip with her finger.

"Quite sure," Gina said with a touch of impatience. "It's about something else, some other business matter they were discussing yesterday, he told me so. Look, he's waiting on the phone, I'll have to tell him yes or no. Is he to come or not?"

Mrs. Parkes nodded. "Very well then, as long as he keeps it short. Actually," she added as if conceding a point, "Mr. Mallinson seems very bright this morning, I think it did him a lot of good to see Mr. Kenneth yesterday." But Gina was already running off down the stairs.

Half an hour later Mrs. Parkes showed the solicitor into old Mr. Mallinson's room.

"What's all this then?" Mr. Mallinson asked. He looked better this morning, the solicitor noted, more colour in his cheeks, eyes bright and alert. "Some query about the will? I thought I made it all plain enough."

Mrs. Parkes drew a chair forward and the solicitor sat down beside the bed.

"One or two small queries," he said smoothly. "Nothing very difficult, just a couple of minor points to be ironed out, details about the minor bequests. You can look at the draft now and we'll go over it, I'll have it typed to-day and I'll bring it over to-morrow or the day after so that we can get it signed and witnessed. But that isn't really what I came to see you about." He glanced at Mrs. Parkes who was fussing with the curtains.

"You can leave that now, Mrs. Parkes," Mr. Mallinson

said with a trace of irritation. She turned and gave the solicitor a level look.

"Please be very careful not to tire Mr. Mallinson. Dr. Burnett wouldn't be at all pleased if——"

"I won't stay long," the solicitor promised. "Ten or fifteen minutes at the most." He waited till the door had closed behind her.

"A good soul," Henry Mallinson said. "But inclined to treat me like a child." He smiled. "Like all nurses." He raised himself against the pillows. "Well now, what was it you wanted to discuss so urgently?"

"The other matter. The money you propose to invest in the business of your elder son. I made a number of enquiries by telephone after I left you yesterday afternoon." He gave a tiny shake of his head.

"What do you mean?" Mallinson asked sharply. "The firm's sound enough, isn't it? Kenneth told me——"

"*Sound* is hardly the word I'd choose. Not by a long chalk." The solicitor's eyes assessed the old man's face, weighing the effect of his words. "Unless your son manages to raise a considerable amount of money within the next day or two, the firm will face bankruptcy. In the circumstances I can hardly advise——"

"Are you absolutely certain?" Mallinson broke in, sitting upright.

"There's no doubt about it, I'm afraid." The solicitor opened his brief-case and took out a folded paper. "I made a few notes of the figures involved. I can go into the matter more thoroughly of course within the next day or two, I can send someone up north to look into matters if you wish." He unfolded the paper and handed it to the old man. "But I have my contacts, you know, and they were very definite. If you'd just run your eye over those figures, you'll see what the position is. I certainly couldn't advise you to make any kind of investment in the firm."

"I see." Mallinson stared down at the figures. Breathing quite steady, the solicitor noted, colour still good.

"I take it you still wish to go ahead with the new will?" he asked. Or does what I have told you make any difference? his tone implied. Do you still wish to leave half your fortune to a son who has clearly shown he cannot manage money?

Thought moved rapidly across Mallinson's face. "Yes, of course I'll go ahead with the new will," he said sharply. "And with the investment. Exactly as I proposed yesterday."

The solicitor uttered a sound of protest. "Surely not——"

"I know what I'm doing," Mallinson said. "What's thirty thousand pounds to me? No son of mine is going into a bankruptcy court. The money will put Kenneth on his feet again, he'll pull out of this situation. It's only temporary, it could happen to any firm without sufficient capital."

It could never have happened to you, the solicitor thought, not even in your early days, you could never have allowed things to come to such a pass.

"Very well, then," he said with disapproval. "If you insist."

"I do insist," Mallinson said. "I most emphatically insist. It's my money, I can do as I please with it." He felt a sudden immense, irrational pleasure in the extravagance of his gesture, seeing it as a handshake between Kenneth and himself, the action that would atone for the past, wipe out in a single splendid stroke all the bitterness, all the resentment.

The solicitor sighed. "I take it you'll wish to attach some conditions to the money?"

"No conditions," Mallinson said, still borne up by that magnificent wave of absurd generosity. "Don't go inventing any fancy restrictions of your own. There are to be no strings attached to the money, so get on with it." His breathing was a little more agitated now, his colour a trifle heightened.

You'll regret this in a day or two, the solicitor thought grimly, recognising the old man's emotion for what it was, a sudden uncharacteristic impulse that would almost certainly die away before many days had passed. He would delay matters as long as possible, give the old man time to come to his senses.

"The will." Mallinson stretched out a hand. "Have you got the draft there? Let me have a look at it. Some query about the minor bequests, you said?" His voice was firm again, his agitation appeared to have subsided.

"Miss Thorson," the solicitor said. "Your secretary. I have a query about her, for one. She is not of course mentioned in your present will as she wasn't in your employment when it was drawn up. And you haven't instructed me to make any mention of her in the new will. I wondered if you had simply forgotten her? You've remembered all the rest of your staff here."

"Yes, it was an oversight. I must leave her something, she's a good hard-working girl. But she hasn't been with me all that long." Mallinson considered the matter. "A couple of hundred pounds should be enough." His generosity appeared to be fading already, the solicitor thought, the old man was reverting to form. "Make it two hundred and fifty. If she is still in my employ of course at the time of my death." He spoke the words now as if the notion of his death had receded into the misty future, as if it were a mere technical term, nothing that would ever translate itself into reality. "Yes, two hundred and fifty will be ample."

"And your godson, young Norman Foster? He's down for a thousand in the present will but you made some mention of increasing the figure. Do you want it increased or not?"

Mallinson made a dismissing movement with his hand.

"No, let it stand at a thousand. A good round figure. It would only spoil him to give him more." Completely back to normal, the solicitor thought, let it go another day or two and I fancy we shall take quite a different view of the investment in Kenneth's moribund firm.

A minute or two later Mrs. Parkes knocked firmly at the door, turning the handle even before the old man's voice had told her to enter.

"Will you be much longer, sir?" she asked the solicitor.

"Doctor Burnett won't be at all pleased if Mr. Mallinson is over-tired."

"I'm just going." He gathered up his papers and slipped them into his briefcase. He glanced at the old man. "I'll be over in two or three days with the will, we'll get it signed then." That would give Mallinson time to regret his instructions about the investment.

Mrs. Parkes came back from seeing the solicitor out.

"Time to take your tablet, Mr. Mallinson. Would you like something hot to drink with it?" She ran a rapid eye over her patient. He looked surprisingly well and spry after his discussion.

"No, I'll just have a glass of water, then I think I'll take a little nap." He gave her a sudden boyish grin. "I want to be fit to take a nice long walk along the corridor after lunch."

Mrs. Parkes handed him a tablet and the glass.

"By the way," Mallinson said, smiling at her, "you're not forgotten in the new will. I thought you'd like to know." He sipped the water, looking at her over the rim of the glass. "It's quite a respectable sum of money. You'll be able to put your feet up and take a good long rest when you get it." He set the glass down on the table with a little bang. "Not that I intend you to get it for many a long year yet."

"It's very good of you, sir." Mrs. Parkes looked down at the coverlet, not wanting her eyes to meet those of her employer. "I hope you'll be spared to us all for many years." What good will a respectable sum of money be to me when I've lost my only son? she asked herself with a treacherous stab of resentment. Mr. Mallinson is old, he's had his life. There is my son, still a young man, my grandsons, scarcely more than babies. And myself, with perhaps a quarter of a century of lonely life ahead of me.

If Mr. Mallinson simply failed to wake up one morning, if he stretched out his hand one sleepless night and took an extra tablet, reached out again, befogged by the wandering half-dozing mind of the old, if he took two, three, four tablets . . . by mistake of course . . . half-doped, not knowing quite what he was doing . . . if he slipped into a long, an endless sleep, into peace and rest . . . who would be the worse for it? . . . Might not many individuals be the better for it? . . . Younger, stronger, more kindly individuals, with a right to a full and happy life, a life without loneliness?

She took a sudden step backwards, appalled by the direction of her thoughts.

"I'll look in a little later on, just to see if you're asleep," she said with over-compensating solicitude. "Then we'll see about some lunch. Cook has some very nice fish. You'll like that. And a hothouse peach."

Mr. Mallinson allowed his eyes to close. Outside in the garden a bird sang, clear and joyful, warning off predators, establishing his right to territory, to air and space and the drifting breezes under a blue and white sky.

"As long as there's no cabbage," Mr. Mallinson said sleepily. "I detest cabbage."

Mrs. Parkes turned the door handle and let herself softly out of the room.

Downstairs in her neat office Gina Thorson sat at her desk. She had attended to the morning's post, had dealt with such matters as she was qualified to handle alone, had placed in an orderly pile the letters which later on she would discuss with Mr. David when he called in on one of his frequent visits. Time hung a little heavily on her hands now, with old Mr. Mallinson temporarily out of action.

There had been time in the last day or two to tidy out all the drawers in the desk, time to go through the filing-cabinets, time to sit and think.

A little way off she heard the small mingling of sounds as Mrs. Parkes showed the solicitor to the door. A new will . . . already made out . . . due to be witnessed to-morrow or the day after that . . . She sat up suddenly. She hadn't been mentioned in the old will, she was quite certain of that, Mr. Mallinson hadn't even known of her existence when it was drawn up. But a new will . . . For the first time the thought ran across her mind, startling, disturbing. Was it possible that she was mentioned in the new will?

No, of course not, another part of her mind answered at once. You haven't been here all that long, you are by no means indispensable, the old man could get a new secretary if he wanted one, simply by lifting the telephone receiver and dialling the number of a Hallborough agency. And you're not all that special, she told herself with wry honesty, not all that remarkably well qualified, not all that experienced, not astonishingly intelligent or poised or even well-dressed. Her thoughts came round again full circle to the nagging question of her wardrobe and her visit to Richard's parents. A visit settled now beyond the hope of escape.

Her ears registered automatically the discreet sound of Mrs. Parkes going back up the stairs. Just suppose she *had* been remembered in the new will . . . and after all, why not? All the other staff had been remembered in the old will and would most certainly not be omitted from the new. The old man had a habit of referring to his bequests from time to time. 'I haven't forgotten you,' he'd say to an employee, 'there'll be something for you when I'm gone.' Strengthening allegiance, banishing restlessness, binding them all together with ties of mutual interest, the powerful weapon of an old, rich man.

Why should she be left out? She did her work well and conscientiously, she never took a day off, pleading a headache or a digestive upset, she was reliable, efficient. She began to play with the notion of the bequest, imagining the amount. A hundred pounds, at least a hundred, a man in Mr. Mallinson's position wouldn't demean himself by dictating a sum so lowly as fifty or seventy-five.

She thought of herself with a whole hundred pounds in crisp new notes, walking in through the door of that exclusive shop in Hallborough, seeing the suède coat, the skirt, the cashmere sweater being wrapped in tissue paper, laid in elegant boxes.

What was a hundred pounds to old Mr. Mallinson? Noth-

ing and less than nothing. No, if he remembered her at all
—and it was now quite inconceivable that he shouldn't, it
would be something more than that, a hundred and fifty, two
hundred perhaps . . . With a hundred and fifty she could buy
new luggage as well, a long dressing-gown of pale fleecy
wool, exquisite nightwear, lingerie . . . With two hundred,
two hundred and fifty, there would be money over, money to
be put away for a trousseau, a reassuring nest-egg to give
her peace of mind.

Mrs. Parkes coming down the stairs again, going out
through the front door into the garden. Gina came out of
her day-dream and glanced at the clock. Still some little
time to go before lunch. That meant that Mrs. Parkes was
taking her daily constitutional in the fresh air, the old man
must be alone now, lying back against the pillows with his
eyes closed perhaps, trying to doze before his tray made its
appearance.

She stood up and pushed her chair back sharply. He was
a very great deal better to-day, the whole household knew
that. There was really no reason at all why he shouldn't be
allowed a peep at one or two of the more interesting letters
from the morning post. He would enjoy the feeling that he
was still in contact with the hectic world of business, still
able to put his signature to a reply, to let people know he
was alive and kicking.

She gathered up a few letters at random. I could ask him
for that rise now, she thought, all notions of the fanciful
legacy vanishing from her mind. It wouldn't distress him in
any way. She'd been at Whitegates long enough to justify
a rise. And he'd be pleased with life at this moment, feeling
so much better, his affairs nicely in order after the visit from
the solicitor, his mind at rest after his reunion with his
elder son. Yes, this was an ideal moment to make her request. It wouldn't tire him in any way. All he had to do was
listen and say Yes.

She walked briskly out of the office, went silently and
swiftly up the stairs.

CHAPTER VI

MR MALLINSON wasn't asleep. He lay with his eyes closed, trying to drift into unconsciousness, but disturbing thoughts flickered across the surface of his mind, destroying the possibility of rest. On the verge of bankruptcy, the solicitor had said, and a man like that didn't utter such words lightly. I'm doing well, Kenneth had said, he'd sat there by the bed and looked his father straight in the eye, telling his lies. Was that why he had come? Not to make peace with his flesh and blood, not to allow old wounds to heal over, but just to grab what he could, a lump sum now to save his tottering firm, half of a great fortune later on when the sheet was drawn over his father's face? Was that what they all wanted? Simply his money? Were they all waiting for him to die? Get what they could while he was alive, share out the proceeds when he was dead?

He clasped his hands together under the sheet. I worked hard for my money, he thought with a wash of pity for that far-off young man driving himself on day and night towards the goal of prestige and riches. I had no advantages, neither birth nor education, nor a single helping hand. I had only my native intelligence, my determination to succeed, the strength of my hands and my brain. And now they are all gathering round me like vultures for the kill, smiling at me, pretending solicitude, but waiting for me to die.

I could do what the solicitor wants, he thought suddenly, I could refuse Kenneth the investment, let the old will stand. Or make a new will, strike out all the legacies, leave the lot to research or charity, cheat them all of their greedy expectations, let them do what I had to do, start from scratch, sweat their own stony way towards the top—if they've got the guts, the nerve, the ambition.

He felt suddenly, appallingly, alone. There wasn't a single living soul who really cared whether he lived or died. Even his wife hadn't loved him. She'd been dazzled for a brief time by his success, his drive, his refusal to take No for an answer. He had snatched her up from her friends and family, almost from the arms of another man, he had put a ring on her finger, borne her off to the altar, allowing her no time to think, to protest . . . but there had been time enough afterwards. Time for the beautiful face to develop lines of unhappiness, of disciplined resignation, an acceptance of the way things were, the way they were inescapably always going to be.

Behind his closed lids he saw the portrait downstairs, over the fireplace, the face turned a little to one side as if attempting by ever so little to avert the gaze from painful reality, the hands loosely clasped, denying any further striving, any positive thrust of action.

Kenneth never even liked me, he thought with a savage stab of sorrow, never liked me, let alone loved me. My elder son. And David—always amenable, always compliant— how much of that compliance was affection? How much was knowing where his bread was buttered? I know Kenneth as one knows an adversary, he thought with sudden realisation, but David I have never known at all. Because I imagined he was on my side. I never turned my head to look him in the face, I have never seen what lies behind those acquiescing, friendly-seeming eyes.

A knock sounded at the door. He moved his lips in a moment's irritation. Mrs. Parkes again with some sudden notion about a sauce or a dessert for lunch.

"Come in," he called irritably.

But it was Gina Thorson, glancing at him with a trace of apprehension.

"I hope I'm not disturbing you, Mr. Mallinson." She gave him a tentative smile. "But Mrs. Parkes told me you were so much better to-day. I thought perhaps you might

like to sign one or two letters. I thought perhaps you'd
want to see these." She gestured with the hand that held a
small sheaf of papers. "In the morning post. Some of the
more interesting mail." She smiled again, even more uncertainly. "I thought perhaps it would do you good."

"Oh, you did, did you?" He gave her a shrewd glance.
"You thought all that?" The girl looked nervous about
something. He extended a hand impatiently. "If you're
going to give me those letters, then give them to me."

"Oh, yes—certainly. Here you are." She handed them
over. "The top one, that's from our Paris agency, they're
putting through the contract——"

"Yes, I can see they are." He ran his eye over the letter,
over the second letter, the third. "This is all routine stuff.
Surely Mr. David can see to all this?"

"Oh, yes, of course, I just thought you'd——" She stood
there at a loss, trying to think of something interesting to
say about the correspondence. Mr. Mallinson suddenly
ceased his rustling of the papers and uttered a sharp exclamation.

"What's this? Why wasn't I told about this?" He looked
up at her with anger in his eyes, he waved a sheet of paper
at her. "This woman—Stallard's widow, I didn't know
she'd been making trouble. You never said a word to me
about this. I should have been told."

A flush appeared on Gina's cheekbones. How unutterably
stupid of her—she'd picked up the papers at random, she
ought to have taken more care.

"I'm sorry, I wasn't supposed to let you see that. Doctor
Burnett said you weren't to be shown anything that might
distress you. Mr. David is dealing with Mrs. Stallard."

"Distress me! I'm not a child! I have a right to know
what's going on! It's a damn sight more distressing to know
things are being kept from me! What is she after? Money,
I suppose." They all wanted money, every last one of
them. He glanced back at the letter again. An unfortunate
affair. No doubt at all now, Victor Stallard had been in-

nocent all along. But to go and commit suicide in that spineless way.

Even now, Mallinson could think of the man only with contempt. If he'd stood his ground, if he'd persevered, taken steps to prove his innocence, persisted with appeals—even if they'd all failed, if he'd had to stay behind bars and serve his sentence, he'd be alive now, he'd be entitled to massive compensation, he could have made something of the rest of his life. Above all things Mallinson detested a man who turned his toes up when things went wrong. If that had been me, he thought savagely, I'd have put up a good fight, I wouldn't have lain down and died.

"I don't know what Mr. David is proposing," Gina said, clasping her hands together. "He has an appointment to see Mrs. Stallard to-day, she's going to see him in the Hallborough office. I believe he's going to discuss the question of compensation—or a pension. Mrs. Stallard has a son, I don't know if you remember."

Oh yes, he remembered all right. He felt suddenly very tired, all at once he lost interest in the sordid Stallard business. Let David deal with it, he certainly didn't want to be bothered seeing the wretched woman, listening to her tearful accusations. Burnett was right after all, he should be spared these distressing matters. He dropped the papers on the coverlet.

"You should watch what you're doing," he said abruptly. "Pay attention to doctor's orders. Burnett knows what he's about. If he says I'm not to be shown things, then I'm not to be shown them."

Gina stooped to gather up the papers, disconcerted by the old man's change of front.

"Yes, I'll try to remember." She took a deep breath, knowing the time was anything but propitious now to ask for a rise but driven by desperation to make her request. If she left it till later it would be too late. He might issue orders that she wasn't to disturb him at all until he was up and about again, he might easily tell Mrs. Parkes to keep her out of the sick-room. And she had to have the money, there was no escaping the fact.

"I wonder," she said, and her voice grew steady with the calm of complete recklessness, "if I could raise the matter of my salary. I've been here some time now, and I feel I might ask you for a rise."

His mouth opened slightly, he was looking at her with something like astonishment.

"There are things I have to buy," she went on, and then abandoned that line at once, feeling it rested on an appeal to pity and not as it ought to, on right and merit. "Secretarial salaries are rising all the time," she said, a little more boldly, surprised and pleased to hear the calm reasonableness of her own tone. "I feel I'm worth more than I'm being paid." She saw at that instant on what shaky ground she stood. He had only to say, 'Then take your things and go somewhere where they'll pay you what you believe you're worth.' But he wouldn't want to be bothered with a change of secretaries now, when he was ill. Aware of the chance she was taking she plunged on. "I could easily get more elsewhere."

In spite of his irritation at being badgered for money by a slip of a girl when he was lying here defenceless in bed, Mallinson felt his lips curve into a smile. She had nerve after all, this Thorson girl, she was prepared to fight for what she wanted, not like Stallard, turning his face to the wall.

Gina saw the trace of a smile and felt immediately heartened.

"I wouldn't have chosen this moment to ask," she said, "but I do rather need some more money right away."

"You have a good home here," Mallinson said. "You have very few expenses that I can see. You're paid the market rate for the job." Mallinson's had never paid less than the market rate, he'd always been proud of that. He flourished his customary weapon. "And there'll be something for you in my will. I haven't forgotten you." He saw her eyes open sharply at that, he saw his shot had registered. "I value your services," he said smoothly. "Quite a respectable little sum I've left you. If you're still in my employment, of course. You understand that?"

Yes, she understood that, and all its implications.

"It's very good of you," she said formally. "I'm very grateful. But about the rise——"

Like a terrier with a bone, he thought, half-admiringly. Not going to let go till she'd got what she wanted.

"And just how much did you have in mind?" he asked on a teasing note.

"Another two hundred a year," she said at once. With an extra four pounds a week she could mortgage her salary, buy the clothes on account, so much down and so much a month, she could easily manage the payments. And with an impressive address like Whitegates, there'd be no difficulty about credit at the shop, they'd let her have the things right away.

"Two hundred pounds!" He was astounded at her cheek, imagining she'd been going to suggest fifty and would have taken twenty-five. "I'll give you another ten shillings a week," he said, letting himself lean back on the pillows to indicate that the matter was now at an end.

Ten shillings a week! Tears came into her eyes, hot and stinging. Ten shillings would buy nothing, nothing at all.

"I do have to buy some things," she said desperately, relinquishing the appeal of right and merit, falling back on pity.

He let out an impatient breath. "Then you'll have to do what everyone else has to do. Save up for them. If you can't afford them, then you'll have to manage without." What things could she possibly be in such need of? Some silly feminine fripperies no doubt, extravagant nonsense, a complete waste of money.

"Always pay cash," he said, unable to resist a sterling piece of advice. "Never get into debt. Pay your way or go without."

All this talk of money suddenly made something click in his mind. He remembered the date on the letter heading. "It's young Foster's birthday to-morrow, isn't it?" he said abruptly.

Gina was jerked out of her misery. "Young Foster?" she asked, puzzled.

"Yes, young Foster, Norman Foster, the gardener's lad, my godson. You know who he is." Mallinson was growing more impatient every second. "Garage apprentice, you know him."

"Oh yes, of course."

"It's his birthday to-morrow. Tell him to come in and see me when he gets in from work. Call in at the cottage this evening and give him the message. I always remember his birthday." He liked the lad, a promising boy, good with his hands, had a natural feeling for engines, might take him into the firm later on. "Eighteen this time, I believe." Might give the lad a pound or two more this year. A bit of a milestone, the eighteenth birthday. Not too much more, of course, wouldn't do to start spoiling the lad, give him fancy notions. Ten pounds perhaps. Or five . . . He'd see.

He turned his head. Gina was still standing there, looking down at him as if she was about to burst into tears.

"Don't forget," he said sharply. "Call in at the cottage this evening."

"No, I won't forget. I'll tell him to come in and see you to-morrow."

"That will be all then." He frowned at her. "I was supposed to be having a nap before lunch." Much chance of a nap there'd be now. Mrs. Parkes would be rustling along the corridor with a tray at any minute. "It's like Charing Cross Station in here," he said crossly. "Be sure to close the door after you."

She saw that it was totally useless. She left the room and went at once into her own room a little along the corridor. She sat on the bed with her cheeks flushed, biting her lip.

Ten shillings a week! Mallinson with his vast fortune!

F

That was what he valued her at! He thought all he had to do was play his old trick, dangle the prospect of a legacy before her and she'd be glad to stay. She sat upright and clenched her hands. The legacy . . . there was, after all, still the legacy . . .

One o'clock. "You can clear off now for your sandwiches, young Norman." The garage foreman wiped his hands on a rag. "You can get back at that gearbox after you've had your dinner, I shall want the whole job finished this afternoon, it's been promised for four o'clock."

"Right you are." Norman laid down the part on which he had been working, setting it with tender care on a newspaper spread out on the floor. He went over to the sink and washed his hands, drying them on a roller towel.

"Not much to say for yourself to-day," the foreman observed. Norman raised his shoulders and let them drop again. He took his jacket from a hook and thrust his arms into the sleeves.

"Worrying about those payments, are you?" the foreman said. All the same, these lads, set their heart on a motorbike or an old car, talked their dads into signing the forms, then found they couldn't keep up the instalments, not on an apprentice's wages. He knew, he'd been an apprentice himself once. He cast a backward look at his first love, the old Norton bike, taken him many a good mile that old bike had before it breathed its last.

"I'll manage," Norman said, uncommunicative. His birthday to-morrow, surely the old man would cough up a tenner at the very least. He was unaware that his face was creased into a massive frown. "I'm not worrying." Not much, he wasn't. "I'll get the money all right."

"You wouldn't go doing anything silly," the foreman said suddenly, not liking the look on the lad's face. "If the payments are more than you can afford, better to turn it in altogether. You can always get another machine later on, when you're out of your time."

Norman flung him an astounded glance. When he was out
of his time! Another three years that would be! Three
whole years without his beloved bike! Impossible to contemplate.

"I'll manage," he said again. "I'll have the money the day
after to-morrow for certain. More than enough." He dug his
hand into his pocket and took out a packet of sandwiches,
strode forcefully off towards the open air, to eat his lunch in
peace and quiet, away from probing questions.

"Where are you going to get it from then?" the foreman
called after him. Young fools, some of these lads. Set their
hearts on something, a bike, a girl, playing the horses, land
up in trouble as soon as look round.

"What's that to you?" Norman said savagely under his
breath. He made his way round the back of the sheds and
sat down on top of an old oil drum, out of sight of the foreman and the other men. He tore open the packet of sandwiches and began to eat, not tasting the good cold beef
smeared with home-made pickle, staring before him at a
vision of old Mallinson looking up to greet him with a smile
and stretching out a hand that held—that *must* hold, surely
—fifteen pounds at the very least.

"Mr. Mallinson is just having his lunch," Mrs. Parkes
said with a note of disapproval. Her patient really shouldn't
be disturbed over his nice plate of white fish and lightly
steamed vegetables, Mrs. David ought to know better, young
as she was.

Carole Mallinson smiled at the nurse. She carried a great
sheaf of flowers in her arms. Always bringing those huge
bunches of blooms, Mrs. Parkes thought with irritation.
As if we didn't have enormous gardens here ourselves, vast
glass-houses, as if we couldn't supply every bud and blossom
anybody could conceivably want.

"Such lovely flowers," she said bending her head and
sniffing delicately at the papery heads. "Shall I put them
in water for you?"

"I'll just slip up for a minute to see my father-in-law," Carole said, smiling with determination. "I won't tire him. I'd just like to give him these myself, and say hallo." She began to move towards the stairs. "I meant to call in earlier but I was delayed in the shops."

Mrs. Parkes knew when she was beaten. "Very well, then," she said, yielding. "As long as it *is* only for a few minutes. We've had the solicitor here this morning, we can't allow Mr. Mallinson to have too many visitors all at once."

Carole paused for an instant. "The solicitor?" she asked lightly.

"Yes." Mrs. Parkes's manner became important. "About the new will." She saw how Mrs. David's eyes flicked a little at that. Mr. Kenneth would be in the new will, of course. And the more there is for him, the less there is for you, my girl, she thought. Didn't altogether care for young Mrs. David, pleasant and polite as she invariably was. An eye for the main chance, young Mrs. David. She'd presided over many a sick-bed in her time, had Mrs. Parkes, used to the ways of anxious relatives, prided herself on being able to recognise genuine feeling when she saw it, able to recognise the other kind too, seen it often enough. It almost always came smiling out from behind great bunches of flowers, quite a trademark really, those flowers. People wouldn't buy them if they knew how it gave them away to the trained eye.

"Not signed yet, of course, the new will," Mrs. Parkes said as they both moved forward again, side by side up the broad stairs. "Two or three days, the solicitor said. He just brought the draft for approval this morning."

"Two or three days," Mrs. David echoed, with an odd note in her voice.

"Mr. Kenneth has been here too, as I expect you know," Mrs. Parkes said smoothly. "Very pleased to see him, Mr. Mallinson was. Quite bucked him up. I expect you've seen Mr. Kenneth yourself, of course." She knew all about the family quarrel, had heard it all many a time from Cook and the other servants, she knew Mrs. David hadn't even so much as met Mr. Kenneth, he hadn't even come to the wedding, though he'd sent a set of goblets, very handsome too, she'd heard.

"No, not yet," Carole said, smiling. "There's plenty of time. I daresay he'll be staying several days."

"I daresay," Mrs. Parkes said. I'd like to be present at that meeting when it does take place, she thought, be interesting to see how they square up to each other. They had reached the door of the bedroom. Mrs. Parkes gave a brief knock and turned the handle.

"Mrs. David to see you, just for a moment," she said as they entered. "With such beautiful flowers, as usual."

The old man gave his daughter-in-law a smile of genuine pleasure, Mrs. Parkes saw. Fond of her he was, really fond of her. She permitted herself the tiniest sniff, drew forward a chair for the visitor.

"Not too long now," she said pleasantly, firmly. She reached out and took the empty dinner-plate. "You liked the fish then?"

"How are you, my dear?" Mr. Mallinson said, paying no attention to the nurse. "You're looking even prettier than usual."

Carole smiled, stooped and kissed him on the cheek.

"How are you?" She patted his hand. "Feeling much better to-day?" She laid the flowers on the table. "Would you be kind enough to see these are put in water, Mrs. Parkes?"

"Certainly." Behaves like a duchess, Mrs. Parkes thought, giving the young woman her due. For all no-one knows where she came from, for all she was a complete nobody as far as anyone can tell, she's got the manner and the appearance, I'll give her that. "I'll see they're attended to right away. I'll bring up your fruit now, Mr. Mallinson." She gave the door a little bang as she closed it behind her.

"And what have you been doing with yourself this morning?" Henry Mallinson was glad to exchange idle chit-chat with his pretty young daughter-in-law. At least she wasn't going to ask him for money like everyone else. She just came to see him because she liked him. Such a nice, sensible, unspoiled girl, his daughter-in-law, so refreshingly open and affectionate in these self-seeking days.

Ten minutes later Carole Mallinson walked out through the front door of Whitegates. She paused by her car, turned and lifted a hand at Mrs. Parkes who was standing firmly in the doorway, watching her go.

"I'm afraid Mrs. Mallinson is out." The uniformed maid held the front door of Tall Trees only half open, not altogether caring for the appearance of the young man confronting her on the steps. Her practised eye made a swift assessment of his face, his hair, his clothes. Not at all the type of visitor usually admitted to the house. In spite of the attempt at a respectable appearance, there was a suggestion of wildness, of the devil-may-care about his looks. The dark suit a couple of sizes too large, the shoes a couple of sizes too small, the hair a little too long and unruly. But it was the eyes that really sounded a warning bell. Hungry-looking eyes, bright and calculating. Gave her quite a turn, as she told Cook later. As if he wanted something from Tall Trees and didn't mean to go away until he'd got it.

Tim Jefford gave the girl one of his charming smiles.

"I can wait," he said easily. Close on one o'clock. Carole would probably return for lunch at any moment. The maid hadn't said her mistress would be out all day. He took a step forward. "I'll just come inside and wait."

The maid withdrew a couple of paces and began to slide the door forward. "I'm afraid not. I can't go letting total strangers into the house. I've never set eyes on you before."

Tim smiled again, more winningly. "I'm not a total stranger, I'm an old friend of Mrs. Mallinson's."

A likely story, the girl thought, allowing the notion to disclose itself in the expression of her face. The door continued its advance, it closed firmly, inexorably. Tim stood for a moment gazing at the hostile wood. No sound of foot-steps moving away at the other side, she was waiting for him to clear off.

He turned and walked noisily down the gravel path, then suddenly darted off into the shrubbery, doubling back round the side of the house. Ah—an open garage over there—Carole would be out in a car, she'd have to drive into the garage, he'd stand over here, a little to one side, out of view.

He took up his position under the branches of a prunus, hoping she wasn't going to be much longer. He was feeling very empty indeed. A great many hours seemed to have dragged by since the magnificent fry-up in the transport café had disappeared before the onslaught of his knife and fork. He had a pretty good idea that the food at Tall Trees would be first-class. Carole had certainly done well for her-self.

He caught the sound of approaching wheels, a car slack-ening speed as it neared the gates, turning into the drive, making for the garage. A nice little foreign car, trim and fast, and Carole's face glimpsed through the glass—as pretty as ever but with a thoughtful, controlled air that certainly hadn't been her habitual expression back in the old days in Chelsea.

He waited till he heard the car door click open, then he stepped inside the garage. She was just extending one slim leg, about to lever herself out from behind the wheel.

"Hallo, Carole," he said softly, "It's been a long time."

CHAPTER VII

CAROLE'S HEAD jerked round, her eyes blinked open in sharp surprise. Her mouth dropped in a look of naked apprehen-sion. Tim took a couple of steps forward. He was beginning to enjoy himself. He put a hand on the car door, drawing it back.

"Allow me," he said graciously.

Carole remained seated. She had got her expression back under control again, he saw. She gave him a long level look.

"What do you want? Why have you come here?"

He raised his eyebrows. "Aren't you pleased to see me? After all this time? I've come all the way from London expressly to pay a call on you."

"I've nothing to say to you." What a lovely jaw-line, she has, he thought suddenly. He'd forgotten that beautiful clear line, the perfect sweep of bone. "I suggest you go right back to London," she said in a cool, precise voice. "I'm not in the least interested in renewing our acquaintance."

He laughed with genuine amusement. "Acquaintance," he said, lingering over the word. "That's a good name for it. Very good." He reached down and took her hand, giving her a little upward pull. "Come on, Carole, give me some lunch. I'm going up to Whitegates to call on your father-in-law later on. You wouldn't want me to have to tell him how remarkably inhospitable you were to an old friend, now, would you?"

She allowed herself to be drawn out of the car. She bent down to pick up her bag and gloves from the seat, she straightened herself and adjusted the set of her jacket about her slim shoulders. Discipline, he thought admiringly, she's taught herself discipline in her new life.

"All right," she said calmly, facing him in the narrow space, "I'll give you lunch. I don't suppose you've had a square meal in many a long day."

He smiled at her. "That's my girl, Carole."

"I'm not your girl," she said softly. "Not any more."

He raised his shoulders. "But it brings it all back," he said. "Standing here, looking at you like this. It all comes back. Your father-in-law might find it very interesting, my simple tale of the old days and the long and happy hours I spent with Carole Stewart, before she found ease and good fortune as Mrs. David Mallinson. I'm not much of a talker," he said deprecatingly, "but I daresay I could hold the old man's interest for an hour or so with my artless reminiscences."

She turned and began to make her way out of the garage, towards the front door. He fell into step beside her.

"Do you have wine with your lunch, Carole?" he asked. "Do funds run to that? I imagine they do. I imagine they run to quite a number of good things."

She pressed the doorbell, making no reply. She stood glancing calmly about her at the garden until the maid opened the door.

"Would you lay another place for lunch?" she asked the girl. Tim followed her inside, giving the maid a tiny triumphant flick of his eyes.

"And now," Carole said briskly, in a very different tone, ten minutes later, when the maid had brought in the soup and left the room again. "Just what is all this about you going up to Whitegates to see my father-in-law?" She lifted her spoon and took a sip of the hot soup. "Come on, Tim, cards on the table. Exactly what are you up to?"

He grinned at her. "That's better. That's more like my old Carole. I thought you were going to keep up the lady-of-the-manor act indefinitely. I was finding it rather wearing." He tasted the soup. "Very good. But I imagined you'd have something a little more exotic. Caviare or some other delicacy. Smoked salmon perhaps."

She gave him a little smile. "But then I didn't know you were coming. You shouldn't have taken me by surprise like this, Tim. If you'd let me know you intended lunching with me, I'd have had time to get you something special."

"I'm staying in Rockley a day or two," he said. "I daresay I'll be lunching with you again. You'll be able to lay on the caviare next time. I have business in Rockley, you see." He raised his eyes to hers, frank and innocent. "I'm staying at the Swan. A quaint old hostelry. But a trifle expensive. Rather beyond my slender means."

"I might be able to do something about the slender

means," she said idly. "I suppose you absolutely *have* to see my father-in-law?"

He pulled a little face. "Well yes, I do. A matter of business, you see. We're both coin-collectors, though I'm in rather a small way, just at present. I'm sure Mr. Mallinson will be very interested in seeing a specimen I've brought him. He will probably want to buy it. Of course how much I let myself go in the matter of reminiscences might depend on exactly what you intend to do about my slender means. I rather thought you might want to help, if you possibly can. You might fancy I could spare the old man too detailed an account of the old days—in return for an active expression of your interest in my welfare."

"H'm, I see." She stretched out a delicate hand and picked up her bag from the chair beside her. "I don't keep a great deal of cash in the house." She opened the bag and took out a notecase of fine tooled leather. His eyes followed her fingers, watching her draw out the notes. "Fifteen pounds. Would that be of any assistance?"

He took the notes and put them away in his breast-pocket.

"As a token, yes. I imagine there will be something more substantial, say to-morrow? I could hold back the reminiscences till then. And the letters."

"Letters?" she said sharply, turning her head and giving him a look that reminded him all at once of the old Carole. "What letters?"

"Oh come now!" He smiled at her, raising his spoon again and beginning to drink the soup with relish. "You don't think I'd have left the letters behind?" He broke a bread roll in two. "Your father-in-law would be particularly interested in the letters, they lend a certain colour—and authenticity—to my tale."

"I never wrote you any letters," she said. She hadn't been such a fool, surely? She cast her mind back, rapidly, trying to remember.

His tone was full of rebuke. "That time you cleared out

and left me broken-hearted. After that tremendous row." He grinned, remembering that row. "When you found you couldn't live without me, when you wanted to come back. Surely you recall those letters you wrote?"

She recalled them now all right. Her jaw tightened, recalling them.

"Passionate letters." Tim nodded, consideringly. "Very lively letters. I made a point of bringing them. I thought the old man might appreciate your literary ability."

She pushed her soup plate away from her. "This is nothing but outright blackmail," she said, abandoning her previous light but wary tone. "I didn't think you'd sink to that, Tim."

He dropped his own air of easy badinage. "A case of have to, Carole," he said in his normal voice. "I'm absolutely on my beam ends. Be reasonable. You've fallen on your feet. You can spare a bit for an old friend. What's a few hundred pounds to you? Let me have it and I'll clear out, I won't bother you again."

"Won't you?" she said, staring back at him. "What about next time you're on your beam ends? And the time after that?"

"Oh come now!" he said. "I'm not as bad as all that. I'm not a professional criminal. I just want enough to let me keep on painting, so I won't have to take a job. You can't see me in a steady job now, can you, Carole? I can wait a day or two for the money."

"I can't lay my hands on a few hundred pounds just like that," she said. "But I'll have some more for you to-morrow. And the rest in a couple of days."

The maid came in to remove the soup plates.

"A fine view you have from these windows," the strange young man was saying. Finished every drop of his soup, the maid noted. But Mrs. Mallinson's plate was still almost full, looked as if it had scarcely been touched.

"Yes, thank you, I've finished," Mrs. Mallinson said in reply to her question. Looked at her as if her mind was miles away, busy with something, working something out.

"No, I'm sorry, I'm afraid it won't be possible for you to see my father." David Mallinson looked across the desk at Mrs. Stallard, neat and composed in her black suit, her face pale and determined under the brim of her black felt hat. "He isn't very well, he's not up to dealing with business matters at the moment, I'm handling everything for him."

"Not very well?" Mrs. Stallard said coldly. "My husband is dead."

David stood up and walked over to the window, turning his back a little on Mrs. Stallard, not caring to go on looking at those clothes of unrelieved black, those accusing eyes.

"I'm terribly sorry, Mrs. Stallard. You must know that." He began to walk up and down between the desk and the window, frowning, looking down at the carpet. "No-one regrets your husband's death more than I do."

Mrs. Stallard sat bolt upright, clutching her black leather handbag, watching Mr. David pacing up and down.

"Does your father regret my husband's death?" she asked.

"Of course he does. He regrets it very much indeed. We propose to make what amends lie within our power."

"Can you bring my husband back to life?" Mrs. Stallard asked. "You and your father? Does that lie within your power?"

David gave a deep sigh. He paused in his pacing. "Be reasonable, Mrs. Stallard," he said on a note of desperation. "There is nothing either my father or I can do except try to see both you and your son are provided for. A lump sum by way of compensation, we thought. And a pension of course. If we could get down to discussing the actual figures——"

"Compensation," Mrs. Stallard said. "You think money will compensate me for the loss of my husband? You think it will compensate my son for the loss of his father?"

David spread his hands out. "What else can we do? The only course open to us is to offer you money."

"I want to see your father. I'm entitled to that much. That much compensation is due to me, at least."

He sat down abruptly in his chair and leaned across the desk. "That's impossible. In my father's state of health—he mustn't be distressed or disturbed in any way. Not now."

"My husband was distressed," Mrs. Stallard said. "He was so disturbed that he took his own life. I want to see your father face to face."

"But why? What good can it possibly do you? It won't bring your husband back to life. And it can't do you any good to keep on brooding about the past. You'll injure your own health. It's far better for you to look on the whole matter reasonably, let me arrange about the money and the pension." His tone lightened. "Perhaps you'd rather I dealt with your solicitor. It would probably be better all round. He'd look after your interests. You could safely leave it all to him. If you'd let me have his name and address——"

"You don't get rid of me as easily as all that," Mrs. Stallard said. "Neither you nor your father. I insist on seeing him."

David let out a long breath. "What do you hope to gain by it?"

"Satisfaction," she said. "My own kind of satisfaction."

He moved his hands in a gesture of conciliation. "I'll have a letter made out. A letter of apology, of contrition, anything you like. I'll see he signs it. Won't that satisfy you?"

"Face to face," Mrs. Stallard said. "I'll see him face to face. I want no letter." She stood up. "I'm staying the night in Hallborough. At the Cross Keys. You can reach me there when you've fixed an appointment."

He followed her to the door. "There's no question of an appointment, you must see that." She opened the door. "If you could let me have the name of your solicitor——"

"At the Cross Keys," she said. "You can phone me. I'll be waiting."

"Your solicitor," he said again. "I think you'd find it

better——" But the door closed behind her and he heard the sound of her steps moving away, calm and forceful, along the polished corridor.

He went back to his desk and sat down, took out a cigarette and lit it. What in heaven's name was he going to do with the Stallard woman? He drew deeply on the cigarette and let out the smoke in a long stream. He frowned down at the desk, drumming his fingers on the smooth surface. He'd always prided himself on his ability to handle people. He knew he didn't have his father's keen business sense, he lacked the instinctive flair and judgment that enabled a man to rise from small beginnings to the lofty peaks of achievement, but he'd always been able to take out his one bright talent and look on it with justifiable pride. Negotiations, contracts, labour relations, any field where it was necessary to handle men and women with tact and diplomacy, in these areas he always felt at his best, speaking the right word, giving the right look, not from training or experience, but from his own native sense of how other people might be expected to react.

And with Mrs. Stallard he'd been at a complete loss. The woman wasn't open to normal approaches, she was deaf to reason, blind even to her own interests. He drew upon the cigarette again and watched the smoke spiralling out in the still air.

There was no question of allowing her to see the old man. Firstly because the doctor would never hear of it and secondly because it would be admitting fair and square that he, David, couldn't handle a really delicate matter without assistance.

What would Kenneth have done, have said? he asked himself. Would Kenneth have hit by chance on the right word, the right look?

And what on earth did Mrs. Stallard want with the old man anyway? If she was looking for a grovelling apology she was barking up the wrong tree. He propped his chin on his fist and stared ahead. Perhaps all she wanted was for the old man, just once in his life, to admit he'd been wrong. Perhaps she simply wanted to savour the experience of standing over Henry Mallinson, the autocrat, the dictator, and watch him eat his own words. As simple as that, nothing more than that.

David smiled suddenly, feeling a momentary stab of sympathy with the woman. Should he after all allow her to see his father? Not mention the visit to Dr. Burnett, just take Mrs. Stallard out to Whitegates, unleash her on the old man for three or four minutes, let her have her way? Afterwards perhaps she'd be ready to discuss the question of money, her pride satisfied, her curious taste for revenge sated.

He sighed and shook his head with a trace of regret. No, it wouldn't do, tempting as it was. He'd have to manage in some way. Just let the matter slide for a day or two perhaps, nothing more complicated than that. Twenty-four hours of her own company in a Hallborough hotel might induce a more compliant attitude in Mrs. Stallard. He stood up with sudden resolution and stubbed out his cigarette. Yes, that was what he'd do—precisely nothing, let the woman stew in her own juice for a bit, let the next move come from her . . . He stood looking down at the squashed stub in the ash-tray, thinking with a last little smiling thought of the scene that wouldn't take place, Mrs. Stallard confronting his father in the bedroom at Whitegates, the old man just once in his long life at a disadvantage.

A discreet knock at the door. His secretary putting her head inside, saying something. David came out of his thoughts with a start.

"Your wife is here, Mr. Mallinson. May she come in for a moment?"

"Oh—yes, show her in, please."

Carole came in almost at once, smiling, looking trim and pretty in her tailored suit. She came round the desk and kissed him lightly on the cheek.

"I hope you don't mind my calling in like this, but I've been shopping in Hallborough and I'm afraid I've run out of money. I left my cheque-book at home. Could you let me have a few pounds? Whatever you've got? I haven't quite finished my shopping and it'd be a nuisance to have to run out to Tall Trees just to fetch my cheque book." She gave him a coaxing smile.

David was mildly surprised. Carole had never done such a thing before. He always thought of her as a very organised person. And she was very good with money, not given to the sudden wild extravagances other men complained of in their wives. She hadn't even asked for her own bank account, she shared a joint account with him, all the details of her expenditure laid open to his inspection every month in the bank statement. He thrust a hand into his breast pocket and took out his wallet.

"Don't you have an account?" he asked. "At whatever shop it is you want to go to? Surely you have accounts at all the stores?"

"Not at every single little shop," she said, laughing at him. "What can you let me have? I know you're busy, I don't want to keep you."

He fingered the notes. "I'd better keep something for myself—just in case. I can let you have sixteen pounds. Will that be enough?"

She pouted, a most unusual expression on her part, one that he saw now with another small thrust of surprise. He gave her a long look as he handed over the notes. Something faintly theatrical about Carole's manner this afternoon, some quality he had never previously been aware of in her, almost, he thought, as if she were acting a part.

"Is that all?" She looked disappointed, then her face brightened. "What about the petty cash? Don't all offices have petty cash? Some great metal box bursting with notes? Haven't you got one?" Again that air of staginess, of slightly brittle vitality.

"I've got my own cheque-book," he said, not returning her smile. "If you tell me the name of the shop and how much you want to spend, I'll make you out a cheque."

She shook her head, laughing. "But you see I don't know exactly how much I want to spend. I might see something else on the spur of the moment and want to buy it."

He frowned slightly. Carole wasn't usually as dense as this about money matters, she usually had her head very well screwed on where finances were concerned. "I don't need to fill in the exact amount," he said patiently. "If I sign the cheque you can fill in the amount later, in the shop, it's perfectly in order."

"Oh, don't bother with the cheque-book," she said, seeming all at once to lose interest in the possibility of unlimited purchases. "I'll make do with the sixteen pounds." She put the notes in her handbag. "By the way," she said a moment later in a totally different tone, the tone she normally used to him, her own, matter-of-fact, sensible tone. "I called in at Whitegates this morning. I picked up a piece of information I thought you might like to know. Your father's making a new will, it's being signed in two or three days."

David put the wallet slowly back in his pocket. She saw that he had totally forgotten about the cheque-book, the store accounts, her request for money.

He gave her a long considering glance. "Do you know what's in the will? The main provisions?"

She shook her head. "No, I didn't discuss it with your father. He never even mentioned a new will. It was Mrs. Parkes who told me, she said the solicitor had been over to Whitegates, that the will was due to be signed shortly. But you can guess what's in it."

He tilted his head back, looking up at the ceiling.

"No, I can't. Kenneth's in it for certain—otherwise why makes a new will at all? But for how much is he in it? A fifty-fifty split?" He put up a finger to his lips. "Or the whole lot?" He heard the little intake of Carole's breath.

"Oh no!" she said. "He wouldn't do that! Leave everything to Kenneth? Why should he? You run the business, you're the one who stayed at home and took charge of everything."

G

David frowned. "My father's an old man, he's not well, he has time now to lie in bed and think. Who knows what goes on in his mind? Kenneth's the elder son. The return of the prodigal. Father may see things in a totally different light now. He might entertain all kinds of fancies. We just can't tell."

She shook her head again. "No, I can't believe it. You've never had a cross word with him in your whole life. Why should he suddenly take it into his head to cut you out of his will? It would be monstrously unfair." Her tone grew suddenly stronger. "The solicitor wouldn't hear of it. He'd never draw up such a will."

David bit his lip. "You may be right. But he might leave Kenneth a controlling interest, more than a half-share."

She drew her brows together, working out the implications. "You mean, he might want Kenneth to take over here after . . . his death? That you'd be answerable to Kenneth?"

He nodded slowly. "Yes. In fact that's probably what he *is* going to do." He raised his eyes to hers. "Exactly when is the new will going to be signed?"

A trace of additional colour appeared in Carole's face. "In two or three days," she said very quietly. "That's what Mrs. Parkes said. I'm afraid I can't be more definite."

"Two or three days. You're quite certain of that?"

"That's what Mrs. Parkes told me. I suppose you could phone the solicitor if you wanted——"

He shook his head forcefully. "No, I won't do that. I'll be calling in at Whitegates this evening. I'll call in on my way home, I'll have a word with my father." His manner changed abruptly. He smiled at Carole, gave her a little pat on the shoulder, kissed her on the cheek, propelled her gently towards the door.

"And now, you go off and spend your money, I've got my work to do."

Carole stood for a moment at the other side of the door. Sixteen pounds—what use was that? She could make out a cheque to-morrow of course, march into the bank and cash it, three or four hundred pounds, simple enough—but in two or three weeks' time when the statement came in, David would look up in astonishment at the breakfast table, he would say, 'What have you been buying, Carole? A new fur jacket? I haven't seen it. Or a diamond ring? What have you been up to, Carole?' He would smile as he asked the questions. But he would wait for an answer.

She gave a tiny shake of her head. No, she couldn't just cash a cheque. What could she do? Sell something? What? A piece of jewellery? Would David notice? Would he say, 'By the way, Carole, you never wear that brooch I gave you. You haven't lost it, have you?' And if she said yes, she had lost it, there'd be a fuss about the insurance, a statement to make, a claim to be put in, lies to be told, to be remembered.

Someone came into view at the far end of the corridor and at once she rearranged the expression on her face, straightened her shoulders and walked briskly off towards the lift.

To-morrow I will get out of this damned bed and put some real clothes on, Henry Mallinson vowed with silent determination. He'd walked about the upper corridors for half an hour during the long afternoon and he'd been perfectly all right. Felt as fit now as he'd ever done. If he lay here in bed much longer they'd turn him into a useless old man between them. He tightened his lips in cold appraisal. They were all ready to take over from him, all ready to step into his shoes. It would suit them all to have him neatly bundled up in pyjamas and a dressing-gown, tucked up under the bedclothes where they could keep an eye on him, control him, prevent him from ever again doing anything he wanted to.

He glared at Mrs. Parkes who stood with her back to him, a duster in her hand, rubbing away at the furniture, removing traces of dust.

He wouldn't ask Burnett's permission before rising from his bed to-morrow morning, he'd simply get up when it suited him and they could all lump it, Burnett and all. And he'd take a bath, a real bath with lashings of hot water, none of this damned nonsense of being washed in bed, being dabbed at with a tepid flannel as if he were a baby.

"There now!" Mrs. Parkes turned to give him a cheering smile. "That's better!" She spoke with professional heartiness. "Not very long now till supper. Cook has some lovely veal."

Veal! Tasteless, rubbery stuff! Mallinson closed his eyes in distaste. He'd have a steak to-morrow, with or without Mrs. Parkes's permission, a huge grilled steak, a little underdone, with mushrooms and onion rings, crisp and golden.

A knock at the bedroom door. David's voice at the other side of the panels. "All right if I come in for a moment, Father?"

"Your son," Mrs. Parkes said, crossing at once to the door. As if he was stone deaf.

"Come in, David!" he called loudly, above the sound of Mrs. Parkes opening the door.

David came in and stood smiling down at him. "How are you, Father? You're looking very spry."

"We had a little walk this afternoon," Mrs. Parkes said. "We've just been having a little rest now after our exertions." She fussed over a chair, running her duster officiously over the back, setting it beside the bed.

"I'm all right," Henry Mallinson said, quite able to answer for himself, thank you, without needing an interpreter to conduct a conversation between himself and his own son. "You needn't bother to stay, thank you, Mrs. Parkes."

David took a few steps about the room, waiting for Mrs. Parkes to finish her fussing and remove herself. He picked things up and put them down again idly. "You don't want to overdo the exercise just yet." He took a book from the bedside table, glanced at the title, replaced the book. "Better do what Doctor Burnett tells you, you'll get better all the sooner." He knocked over some small object on the table.

"Do stop fidgeting!" Henry said.

"Sorry, Father." David crossed to the window and stood with his back to the room, looking out.

"Not too long now." Mrs. Parkes at long last seemed ready to remove herself from the room. "We mustn't get overtired."

Henry let out a long breath of exasperation as the door closed behind her. "Irritating woman," he said. Then justice prompted him to add, "No, she's very good, really." Any nurse got on your nerves when you were stuck in bed all day, wanting to be up and about. He immediately forgot all about Mrs. Parkes and her fussing.

"What's all this about Stallard's widow?" He levelled the words sudden and sharp at David's back and had the satisfaction of seeing the lad's shoulders stiffen into alertness. "Thought I didn't know about it. But I do. What's the woman after? Money, I suppose."

David turned and gave his father a quick glance. How on earth did the old man know about Joyce Stallard's visit to Hallborough? Surely he hadn't been downstairs, ferreting through the mail?

"Don't worry about Mrs. Stallard," he said easily. "I'll see to all that. I can deal with her."

"Have you seen her?" Henry asked. "Have you settled on a figure?"

David resumed his tour of the room, reverting to his trick of lifting things and putting them down again. "Yes, I've seen her, she's staying on for a day or two. I told her I'd prefer to deal with her solicitor. I'll let you know what we decide." His voice took on a note of authority. "I'm sure you're not supposed to be worrying about business matters. You can safely leave it to me, I can handle it."

Yes, I suppose he can, Henry thought, suddenly tired of

Mrs. Stallard and her claims. Let the boy deal with her, let him earn his salary. "Have you seen Kenneth yet?" he asked and David's ears caught a different note in his voice. Malice? Or simple embarrassment? He couldn't be sure.

He shook his head. "Not yet. He'll be here for some little while, I understand. I'll look in at the pub and ask him over to Tall Trees for dinner. To-morrow, probably." He wasn't at all anxious to stand face to face with Kenneth again. It would have to be done though, there was no escape that he could see. "I've been rather busy, what with one thing and another." With your illness, his tone implied, with all the extra work it has laid on my shoulders.

"Your own brother," Henry said. "Your only brother. I should have thought you'd have made time to see him." His voice took on a keener edge. "I saw the solicitor again to-day. I'm changing my will."

David's fingers strayed over the surface of the chest of drawers. "I rather thought you might."

"The will's being signed in a couple of days," his father said, a shade too loudly. There was a tiny silence. "Don't you want to know the provisions of the new will?" he said, not altogether certain of his own motives in framing the question. "Aren't you curious?"

David didn't turn to look at him. "I'm sure you'll be fair in whatever you decide." A steady, expressionless tone, giving nothing away. Henry rather liked that. He moved his head and saw that the lad had his hand on the neck of the whisky decanter.

"Leave that alone!" he said sharply. "That's my whisky!" His own particular brand, superior, appallingly expensive. "Plenty of whisky downstairs if you want a drink."

"Oh—I'm sorry—no, I don't want a drink, I was just fiddling about, I didn't realise——" David came over and stood by the bed. "Is there anything you want me to do? Anything I can get you? Or anything Carole can do? You know we're both only too anxious——"

"No thanks, I'm all right," his father said brusquely. "Kind of you to ask. I have enough people here to see to what I want. Too many people. Running in and out all day long. You'd think you could expect a bit of peace in bed."

David smiled. "I'll be running along then and let you have some peace now. I'll look in again to-morrow. And don't go worrying about the firm. I'll see to everything."

He was gone. Henry lay with his eyes closed, washing them all out of his mind, David and Carole, Kenneth and the solicitor, Dr. Burnett and Mrs. Parkes, Gina Thorson and Mrs. Stallard, willing himself into emptiness and blankness, into rest and peace.

But peace eluded him. Disturbing thoughts flicked into his consciousness, skirted the edge of his brain, refusing to be dismissed. 'I've been too busy to call and see Kenneth,' David had said. His own brother. Staying in the Swan, no distance at all from Tall Trees. David would have to drive past the pub at least a couple of times a day. Too busy, indeed! A man was never too busy to do what he wanted to.

The door opened softly and Mrs. Parkes came in.

"Are you all right, Mr. Mallinson? Not too tired, I hope?"

He opened his eyes and looked at her. "I want you to ring the solicitor. Now. Right away. Tell him I'll sign the new will to-morrow morning."

"Oh—but I thought—surely it was arranged——"

"To-morrow," he said again, more loudly. "I'm an old man." He felt a huge wave of self-pity. "I could die at any moment." And not a soul in the world to care. "Tell him I'll sign the will to-morrow. Without fail. Get along now and ring him. If he's left the office ring him at home."

She turned towards the door, hesitated "If you're sure ——"

"Of course I'm sure! I'm not a child! I know my own business!"

"Very well." The door closed behind her. He drew a deep breath and clenched his hands under the covers. Perhaps I won't get up and dress to-morrow after all, he thought, perhaps I'll stay in bed another day or two. Get a little rest, a little peace. That was what Burnett had advised . . . and presumably Burnett knew what he was about. . . .

CHAPTER VIII

"I'LL BE LEAVING here just after lunch to-morrow," Dr. Burnett said. "It's a long drive. I'll be back sometime in the early hours."

"Why not stay over in a hotel?" Richard Knight suggested. "No need to drive all that way back after the dinner. I can hold the fort here."

Burnett shook his head. "No, I'll drive back. I'll be home by three or four o'clock. No traffic at night worth mentioning. I don't like strange beds." He gave a little smile. "Too old for them now." He contemplated without pleasure the speech he had promised to make at the Society's annual dinner. He'd promised months ago in a moment of goodwill when the dinner seemed light years away.

And now time had caught up with him and the speech would have to be delivered to-morrow evening. Far too late to cancel it now, they'd never get another speaker in the time. And it was an honour to be asked.

"I'll have to prepare something," he said. "To-night, before I go to bed." He'd jotted down a few ideas months ago, when he'd accepted the invitation. The notes lay in a drawer of his desk, he'd have to go over them, work on them, add a few touches of humour. He sighed at the prospect.

"I should detest having to make a speech," Richard Knight said.

"Does Henry Mallinson know you're going?" he asked

suddenly. "Do you want me to look in on him to-morrow for you?"

"No, no need to bother—unless you're sent for, of course."

A conservative old man, Mallinson, didn't like a change of doctors, didn't care for a young man anyway, preferred to trust himself to older, more experienced hands, preferred an old friend, a wiser head. "I'll look in on him in the morning, I'll tell him I'll be away the rest of the day. I'll speak to Mrs. Parkes. There shouldn't be any trouble. Everything's going along smoothly."

"You never told me you had this dinner," Mallinson said with a hint almost of accusation. "I'd no idea you were going to be away." The absorbed egotism of those who are wealthy, old and ill, Dr. Burnett registered on the surface of his mind.

"To tell you the truth," he said with a trace of genuine irritation, "I forgot all about it myself, until the fellow wrote and reminded me. I'm not at all anxious to go, I can assure you."

Mallinson made an abrupt gesture with his hand, striking the drum of tablets on his bedside table. He gave a petulant exclamation and caught the drum as it toppled over. "Then why not ring up and cancel it? I might have another attack, I might need you." He took the lid off the drum and peered inside unseeingly "I would have thought——"

"You won't have another attack," Burnett said soothingly. "You're a very great deal better and you know it." He smiled a little. "Romping about the corridors yesterday afternoon. Mrs. Parkes told me you'd have got dressed and gone downstairs if she hadn't stopped you."

"Well, I'm not getting dressed to-day." Mallinson half-jammed the lid back on the drum. "I don't feel very fit to-day," he added aggressively. "I might very well have a relapse."

"In that very unlikely event," Burnett said with professional cheerfulness, "Mrs. Parkes can always send for Richard Knight. He'd be over in a jiffy."

"Knight!" Mallinson said with contempt. "A lad! A mere puppy! What does he know?"

"Come now, Knight's a very good doctor. Youth isn't a crime. You're just envious of him."

"Envious? Of Knight?" Mallinson was astonished. "Why on earth should I be envious of a young whipper-snapper like that?"

"Because he's young," Burnett said quietly. "Because he has forty good years ahead of him with luck. Because he's thinking of taking your pretty little Gina away from you and marrying her."

Mallinson flicked up his eyes. "Marrying her? Has he told you that? Definitely?"

Burnett shrugged. "No, he hasn't actually said anything."

Mallinson snorted. "Well then——"

"He doesn't need to say anything. I have a pair of eyes in my head. You mark my words, you'll be buying Gina Thorson a wedding present before the year's out."

Mallinson looked thoughtful. "H'm, perhaps you're right. I wonder if that was why she——" He broke off, remembering his grievance. "So you won't cancel your precious dinner? You're going to leave me to the tender mercies of Richard Knight?"

Burnett stole a discreet look at his wrist-watch. "Of course I can't cancel at the last moment. You're well aware of that. One has obligations. When one has given one's word——"

"Ye-es." Mallinson nodded, acknowledging the most powerful element in Burnett's nature, the sense of duty, loyalty, obligation; he felt obscurely comforted by the knowledge. "I suppose it can't be helped. And I daresay I shan't need young Knight's services at all." He grinned. "I'll probably manage to survive till you get back." He rattled the drum of tablets. "Quite effective, these things. Haven't had a twinge of pain since I started taking them."

Burnett stood up and moved his shoulders. "Then keep on with them. Exactly as I told you." He walked over to the chest of drawers and lifted the whisky decanter, held it up, looking at the level of the spirits, removed the stopper and sniffed appreciatively.

"You remember what I told you about the tablets—never with alcohol? You wouldn't be such a fool, I hope? If you feel you really want a drink——"

"Yes, I remember," Mallinson said impatiently. "I do take a drink occasionally at night. But only if I haven't had a tablet after four o'clock. Mrs. Parkes sees to that." His tone changed abruptly. "Have you seen Kenneth yet? He's at the Swan."

Burnett had his back to him, he couldn't see the expression on his face. "Yes, I saw Kenneth," the doctor answered in a level tone. "He called in to see me yesterday. We had quite a long chat. And now, I'd better have a word with Mrs. Parkes." He replaced the decanter, fussing over the stopper. He crossed to the door and threw it open.

"Mrs. Parkes——" he called into the corridor. She came in at once and stood with her hands folded while he told her about his trip, gave her instructions.

"I'll be off then," Burnett said, going over to the bed and stretching out his hand to Mallinson. He caught sight of the drum still in his patient's fingers, the lid half off. He clicked his tongue. "Give me that—you should know better than to play about."

Mallinson grinned and raised his hand in a thrust of elderly mischief. The lid flew off the drum and the tablets cascaded in a little stream, on to the bedcover, spilling down over the carpet. Burnett uttered an exclamation, unable to prevent the momentum of his advance on to the bed from bringing his foot down on the scatter of tablets, feeling them grind to powder beneath the sole of his shoe.

"Look at that!" he said, raising his foot and frowning

down at the floor. "You're worse than a child!" He stooped and picked up a few tablets that had escaped the pressure of his shoe, straightened himself and ran his fingers over the bedcover looking for any other survivors. Mrs. Parkes joined the search, ashamed of her patient, of his silly behaviour.

"I've got half a dozen here," she said, extending her hand to tip them into the drum. Mallinson assumed a look of innocence.

"No need to make a fuss. There are still plenty there. You can let me have some more when you get back."

Burnett cupped his palm and let the remaining tablets trickle into the drum. Mrs. Parkes spied the lid at the foot of the bed and clapped it on tightly.

"I'm sorry about this, Doctor," she said, assuming responsibility for her patient and his tantrums. "I'll get a dust pan and sweep up the mess."

Burnett flicked his fingers free of the traces of powder.

"I'll be off then," he said for the second time. He shook hands with Mallinson. "Behave yourself while I'm away."

"I'll do my best." Mallinson grinned up at him. "Don't bore your audience to death with your speech, will you?"

Mrs. Parkes escorted the doctor from the room. Mallinson lay back against the pillows with his hands linked behind his head. There was no trace now of mischief in his expression, he frowned up at the ceiling, assessing the day ahead. At ten-thirty the solicitor would be here with the will, bringing a couple of clerks with him to act as witnesses, for all the employees at Whitegates would benefit under the will and so would be barred from acting in that capacity.

There was the burning question of the investment in Kenneth's firm. He bit his top lip, pondering the distasteful matter. One wild extravagant gesture in a lifetime of business shrewdness? Hand over the thirty thousand pounds and to hell with caution? Or probe into the affair much more deeply, let reason and common sense be his guides as always, listen to the solicitor, even if it meant temporary ruin for Kenneth?

Mrs. Parkes came back with the dustpan and brush, she knelt primly by the bed and dabbed at the carpet with little mincing strokes, emphasising the generosity of her nature in performing a task normally allotted to a housemaid. Mallinson closed his eyes, tired, unable to make up his mind.

He jerked his lids open again as a thought struck at him —the solicitor would be anxious to drive back to his office with his cargo of clerks, it would be inconvenient for them all to be absent from their duties at the same time, he wouldn't want to spend time arguing the question of the investment, and in any case it wouldn't do to raise it in front of juniors. He let out a breath of relief, aware at the same time of his own cowardice in postponing the affair. He'd let it stand over for a day or two. If he left it alone, didn't brood over it, his mind might make itself up, absolving him from the necessity for tedious thought.

Mrs. Parkes rose stiffly to her feet. "I'd like some coffee," Mallinson said suddenly. He'd sneak a cigarette with the coffee when she was out of the room. He wasn't supposed to smoke since his attack but he longed all at once for a cigarette. That means I'm a lot better, he thought with a little nod of his head, a couple of days ago I wouldn't have taken a cigarette if Burnett had offered me one himself. He still had a dozen or so hidden away in his cigarette case—in the small drawer of the bedside table, surely?

"Very well," Mrs. Parkes said, with one hand on the door-knob. "But not too strong. You're not supposed to have very strong tea or coffee. Doctor said so."

He sighed, resenting his invalidism. Still, weak coffee was better than none at all. "And a couple of biscuits," he said, feeling appetite begin to return. "Some of those fancy ones, with sugar on top."

He's getting childish, Mrs. Parkes thought grimly, making her way downstairs towards the kitchen. Wanting sugary biscuits at his age. It'll be ice-cream and jelly-babies next, I shouldn't wonder.

Mallinson raised himself in the bed and reached out for

the morning papers still neatly folded. He began to glance over the columns, the first time he'd concerned himself with the world at large since his illness. He was surprised to find how rapidly one lost touch with events. There had been an election up North, student riots in London, a new strike in an engineering factory . . . he gave a wry smile. The world didn't stop turning because one old man took to his bed in an obscure English village.

He crushed the pages together and stared at the wall. The world wouldn't stop turning when he closed his eyes for the last time, either. Someone would press the button that sent a new rocket rushing into space, buildings would catch fire, thieves would break into warehouses, athletes would win gold medals. He felt a wave of black depression sweep over him.

What is it all for? he asked himself. What is the point? For what end did I strive all my life? To lie here at last waiting for a cup of weak coffee and an illicit cigarette while the uncaring world goes on its way?

The door opened and closed again, softly. He turned his head expecting to see Mrs. Parkes balancing the coffee cup and the plate of biscuits—and found himself staring up at a total stranger, a woman dressed from head to foot in black.

He opened his mouth to speak but no words came. He had a confused notion of crying out for help—there was something vaguely sinister, threatening, about the woman's attitude, about the expression on her colourless face. She took a couple of steps forward. He heaved himself up in the bed, putting out a hand as if warding off an attack.

"Henry Mallinson," the woman said in a flat dull voice. "Joyce Stallard." She gave the tiniest inclination of her head as if acknowledging a formal introduction. "I've been wanting to meet you. It's been a long time."

A chaotic whirl of thoughts rose in his brain. The solicitor, he thought, he will be here at any moment. He made a strong effort to banish the fear that washed through him, recognising its absurdity, registering with some de-

tached part of his mind the way in which his treacherous
heart had begun to pound, the tight feeling clenching the
muscles of his chest.

"You can deal with my solicitor," he said, striving to
recall the man's name which had totally vanished from his
mind.

She shook her head, she continued her slow advance upon
the bed. "I want no solicitors. Nor your son. I came to see
you. No-one else will do."

"I haven't got any sugary biscuits," Cook said crossly.
"We don't keep any sugary biscuits in the house. I'm sure
I don't know which ones Mr. Mallinson means, anyway.
I don't know how long it is since he wanted biscuits."

"Well, what have you got?" Mrs. Parkes asked impatiently. "I'll have to take him something."

Cook moved her shoulders. "There are some of those
chocolate ones we keep for Mrs. David when she comes to
tea. Or plain water biscuits—or digestive or——"

"I'll take the chocolate ones," Mrs. Parkes said, interrupting the catalogue. "Hurry up or the coffee will be stone
cold."

She carried the tray carefully upstairs and along the corridor, gave a single knock at the bedroom door and let
herself in without waiting for an answer.

Mr. Mallinson was lying back with his eyes closed. He
didn't stir at her entry and she thought for a moment that
he had grown tired of waiting, that he'd fallen asleep.
She set the tray quietly down on the chest of drawers.

"Mr. Mallinson," she said softly, and saw his eyes flick
open with a strange expression—almost of fear. "I'm sorry
to have been so long," she said, "but Cook didn't have——"

"Has she gone?" he asked, raising himself on one elbow.
"Did you see her? You must have seen her!"

She drew her brows together. "Who?" Gina Thorson?
Mrs. David? "I saw no-one. Who was it?"

He gave a little shivering movement of his head and

shoulders. "That woman. Dressed all in black. You shouldn't have let her come. I'm a sick man." His voice trailed away. "You're supposed to keep people out, you're supposed to look after me." She had a sudden horrid notion that he was about to burst into tears.

"Here." She carried the coffee and biscuits over to the little table. "Drink this. It'll do you good. And the biscuits are nice, look, they're fancy chocolate ones, they're the best we could find." She spoke soothingly, kindly, as if to a child woken from a bad dream. "You can take one of your tablets with the coffee, it's time you had one."

He stared up at her. He took the cup she urged on him, he sipped at the hot coffee.

"You had a dream," she said. "You dozed off while I was gone." She smiled down at him. "There now, you're beginning to feel better, aren't you? Lady in black, indeed!" She gave a little laugh at the absurdity of the notion.

He felt vitality begin to surge up again under the influence of the coffee. "*Was* it a dream?" he asked. Could it have been? He strove to recall what had happened. He'd been lying here with his eyes closed and the door had opened softly—

"Of course it was a dream," Mrs. Parkes said briskly. "Now eat your biscuits. We want to be fresh and alert when the solicitor comes, don't we?" Second childhood beginning, that's what it is, she thought, taking a tablet from the drum, remembering a patient she'd nursed a few years back, staring at the walls all day, bursting into irrational tears, refusing to be washed. "Here you are now, take this, it'll calm you down."

CHAPTER IX

"Stand still and let me brush your jacket, do!" Mrs. Foster whisked invisible specks from Norman's best dark suit. "You can't go up to see Mr. Mallinson looking like a tramp!" She raised a hand and fingered aside a lock of hair that had fallen over his brow. "What time did Miss Thorson say you were to go up to Whitegates?"

"This evening, Mr. Mallinson said." Norman moved protestingly as his mother adjusted the set of his jacket about his shoulders. "But I told her it was my half day so she said it would be all right to go up this afternoon. Three o'clock, she said, give him time to have a nap after his lunch."

Mrs. Foster glanced at the kitchen clock. "Five to." She gave him a last pat, pursing her lips, considering the effect of her endeavours. "Better get going then. And mind you thank him nicely, whatever he gives you."

Norman's eyes looked nervously back at her. Ten, he thought, at the very least, fifteen or twenty with luck. His mother caught the expression. "Don't go showing disappointment, if he forgets to give you anything at all." An old man now, Mr. Mallinson, and a sick one, might very well forget why he'd sent for the lad at all. A look of acute anxiety flickered across Norman's face.

"He couldn't!" he cried in anguish. "He couldn't just forget!"

She raised her shoulders. "He might. Take it in good part if he does." Couldn't last very many years longer, the old man, there'd be something for Norman after he'd gone, he'd indicated as much to her many a time. "You're lucky to have him for a godfather, you just remember that and be polite. Ask him how he is. Tell him we're all thinking about him." She crossed to the back door and flung it open. "Now, off with you! And mind your manners!"

Gina Thorson was sitting in her office writing down figures on a piece of paper, adding them up, wrinkling her fine brows at the inexorable total. Suppose she could somehow manage just the suède coat and the shoes? She crossed off the remaining figures and contemplated the reduced sum without hope. And the coat and shoes would serve

H

only to heighten the contrast with the rest of her clothes. She scribbled angrily through the little columns and started again.

Do without the coat and settle for the cashmere sweater and the good skirt? But what if Richard's parents saw fit to hold a cocktail party to introduce her to their friends? What if they all went out to dine at some smart hostelry? She would need at least one good dress.

A timid knock sounded at her door. She stood up and crumpled the piece of paper, flinging it with contempt into the waste basket.

"Come in." It would be young Norman Foster of course, dead on time, nervously ready to pay his ceremonial call on Mr. Mallinson.

He opened the office door, didn't come inside, remained on the threshold, staring in at her without smiling.

"It's three o'clock, Miss Thorson. Hadn't we better go up?" He couldn't take a chance on being so much as a minute late, couldn't risk offending the old man by a display of unpunctuality. Mallinson might turn whimsical in his illness, refuse to see him at all, sending out a message about the younger generation and their slack ways.

Gina ran a hand over her hair, peered in the mirror over the fireplace, settled the collar of her neat dress about her slim neck, tightening Norman's nerves still further with her silly female fussing. His eyes implored her to get a move on but he didn't waste energy in unnecessary speech, holding his forces in reserve for the interview upstairs.

Gina gave him a brisk abstracted smile. "Right, Norman, I'll take you up now." She crossed to the door and he stepped back to let her through. "No need to look so anxious. He won't eat you." She walked through the echoing hall with the boy a couple of paces behind her. "He's a lot better to-day," she said over her shoulder, making conversation out of professional politeness. "The solicitor came in this morning and he signed the new will." She flashed a little smile at Norman. "I expect you're down for a legacy, aren't you? His godson, he wouldn't be likely to forget you."

A slow flush appeared along Norman's cheekbones. He was walking beside her now, up the broad stairs. He threw her a sudden upward glance.

"Do you know how much he's left me?" he asked in a low intense voice.

She shook her head. "No, I'm sorry, I don't know." Their eyes met. "I don't know how much he's left me either." He seems very anxious about it, she thought, touched by surprise. A lad of Norman's age, what could he want with legacies? What could he know of the urgent need for ready money, the things it could buy? His apprentice's wages, low as they probably were, would be large enough to cover every expense a lad like Norman might conceivably have. Too young, too quiet for a steady girl-friend, reared in circumstances too humble to prompt extravagant tastes, he would probably be overjoyed if the old man handed him a birthday fiver, pocketing it with pleasure, wondering how on earth he was going to spend his little fortune.

"He's in a good mood," she said lightly. "I expect he's feeling generous." She thrust down a stab of angry resentment at the memory of the old man offering her another ten shillings a week. Ten shillings! The meanness of the sum burned in her mind. She would almost rather he had offered nothing at all. Almost but not quite. Even ten shillings a week would help to buy *something*.

They had reached Mr. Mallinson's door. She knocked lightly and gave Norman an encouraging look.

"Just speak up when he talks to you." The old man couldn't bear mumbling. "Don't be frightened of him." Mallinson despised nervousness, it always brought out a touch of the bully in him.

Norman gave her a quick nod of acknowledgment.

"Come in." Mr. Mallinson's voice, clear and impatient behind the door. Gina turned the handle.

"Your godson to see you, Mr. Mallinson." She jerked her head at Norman still hesitating on the threshold. "Come along, Norman." He followed her into the room, unable to refrain from twisting his hands together.

"Ah yes, Norman. Come in and sit down. Bring up a chair, Gina." The boy looked ill at ease, shifting his weight from one foot to the other. His hands, large and competent, recently scrubbed bright pink to remove all traces of oil and grime, clasped and unclasped themselves. As always, Mallinson felt irritated by a manifest air of unease in a subordinate. He caught the little conspiratorial look Gina threw the boy and the tiny answering blink of a smile on Norman's tense face.

Something like anger stabbed at him. He could quite clearly imagine the two of them mounting the stairs to his room a few moments earlier, the lad saying, 'I wonder how much the old boy will hand over?' and Gina smiling, shrugging, saying, 'Who knows? This might be your lucky day. A fiver, a tenner, twenty maybe, after all it's your eighteenth birthday, quite a milestone, and old Mallinson's made of money, he could slip you fifty and never even notice it, it'd be the same as a sixpence to you or me.' As if his money hadn't been made the hard way, every penny of it, as if the accumulation of wealth somehow entitled every Tom, Dick and Harry, every vulture in the neighbourhood, to a share of it.

His mouth hardened, he felt old, sour, weary. Let them do as he had done, let them work all day and half the night, piling one difficult pound on another, and then let them see how willing they'd be to stretch out a hand to every idle petitioner.

"Come back in—" he glanced at the bedside clock— "five or ten minutes," he said to Gina. "Then you can take Norman down to the kitchen and give him some tea."

"Very well." He shot a swift look at the girl, expecting to see resentment or sulkiness on her features. But she gazed down at him calmly and pleasantly. She seemed to have forgotten her request of yesterday and the way he had countered it. A try-on, that was what it was. Thought all she had to do was demand another couple of hundred a year and he'd say yes. He gave a little snort. A couple of hundred! More than he'd made in a year when he first started.

He came out of his thoughts of the old days to find that Gina had left the room and Norman Foster was still standing awkwardly beside the bed.

"Oh, sit down, do!" Mallinson said abruptly. The boy lowered himself on to the edge of the chair, remaining stiffly upright, as if poised for flight.

"Well, now, and how are you getting on at the garage?" Mallinson began to soften. After all it was the lad's birthday. "Eighteen now, aren't you? A good age, everything before you. See you work hard, make the most of your opportunities."

For a few minutes he conducted a rather one-sided conversation, himself firing questions, which was the only way he knew of communicating with the young, and Norman giving brief replies. From time to time the lad glanced at the clock, astonished each time to discover by how little the hands had advanced.

"And now," Mallinson said with a touch of formality. "I'd like to wish you many happy returns of the day."

"Thank you, sir." Norman spread his fingers out on his knees. The moment was drawing near. Mallinson raised himself in the bed, leaned out, away from Norman, and fumbled with the lock of a little cabinet at the other side of the bed. He turned his head, glancing at Norman.

"Would you mind?" A command, not a request. "Just go over and stand by the window for a moment." His lips moved in a fractional smile but the eyes remained cool, cautious, one didn't go round flashing cash-boxes in front of young lads, even well-behaved, well-brought-up lads like Norman.

"Oh—yes, of course, sir." Norman rose at once to his feet, almost knocking over the chair in his awkwardness. He crossed to the window and stood in front of the dressing-table, listening to the small sounds behind him, interpreting them, the clink of a metal box, the scrape of a key, the creak of a hinge, the whisper of notes. He moved his head a trifle and remained rigid.

In the dressing-table mirror he could see the old man clearly reflected, sitting upright now against the pillows with the red and black cash-box open on the coverlet. Norman's heart began to beat in rapid, painful thuds.

The old man had a thick wad of notes in his left hand. With the other hand he was removing notes from the bundle, hesitating over them, looking down at them, pausing, considering. One note, two notes, three—impossible from here to see their value—suppose they were fivers? Tenners even? Norman opened his mouth to gulp in a deep breath of air. Four notes, five. If they were tenners that would be a cool fifty! He exhaled the breath slowly, feeling the muscles tighten at the back of his neck. The old man was fingering yet another note, pursing his lips, closing his eyes in a moment's thought.

A soft tap at the door and Gina Thorson came in without waiting for an answer, smiling at Norman in a friendly way, saying, "Ten minutes, Mr. Mallinson, as you said. Cook's made Norman some tea and she's put out a nice plate of cakes."

Norman threw her a frenzied look. Couldn't she see she'd interrupted them? Behind him he heard the little flurry of movement as the old man stuffed the money back in the box, snapped the lid shut.

"Wait outside for a moment," he said sharply to Gina. "You ought to knock before you enter a room."

"Oh—I'm sorry. You did say ten minutes. I'll wait outside, of course."

As soon as she had vanished Norman saw the old man lean over and replace the cash-box in the cabinet, turn the key, leaving it in the lock. If only Miss Thorson hadn't chosen that moment to come in! He felt certain old Mallinson had been about to add another note to the pile—another ten pounds, most likely! That would have made a difference to the course of the next few months and no mistake!

"You can come back and sit down again now," Mallinson said affably. "As you know, it is my custom to mark your birthday with a little gift." Norman allowed his features to relax into an expression of gratitude. Mallinson frowned. "I hope you're sensible with your money. I don't intend my gift to be taken out and spent on any rubbish that you catch sight of in the shops. Put it away in the post office——" He indulged himself for another couple of minutes, delivering one of his ritual lectures on the value of saving, of encouraging money to make money.

Norman felt his face beginning to ache from the effort of keeping the grateful, unassuming look in place. I wish he'd get it over and come to the point, he thought.

Suddenly the old man stopped speaking, taking Norman by surprise. He nodded eagerly, indicating fervent agreement with anything that had been said.

"Yes sir, I'll remember."

Mallinson stretched out his hand and discreetly slipped the rolled notes into Norman's palm. He smiled.

"A very happy birthday, Norman. Now run along to the kitchen and see what Cook has found for you. Gina will take you down."

The boy sprang to his feet with relief. "Thank you very much, sir. I hope you'll be better soon."

Mallinson nodded, bored now with the visit. "Yes, thank you. As a matter of fact I'm going to get up and get dressed in a few minutes, I'm going to take a look downstairs, see how they've all been behaving themselves while my back's been turned."

"Are you allowed to do that, sir?" Norman was surprised. "I thought you'd have to stay in bed, I didn't think the doctor would let you——"

"I don't tell the doctor everything I intend to do." Found his tongue all right now, when he'd got his fingers on the money, Mallinson thought sourly. Ready to chatter all day now he'd got what he'd come for. "Gina!"

At his call the girl came in. "You can take Norman down for his tea. And tell Mrs. Parkes I want her. I'm going to get up and take a prowl round, I'm going to get dressed in some proper clothes." He tugged at the cord of his dressing-gown, tired of the garment, tired of playing the invalid.

"Are you sure that's wise? Did Dr. Burnett say——"

He clicked his tongue at her. "I know what I'm about." Once you stepped back from the struggle for an instant, once you let go and took to your bed, every chit of a girl thought she was in a position to proffer unwanted advice. "Send Mrs. Parkes here." He closed his eyes, tightened his lips, waiting for them to go, to clear out and let him get up.

"Very well," she said. "Come along, Norman." He drew a deep breath, hearing the door close at last behind them. He flung back the covers, swung his legs out of bed, fumbled for his slippers, stood up and stretched his arms wide in a gesture of freedom.

"I feel fine," he said aloud. "As fit as ever I did."

"Could I wash my hands first?" Norman asked as he walked down the stairs beside Gina. He still held the little wad of notes tight in his palm and he couldn't wait another minute to unroll it and find out once and for all how much it was. Pride prevented him from simply opening his clenched hand and counting out the notes with Gina there to watch curiously, to see his reaction—whether of blinding relief or crippling disappointment.

"Yes, of course." Gina nodded back towards the bathroom they had already passed in the corridor. "You can go in there. I'll wait for you here."

As soon as the door was safely closed he uncurled his hand, dropping the little bundle on the tiled floor in his awkward haste, flinging himself down on his knees, fingering the notes apart with savage disbelief.

Five single one-pound notes! He smoothed them out, staring at them, turning them over as if they might somehow be playing a trick on him, would all at once transform themselves magically into fives or tens.

But they remained obstinately themselves. Tears came into his eyes, hot angry tears. He squashed the notes together and stuffed them into his breast pocket, ran the taps furiously, splashed the water about, dried his hands on the thick-piled towel.

Five miserable oncers! Not enough to make the slightest difference to his finances! He thought of his beautiful bike oiled and polished, standing patiently in the shed . . . how much longer now before he would have to ride it back to the garage in disgrace? Hand it over, unable to discharge his obligations, say good-bye to it for ever?

He glanced in the mirror over the wash-basin and saw the marks of tears on his cheeks. He dabbed at them with the towel, straightened his shoulders, looking back at his reflection, steadying his expression till he was certain it would reveal nothing of his tumult of feelings to Gina or any other casual observer, folded the towel neatly from long habit, opened the door and ran down to where Gina stood tapping her fingers on the banister rail.

"I'm hungry," he said with strong cheerfulness. "I hope the cakes are good."

Gina slid him a little glance. "By the way," she said lightly as they resumed their progress towards the kitchen, "did the old man cough up a good present?" Ten bob a week he'd offered her. Had returning health and vitality prompted greater generosity towards his godson? She didn't really grudge Norman any good fortune that might have come his way in the upstairs room. He was a decent lad, always good-natured and courteous, she hoped he'd got a few pounds to take himself off to the pictures or have an evening out with his mates.

"Quite a handsome one, thanks," Norman said stoutly. He smiled with sudden pleasure, a brilliant idea having just arisen in his brain. "Could I spend a little time in the library after tea? I'd like to look up one or two things in the reference books." Henry Mallinson had an impressive collection of engineering manuals and textbooks housed in glass-fronted bookcases in a peaceful room on the ground floor. He'd encouraged his godson to make use of them more than once in the past. "I wouldn't get in anyone's way. And I'd leave the room tidy."

"Yes, of course, I'm sure that would be all right." Gina was pleased to see the lad looked happy. The old man had probably given him fifteen or twenty pounds. Good luck to him, she thought, I'm glad someone's managed to pry some of that vast wealth loose.

"I'll have a cup of tea with you myself," she said, throwing open the kitchen door. "I'm rather partial to cream cakes."

An hour and a half later Gina sat down at her desk and glanced at her watch. A quarter to five. Her face was a little flushed, her eyes bright and sparkling. The dress shop would still be open. She was aware of her heart beating with pleasurable excitement. She lifted the phone and dialled a number, hearing the receiver lifted at the other end, the smooth voice announcing the name of the shop, asking if it could help.

"I was in the shop yesterday," Gina said. She mentioned the name of the assistant who had dealt with her, and sat waiting till the girl came to the phone.

"Yes, Miss Thorson. Have you made up your mind yet about the purchases? I put the articles aside, as you requested."

Gina smiled at the opposite wall. "Yes, I've made up my mind. I'll take all the things I chose. I'll probably want one or two other things as well, a dress and a wrap of some kind."

"Very good." The girl was pleased, savouring a nice

little sum in commision. "Will you be coming in within the next day or two?"

Gina thought rapidly. "What time do you close? Half-past five?"

"Normally at half-past five, but this is our late evening. We're open till seven to-night. Will you be coming in this evening?"

No time like the present, Gina thought. She made a swift mental survey of the buses into Hallborough—or she could get round the chauffeur, surely, to run her in in one of the smaller cars . . . With Mr. Mallinson out of action the chauffeur was eating his head off in idleness, he'd be glad of something to do.

"Yes, I'll come in right away," she said, a little breathlessly.

"Very well, Miss Thorson, I'll look out for you."

Gina replaced the receiver and stood up, her eyes shining. She clasped her hands together and executed a few dance steps about the room. A short evening dress . . . black perhaps? Or something gayer, less ordinary . . . but still well-bred, tasteful? And a stole? Or a short jacket? She frowned in happy anxiety, trying to visualise the dress and the best sort of wrap to wear over it.

She crossed to the door, opened it and stood for a moment listening, looking about her. No-one in sight, no-one moving about the hall and corridors. She ran lightly, silently, up to her room. She was going to enjoy her visit to Richard's home after all. She hummed a little tune as she drew a comb through her hair and dabbed at her face with a powder-puff.

A couple of miles away Norman Foster, still in his best dark suit, his crash helmet crammed incongruously down over his brow, whirred smoothly along the road towards the garage and the petrol pumps standing like sentinels. As he swung on to the forecourt a car turned off the road and halted by one of the pumps. An overalled lad came out of the kiosk and unhooked the hose.

"Norman!" he said, catching sight of young Foster swinging his leg off the bike. "What are you doing here? Thought it was your afternoon off."

"It is." Norman offered no explanation. He left the bike standing by the low wall, removed his crash helmet and walked towards the office.

The manager was sitting at his desk, running a pencil down a row of figures in a ledger. He looked up as the door opened.

"Hallo there! Didn't recognise you for a moment in your glad rags. You off to the pictures? Did you want something?" He ran his eye down the column for the third time, hunting for an elusive shilling.

Norman thrust his hand into his breast pocket. His face wore a bright, excited look, his cheeks were slightly flushed.

"I want to settle up. About the bike."

The manager threw down his pencil with a sigh of exasperation, having failed again to locate the missing shilling.

"Ah yes, the monthly instalment. I'm glad you could make it. Thought we might have to take the bike back. Wouldn't want that." He reached up to a shelf and pulled down another ledger. "Let me see now, how much is it?"

"Not the monthly instalment," Norman said in a light, brittle voice. "The whole lot, the outstanding sum. All of it. I want to pay it all now. Then the bike'll be mine." For always, for ever and ever. Belonging to him permanently and absolutely, no other soul in the wide world having a breath of claim to it.

"Come now!" The manager looked up with a grin. "You haven't come into a fortune or something, have you? Do you know just how much is still owing?"

"One hundred and five pounds, more or less," Norman said, taking the elastic band from the roll of notes in his hand. His voice grew even bolder. "But there might be something to come off that, seeing as I'm paying it earlier than arranged. The interest, you see, there shouldn't be so much interest to pay."

The manager frowned. "Where'd you get that money? You haven't saved all that, surely? Not on your wages."

"It's mine," Norman said stubbornly. "I want to pay off my debt. What's it to you how I managed to save it?"

"No, I suppose not." But the manager was still frowning, opening the ledger, turning the pages, finding the entry relating to the purchase. "Ah, here we are."

"Can you make me an allowance?" Norman persisted. "About the interest? I don't see why I should have to pay it all——"

"Strictly speaking, we're not compelled to," the manager said, still with a line between his brows. "But in the case of one of our own employees I daresay——" He made pencilled calculations on a scrap of paper. "Say, ninety-three pounds, seventeen shillings and sixpence." He flung the lad a sharp upward glance. "That suit you?"

"Yes, sir." Norman nodded, suddenly polite again, a little more relaxed. "Ninety-three pounds." He peeled off the notes, counting them aloud, carefully. A few tens, quite a lot of fives, three singles, the manager noted. Norman glanced up. "I haven't got the exact silver." He added another single to the pile. "Have you got half a crown?"

"Yes, somewhere." The manager slid open a drawer and took out some coins. "Here you are. I suppose you want a receipt now? You'll get the papers later, head office see to that."

"Yes, please, I'd like a receipt." Norman waited while the manager wrote it out. He stood in a posture of ease, not making conversation, glancing out once through the window at his bike gleaming dully by the wall.

"Your father know you're paying the bike off?" the manager asked suddenly.

Norman raised his shoulders but made no reply. None of your business, his gesture implied as clearly as if he had spoken the words aloud.

No, I suppose not, the manager thought. Or is it? One of my lads. Only an apprentice's wages. The father just a gardener at Whitegates, no money to spare there, I should imagine. Still . . . He handed over the paper.

"Thank you, sir." Norman placed it carefully in his breast pocket and turned to go. "I'll see you in the morning as usual."

The manager watched him stride off across the forecourt, swing his leg over the bike, drive off with a challenging roar from the exhaust. He scratched his head with his pen, frowned, bit his lip in thought, and then remembering the missing shilling, sighed and returned to his columns. Two minutes later he had forgotten all about Norman Foster and his precious motor-bike.

CHAPTER X

"OH, VERY MUCH better, thank you," Gina Thorson said to Carole Mallinson who was cradling as usual a great bunch of expensive blooms. "He's gone back to bed now. Mrs. Parkes had quite a little set-to with him to make him get back into his pyjamas and dressing-gown. He was as pleased as a child to be really up and about again." She led the way towards the stairs.

Carole frowned. "I hope he didn't stay up too long. I don't know what Doctor Burnett would say——"

Gina laughed. "I don't think he cared what Doctor Burnett would say. He was just weary of staying in bed. An active man like that, I suppose it comes harder to him than to most men of his age. Anyway, Doctor Burnett isn't here to-day."

"Not here? What do you mean?" Carole paused on one of the wide stairs.

Gina halted and looked back at her. "He's gone off to some dinner, miles away. He has to make a speech, I believe. Richard—Doctor Knight——" she blushed faintly—"told me when he looked in earlier. He didn't go up to see Mr.

Mallinson, he just looked in to ask if he was all right." Her voice took on a trace of defensiveness. "Mr. Mallinson doesn't really trust young doctors, I don't know why, Doctor Knight is a very good doctor, everyone says so."

All right, all right, Carole thought with a touch of amusement, no-one's attacking your precious Richard Knight. We all know how the wind blows in that quarter. Knight was for ever running in and out of Whitegates, with or without a professional excuse. Something highly-strung and over-wrought in Gina's manner to-day, Carole's sharp eyes noted. Perhaps Knight has proposed to her. A step up in the world for the girl. Nicely-spoken, well-mannered, but no background all the same. Carole could spot the signs a mile off, knowing them from harsh experience. The lack of any real sophistication, the permanent air of slight diffidence, the clothes, neat enough, discreet enough, but obviously bought in one of the large chain stores.

I hope she pulls it off, she thought with a sudden flash of casual good-will. Gina's good fortune wouldn't be any skin off young Carole Mallinson's nose, she could afford to wish her well. And the girl would make an excellent wife for a young doctor. Hard-working, malleable, compliant, anxious to learn. Carole gave a tiny nod. Yes, Gina would play her part well as Mrs. Richard Knight.

"When will Doctor Burnett be back?" Carole began to walk up the remaining stairs.

"Not till the early hours of to-morrow morning, I believe. Richard—Doctor Knight——" again that faint rise in colour—— "wanted him to stay the night in the hotel, but Doctor Burnett wouldn't hear of it. He's terribly conscientious. I imagine he felt that if Mr. Mallinson were to be taken ill again——"

"I don't see why he should," Carole said sharply. "He's making excellent progress. And in any case it was only a mild attack."

"Yes, but you know how it is. Doctor Burnett and he were boys together, here in Rockley. He takes much more

than a professional interest in this particular patient. He'd
never forgive himself if anything went wrong and he wasn't
here." They had reached the bedroom door.

"Don't stay too long, will you?" Gina said in a low voice.
"We mustn't encourage him to overdo things." She gave a
little knock on the panel.

"You can safely leave that to me," Carole said stiffly
Really, the girl behaved sometimes as if she were a member
of the family and Carole an outsider. Her momentary thrust
of good-will dissolved and vanished. "No need to come back
for me. I can see myself out." She smiled without pleasant-
ness. "I ought to know my way by this time." She gave a
little nod, dismissing Gina, going into the room on the old
man's call.

He was sitting up in bed fingering one of his coins. A
couple of trays holding other mounted coins were spread out
on the coverlet.

"How are you?" Carole stooped to kiss his cheek, ex-
periencing a little stab of panic at the sight of those coins.
Why had the old man chosen this evening to fondle them?
Had Tim Jefford been in contact with him?

"Oh, very spry, thank you, my dear." Mallinson waved
her to a chair. "I'm getting up again to-morrow. It did me
all the good in the world, much better than lying here in
bed bored to death."

He had caught her sharp glance at his treasures. He
smiled at her. "I'm just looking over part of my collection.
I'd forgotten I had some of these." He gazed fondly down
at the trays. "Not at all a bad collection, though I say it myself." Was that all? she wondered with unease. A sudden
whim to gloat over his possessions? She allowed herself to
relax a little. His next words took her by surprise, so that
she didn't quite have time to mask her change of expression.

"Gina had a call from a young man this morning. Jefford, or some such name. He's staying at the Swan." He gave
her an alert glance. "Anything wrong, my dear?"

She shook her head, in control of herself again. "No,

nothing wrong, what should there be? What did this young man want?" An easy tone now, the right air of casual enquiry.

"He has some coins he wants to dispose of. He heard I was a collector specialising in coins of that particular period." He was pleased at the notion of his name being mentioned by London dealers as an authority, a respected connoisseur. "He's coming in this evening, Gina made an appointment. I might buy a couple if he has anything of interest, time I added to my collection, I haven't done much with it lately."

Carole stood up and laid the flowers on the chest of drawers, fussing with them, moving the heads of the blooms.

"Why not leave it for a day or two?" she asked lightly. "You don't want to tire yourself out." Her voice took on a teasing note. "All this gadding about downstairs. You could see this Jefford man in two or three days, if he's staying in the village."

"Ah, but you see he might not be here all that long. He's here on some little local matter of business, he told Gina. I daresay he'll have to rush off again elsewhere. You know what these young men are." Yes, I know what this particular young man is all right, Carole thought grimly. "I don't want to miss a good specimen," the old man said, "for the sake of a day or two. Don't worry about me, my dear, I'll watch it that I don't overdo things." He gestured at his bedside table. "I have my tablets, they're very good, Burnett knows what he's at."

She turned and moved idly towards the little table, picking up the drum of tablets and regarding it, lifting the lid and staring down at the contents.

"What effect do they have? Calm you down? Or buck you up?" She smiled, took out a tablet and looked at it with curiosity.

"If I get a twinge of pain they take it away. That's all I know and all I care about. I don't know what they're sup-

posed to do technically. I leave all that to Burnett." He
made a dismissing gesture with his hand. "Have you seen
Kenneth yet?" he asked with an abrupt change of subject.
"I should have thought you and David would have invited
him to dinner by this time. He may not be down here much
longer."

An idea rose whole and complete in Carole's brain.

"As a matter of fact I'm just going to call in at the
Swan now, after I leave you here."

The old man nodded, satisfied. "Yes, do that. You've
never met Kenneth, have you? Not a good thing, coolness
between relatives." How he has the nerve to say that!
Carole thought with a rush of feeling that surprised herself.
After all those years——

"Blood's thicker than water," Henry Mallinson went on.
"You realise that when you're——" When you're old, he
added, finishing the unwelcome sentence in his mind, when
you lie in bed and contemplate the idea of your own end.
He smiled at his pretty daughter-in-law. "Bury the hatchet,
my dear, ask him to dinner. Easier for you than for David,
there's less to forget."

Carole returned to the chest of drawers and picked up her
flowers. "I'd better call Mrs. Parkes and ask her to put
these in water." She glanced at her wrist-watch. "And I
mustn't stay much longer, not if I'm going to call in at the
Swan." She opened the door and called, "Mrs. Parkes!"

"What time is your coin-collector coming to see you?"
she asked, stroking the delicate head of a bloom.

"After I've had my supper. Eight o'clock. Gina fixed it."

Her manner grew brisk. "I'll be off then and let you have
a rest before supper. We can't have you getting overtired."

Mrs. Parkes came into the room, a little stiff in her
attitude, not altogether approving of so many callers, so
much excitement, gadding about upstairs and down. Her
responsibility, after all, with the old doctor away.

Flowers of course. Always flowers with Mrs. David.

"You'd like me to put those in water?" She managed to

imply that it was a bit much, on top of all her other duties.

Carole thrust the flowers into her arms. "Yes, please." She turned and kissed her father-in-law on the cheek. "Look after yourself, I'll be in to-morrow to see you."

Eight o'clock she thought, crossing the hall. Where could Tim be now? In his room at the Swan? Hardly likely. What would he find to do alone in his room? He'd probably be out somewhere, in Hallborough perhaps, in a café, or a cinema, or just walking about the streets, killing time. If he was in the pub at all he'd be in one of the public rooms, talking to some casual acquaintance. In all probability he wouldn't enter his own room again until just before dinner. She opened the door of her car and slid into the driving seat.

The letters—he'd leave them behind in his room, in a suitcase perhaps. She smiled into the rear-view mirror. A suitcase without a lock, most likely. No suitcase Tim Jefford was likely to possess or borrow would boast a pair of keys. She could visualise the case, tied round with an old leather strap, thrust under the bed.

All she had to do was find his room. She frowned, turning the car out on to the road. She couldn't just march into the Swan and ask for Mr. Jefford's room, that was totally out of the question. She strove to recall the lay-out of the upper floor of the public-house. She'd been upstairs more than once, bound for the ladies' cloakroom.

In the distance she could see the yellow glow of the Swan's lights. They'd be busy in the bars now, a last-minute effort before opening-time. No-one would notice if she went silently up the stairs. If anyone did see her she could always seek temporary refuge in the cloakroom.

Only four or five bedrooms, surely? She screwed up her face in thought. Four, actually, she was pretty certain there were only four, three larger rooms on the right of the corridor and on the left, the bathroom, the ladies' cloakroom and one small bedroom. A single room, the others would be double. She bit her lip. The single room, most probably, its situation would make it the noisiest and least desirable and so the cheapest. Tim couldn't afford to be choosy, he'd have taken the single room—unless it was already occupied before he arrived.

She parked the car and walked without obvious haste through the little side door. No-one about. Her heart began to beat a little faster. Just suppose by some wild chance Tim *was* in his room? In that case she couldn't lay her hands on the letters, but at least she'd be able to spy out the land.

Up the narrow stairs, past the bathroom, past the ladies' cloakroom. From downstairs she could hear the rattle and clink of glasses, a door opening and closing, the sound of voices.

She reached the door of the single room. It wasn't locked, the handle turned easily in her grasp. She drew a little breath of relief.

Then suddenly, behind her, she heard a door open, someone stepping out into the corridor from one of the double rooms. She had a sudden wild impulse to push open the door and vanish inside but common sense restrained her. She let her fingers drop from the handle, turned with a slight smile arranged on her features.

Kenneth Mallinson! She knew him at once from the family photographs, from his likeness to the old man, the same chin, the same nose.

"Kenneth!" she said, recovering herself, taking a step towards him. "It *is* Kenneth Mallinson, isn't it? I'm Carole, David's wife."

He remained where he was, looking levelly back at her, not smiling, not holding out his hand.

"Were you looking for me?" he asked.

"Yes, I made a mistake, I thought that was your room," she cried in a little rush, jerking her head back at the door of the single room.

"No," he said. "That room is occupied by a Mr. Jefford."

She drew a small breath of disappointment. If she'd been five minutes earlier she could have been in and out of the room with not a soul the wiser. But there was no help for it now.

"I wanted to ask you to dinner," she said. "This evening, if you're not doing anything else, that is."

"No, I'm not doing anything else."

"You'll come then? Half-past seven? We would have asked you before—but we've been so busy. You know how it is."

"Yes, I know how it is." He appeared to consider the matter, to reach a decision. He tilted his head back slightly and gave her a long, thoughtful look. "Yes, thank you, I'll come. Half-past seven." He seemed to recollect his duty of hospitality. "Won't you come down to the bar and have a drink?"

She shook her head. "No, thank you, I must be getting back." She made a vague gesture with her hand. "I have things to see to. I've just been into Whitegates——"

"I called in there myself before lunch. I thought my father looked surprisingly well."

"Yes, he seems quite energetic to-day. I gather he went downstairs earlier. He's beginning to take an interest in the business again." She slid a little calculating look at him. "You know he's making a new will? He's had the solicitor in, he's going to sign it in a couple of days."

But it's been signed already, Kenneth thought, it was signed this morning. The secretary had told him so, quite definitely. Was Carole in ignorance of the fact—or was she only pretending ignorance, for some devious reason of her own? Did she want him to think the will had not yet been signed?

"Yes, I know about the will," he said, waiting for her to go on, to show her hand.

I wish he'd take himself off to the bar, Carole thought desperately. If Tim Jefford was in his room he might emerge at any moment. If he was out, or downstairs, he might round the turn of the stairs, might cry out, "Carole! What are you doing here?" Disclosing the fact that they knew each other. She experienced a thrust of panic at the thought.

But Kenneth made no move, he looked as if he were quite content to stand there for half an hour, making stilted conversation. Exasperation washed through her.

"Well then," she said brightly, "I'd better be getting back to Tall Trees." Still he stood rigidly unmoving. She stepped back a pace and looked along the corridor at the doors. "I'll just pop in there for a moment." She indicated the door of the ladies' cloakroom. Surely he wouldn't be so unmannerly as to remain where he was while she went inside?

To her immense relief he took a step away from his own door. "I'll see you later on then," he said. "I'm just going down to the bar for a drink. You're sure you won't join me?"

She shook her head and smiled. "No thanks, I really don't have the time."

He made a little formal movement of his head, said, "This evening, then," and walked away down the stairs.

As soon as he had disappeared she moved swiftly back to Tim's room and gave a low knock on the panel, hoping fervently that there would be no reply, that she could slip in and out again.

But there was a sound of movement within, the creak of bedsprings, feet shuffling across the carpet.

The door opened a little and Tim Jefford's face appeared round it. He looked half asleep. His tie was loosened and he wore no jacket. His eyes blinked open at the sight of his caller.

"Carole! I wasn't expecting you!"

"Let me in." She pushed past him without ceremony, swept his hand from the doorknob and closed the door behind her. "I want to talk to you, and I don't want to advertise the fact." No hope now of filching the letters but she made a rapid survey of the room all the same. She might be able to slip back another time.

"I was having a kip," he grumbled. "Nothing to do in this hole." He yawned widely and rubbed his eyes. "Until eight o'clock that is." He grinned at her. "I have an appointment at eight."

"Yes, I know. That's what I want to talk to you about." A small chest of drawers, no lock in any of the drawers, a wardrobe with a lock but no key visible. Lost years ago, most likely. "I've just been talking to my father-in-law, he told me you're going to show him some coins." No bureau, no bookcase. "He's by way of being something of an expert, you realise that? If you're trying to palm some valueless imitation off on him——" Ah, a suitcase peeping out from under the bed. The letters would be in that no doubt. A battered-looking object, from what she could see of it.

Tim flung himself down on the crumpled coverlet, and linked his hands behind his head. He wore no shoes; a toe stuck out from a hole in one of his socks.

"I've only got one coin." He grinned at her. "But it's a good one. Spent damn near every penny I had on it." He raised his foot and gazed critically at his toe. "Of course old Mallinson doesn't know it's the only one I've got. I let on I'd got a dozen or so. Interesting voice, that secretary of his. What's she like? Pretty?"

"Pretty enough." Carole lowered herself delicately on to an upright chair in front of the wardrobe. If the suitcase ever had a lock she'd like to bet good money the lock wouldn't function now. She tilted her head back and was able to discern the edge of a leather strap. Her face relaxed into a smile.

"You're going to be a good boy, Tim, aren't you? You're not going to queer my pitch? You wouldn't be so mean." She considered the appeal of sentiment. "Not after the old days."

Tim was amused, recognising her tactics. "I remember the old days very well." He smiled at her. "The rows. And the reconciliations. Some of the reconciliations weren't bad." He sat up suddenly and reached out a hand towards her. She allowed him to take her fingers into his grasp.

"But you'd be surprised how mean you can get when you're on your beam ends," he said softly, pressing her fingers. "You can get very mean indeed."

She raised her eyes. "You wouldn't say anything to the old man?"

He began to play with her unresisting fingers. "Well now, that depends on whether or not you've got anything for me. Just a little something to keep the wolf from the door. He gets to howling awfully loud some days."

She thrust his hand away from her and snapped open the catch of her bag. She took out a leather notecase. He was pleased to see the promising way its sides bulged.

"This is all I can manage, just at the moment," she said with a business-like air. "It isn't as easy as you think."

"Easy enough," he said. "A lady in your position. Count it out, my dear. Let's see what we've got there."

"A hundred pounds." She didn't count out the notes but thrust them at him with a contemptuous gesture. "It took a bit of getting."

He looked down at the roll, ran a finger caressingly over them. "Acceptable," he acknowledged. "But not enough, not by a long chalk." He stood up and stuffed the roll into the pocket of his trousers. His manner changed abruptly, lost its teasing edge. "I should start thinking in larger sums if I were you, my dear. Something a little more substantial." He looked down at her, his blue eyes none too friendly behind the little smile.

She snapped her bag shut. "I'll get you some more. But it will take a few days. You must realise that. Just don't say anything to the old man, please! I can meet you—in Hall-borough, at a café, we can fix a place. Say the day after to-morrow. I'll have some more by then."

He narrowed his eyes reflectively. "Very well," he said at last. "The day after to-morrow. Which café? And what time?"

She thought rapidly. "Better make it the buffet at the

railway station." No-one she knew was likely to visit the buffet. "Four o'clock. I'll be there."

"You'd better be," he said softly.

She stood up and smoothed her skirt. Tim slid an arm round her shoulders. She made no move to push him away.

"I miss you sometimes," he said. "In the middle of the night sometimes I get to thinking about you."

"Open the door and take a look out," she said. "I don't want anyone to see me leaving this room."

He relaxed his grip, flashing her a look she couldn't quite interpret. He crossed to the door, opened it softly and glanced out. He extended a hand, beckoning her forward.

"All right," he whispered. "All clear."

"Close the door as soon as I've gone," she said in a low voice. "If anyone sees you looking out after me they'll know what room I've been in."

He inclined his head in a moment's admiration at the way she thought of everything. "Very well."

She went swiftly and silently past him, out into the deserted corridor, hearing the little click as he obediently closed the door. Down the stairs, past the cheerful hum of voices in the bar, through the side door out into the breezy car-park, not allowing herself to draw a deep breath till she was safely behind the wheel once more, pulling out on to the road.

CHAPTER XI

"OH! A BEAUTIFUL specimen!" Henry Mallinson's business sense deserted him temporarily at the sight of the coin. "Very fine indeed!" He was suddenly aware that his unmasked enthusiasm had probably put another ten or twenty on the price but for once he didn't care. It was a couple of years since he'd added to his collection. A surge of the old passion rose inside him. He picked up his magnifying-glass and studied the head, the inscription, running his finger along the edges, turning the coin over to examine the other side.

"What else have you got? Let me see the others." He stretched out an impatient hand.

"Well now." Tim Jefford put up a finger and scratched his head. "That's the only one I've brought with me this evening." He gave a little deprecating movement of his head. "I wasn't sure if you'd be interested——"

"Interested?" the old man said sharply. "Of course I'm interested . . . My period, my speciality. I'm always interested in a coin in this condition." He ran his finger lovingly over the clearly-incised head. "Where have you got the others? At the pub? When can you bring them?"

Up to London to-night by the late train from Hallborough, Tim thought swiftly. Carole's hundred pounds in his pocket. Might as well make what profit he could on the side. A vista opened out all at once before him—might be something in this coin lark after all, might make a good thing out of it, buying and selling, looking up other wealthy collectors. He jerked his thoughts back to the present moment of urgency. Lay out, say seventy-five of Carole's money with the same dealer, a good man obviously, knew what he was about. Take the train back again in the morning, say at ten or eleven, in Rockley shortly after lunch.

"I could come in again to-morrow afternoon," he said. "Would that suit you? I have appointments in the morning, I can't manage it till the afternoon."

Mallinson grunted. "All right. Half-past two?" Tim nodded. "And now, what are you asking for this one? Might as well settle up now." He wanted the coin to be his, now, at once, he wanted to be able to fondle it, examine it, after Jefford had left.

Mallinson leaned out of the bed and unlocked a little cabinet on his right. He took out a metal cash-box.

The old boy's actually going to pay me in cash, Tim

thought in surprise. What is he? Some kind of miser? I'll ask seventy-five, he'll beat me down to fifty, he decided rapidly.

With the fifty he could buy another couple of coins. He'd discuss the matter very carefully with the dealer, lay out his money to the best possible advantage. He felt exhilarated, gay and expansive, forgetting for the moment the errand that had brought him to Rockley, seeing himself now as a dealer in old coins, branching out later on perhaps. Who could tell? Small objets d'art, larger stuff in time. Pictures! He'd know what he was doing with pictures! He cursed silently at all the wasted years behind him. By Golly, he'd more than make up for them now! He had totally forgotten that the only reason he'd bought the coin in the first place was to gain access to Whitegates, to enable him to pursue a course of blackmail.

"Seventy-five, I thought," he said smoothly. "Guineas, that is."

The old man frowned. "A bit steep." He made a swift assessment of the young man. A determined-looking customer, something a trifle wild, buccaneering about his appearance, the face of a man who meant business, young as he was. And Mallinson had to have that coin.

"Sixty's plenty," he said.

Tim was beginning to enjoy himself. "I don't think you quite realise." He raised his eyebrows. "Values have gone up a good deal in the last year or two. I have other contacts, naturally. I know someone who'd be very glad indeed to pay seventy-five for that coin."

Mallinson sighed. "All right," he said abruptly. "Seventy-five pounds." He opened the metal box.

"Guineas," Tim said. "I never deal in pounds."

The old man uttered a sharp exclamation and for a moment Tim thought he'd gone too far, that Mallinson had lost patience with him, that he was about to fling the coin back and tell him to go to hell.

But the old man was staring down into the cash-box with disbelief. "The money!" he said, almost in a whisper. "It's

gone! Every penny!" He raised his head and sat looking at
Tim with his jaw hanging open. "It's gone!" he said again
and Tim had a startled notion that he was about to burst
into tears.

Disappointment struck at Tim. He wouldn't have the
seventy-five in cash now for to-morrow's venture. Wait a
moment though—if the old man gave him a cheque, made
out to Cash, he could take it into the London bank to-
morrow as soon as it opened. Yes, that would be all right,
better in a way, save him having to carry all those notes
about in his pocket.

"Don't you think it's possible you made a mistake?" he
asked. An old man, forgetful, stuck away in bed, probably
had the money there for weeks, months even, had taken it
out for some purpose, forgotten all about it. "You may have
used the money for something else. It may have slipped your
mind."

The old man stared at him. "Nonsense!" he said, suddenly
not seeming at all an old man. He sat bolt upright, frowning in sharp thought. "I had the box out earlier to-day. My
godson's birthday, gave him a present." Norman? No, the
lad had never been anywhere near this side of the bed,
hadn't even seen the cash-box, didn't know it existed, let
alone how much it held. And in any case the lad was no
thief, son of his own gardener, strictly brought up, a decent
well-behaved lad.

He shook his head, dismissing the idea of Norman, and
suddenly caught his breath, seeing again the door opening,
Gina Thorson coming in without knocking—or knocking so
quietly that he hadn't heard her—she'd seen the box all
right. He remembered the way her eyes had opened at the
sight of it.

"Gina!" he said aloud. "That's who it was!" What did
he know of the girl? Nothing. And she'd asked him for a
rise only yesterday, cool as a cucumber she'd opened her
mouth and asked—no, demanded—another couple of hundred a year! That look she'd levelled at him when he'd

refused, he could see it now. A calculating, hostile look. Things to buy, she'd said, needed the money urgently. He snapped the cash-box shut.

"Tell Mrs. Parkes I want her," he said sharply to Tim.

"About the coin," Tim said, striving to keep the situation under control. "I could take a cheque."

Mallinson frowned. "Never mind the coin." He glanced down at it, lying on the coverlet, he picked it up. "I'll keep it of course. I'll settle up with you when I've seen the other coins. No point in making out two cheques if I decide to buy something else. You're not short of money, are you?" he asked fiercely, glaring at Tim. "You can wait a day or two, can't you?"

"Yes, certainly." Tim allowed himself a small laugh. "I just thought you were anxious to have the matter settled."

"It is settled," Mallinson said. "Stick your head out and call Mrs. Parkes. The nurse, go on, call her! I want Miss Gina Thorson up here right away!"

Tim saw that it was no good. There was going to be an almighty uproar about the money and no chance at all of cash or a cheque to-night. He got to his feet.

"I'll call her. Then I'll be getting along, back to the pub. I'll see you to-morrow, half-past two."

The old man said nothing. He opened the cash-box again and stared down into the empty interior.

Tim opened the door and called "Mrs. Parkes!" not knowing in which direction to shaft his voice. I bet the old man spent it on something else, he thought—if he had it in the box at all. All the same, he thought, remembering those fierce eyes under the heavy brows, I wouldn't like to be in Miss Gina Thorson's shoes.

The room next door opened and a neat, middle-aged woman dressed in a nurse's uniform stepped into the corridor.

"Mr. Mallinson wants you," Tim said. "I'm just leaving. I can find my own way out." As he went off towards the stairs he heard the sound of voices, the old man's raised in anger and the nurse answering him in a low, soothing tone.

In her room along the corridor Gina was listening half-heartedly to a talk on the radio. She wouldn't be able to see Richard this evening, he was on call as Doctor Burnett was away. She raised a hand and touched her lip with a finger. Was the imitation fur wrap a mistake or not? She couldn't make up her mind. It had certainly looked very handsome in the shop. Gina hadn't been able to tell it from the real thing. But it might look very different beside the fur wraps and jackets she was quite certain would adorn the shoulders of Richard's mother and her friends, if they should all happen to go out somewhere really smart. Would it pass muster—a young girl's fur? Or would they slide glances at each other . . . 'My dear, did you see her jacket?' She bit her lip in thought.

About the other garments she had chosen she was more than happy. They lay now, wrapped in tissue-paper, folded into elegant boxes, in the despatch room at the shop, await-ing delivery later in the week. She was particularly pleased with the short evening dress, a beautifully-cut understate-ment in dull-surfaced black crepe. No-one could criticise that dress, it was perfect, totally right. But the wrap . . . she frowned again, considering the alternatives. A brocade jacket perhaps? A silk theatre coat?

She became aware of some kind of commotion not very far away. She turned her head, listening. Mr. Mallinson's voice raised, sounding highly displeased. Mrs. Parkes an-swering him in an even tone. Had Mrs. Parkes displeased the old man in some way? Not like her, she was usually able to deal with shifts and changes in his moods, able from long experience to handle a patient with tact.

A door opening, Mr. Mallinson's door, the sound of voices ceasing suddenly. It was all over then, whatever it was, a storm in a teacup no doubt. Gina relaxed into the easy chair. Yes, perhaps a silk jacket or coat of some kind might be better than the fur. It would probably cost less too, there would be the difference to spend on stockings, underwear, even a new dressing-gown.

Footsteps going along the corridor, halting outside her own door. She sat motionless, waiting for the knock. Mrs. Parkes wanting to unburden herself no doubt, to enjoy a little grumble about her employer's unpredictable temper.

When the knock sounded Gina stood up and crossed to the door, throwing it open, smiling out at Mrs. Parkes who stood looking back at her with a gaze that was less than direct. A veiled quality as if the nurse was entertaining some thought she was anxious not to reveal in its entirety.

"May I come in for a moment?"

"Yes, of course, I'm just listening to the radio. It's not a very interesting talk, anyway." Gina reached down and switched off the sound. She straightened herself and smiled at the other woman.

"Do sit down. What was the matter with Mr. Mallinson? He sounded upset about something just now. I could hear him from here."

Mrs. Parkes dropped suddenly into a chair. "When you were in Mr. Mallinson's room earlier to-day—when young Foster was here—did you see the old man take out a metal cash-box?" She spread her hands in a gesture. "About that big—black and red."

"A cash-box?" Gina wrinkled her brows. "Let me think . . . Yes, I believe I did. I went into the room thinking Mr. Mallinson had finished with Norman, I was going to take him down to the kitchen for some tea, and the old man was quite sharp with me, told me to go outside and wait till I was sent for, he hadn't heard me knock. He was holding a cash-box, he had it open on the bed." She nodded. "Yes, I'm quite certain now, I remember it, black and red. He had some notes in his hand, quite a thick roll." She sat down and looked at Mrs. Parkes. "He was taking it out to give Norman a present, I suppose. Why do you ask? Has he mislaid the box?"

Mrs. Parkes opened her mouth and expelled a long breath. "No, the box is there all right, but it's empty."

Gina stared at her. "Empty?"

"Yes, all the money is gone. He did give Norman a present, but only five pounds, apparently. He says there was over a hundred left in the box and now there's nothing."

Gina smiled and leaned back in her chair. "Then I expect the money's in the drawer of the cabinet or stuffed away at the back of a shelf. He probably forgot to put it back in the box. He's old, he's not well, he's likely to forget things. He probably closed the box and put it away and then saw he still had the roll of notes in his hand, opened the cabinet and just shoved it inside. I expect you'll find it if you look."

"I have looked," Mrs. Parkes said. An odd sort of note in her voice. "I've looked everywhere, all the drawers and shelves, the pockets of his dressing-gown, I even turned up the end of the mattress and looked there."

A slight look of unease began to manifest itself on Gina's face. "He went downstairs this afternoon," she said suddenly. "He put on that dark grey suit with the thin stripe. He may have picked up the roll and put it in the pocket of his jacket."

"I looked there too," Mrs. Parkes said, shaking her head.

"He may have carried it with him in his hand, put it down absent-mindedly somewhere downstairs." Gina stood up. "Shall I go and look?"

Mrs. Parkes gave her a long, considering look. "Yes," she said at last. "You go down and look for it. Look everywhere you think at all likely." She lowered her eyes. "I think perhaps you may find it. It would save a great deal of unpleasantness if you did."

"What do you mean?" Gina asked with a trace of heightened colour. "I didn't altogether like the way you said that. As if you were implying I had something to do——"

Mrs. Parkes got to her feet. "I'm implying nothing," she said in an expressionless voice. She seemed to make up her mind suddenly. She met Gina's eyes fair and square. "I may as well tell you, Mr. Mallinson is convinced you took the money."

Gina took a pace backwards. "Me?" she cried. "Steal from Mr. Mallinson?" Her face was pale now, with a tight strained look.

Mrs. Parkes nodded. "He said you went to him for a rise and he refused to give you as much as you asked for. He said you indicated you were in need of money."

"But I didn't steal it! You must believe me!" Gina clasped her hands together. Mrs. Parkes turned her head, listening.

"I can't stay, I must go back to him, I can't have him working himself up into a state, he might bring on another attack." She leaned forward and put a hand on Gina's arm. "Take my advice, my dear, if by any chance you did take the money——" she raised a finger for silence as Gina opened her mouth—— "you might have been tempted, seeing all that money, you might have done something you regret. My advice is to go downstairs now, make a show of searching, then come back and say you found the money—oh anywhere, in one of the rooms you know he visited this afternoon. If the money is returned there'll be no more questions, he may not believe he mislaid it but he can't prove otherwise."

"I didn't take it," Gina said despairingly. "So how can I know where to look for it?" She raised her hand to her head as a thought struck her. "If I do find it—by sheer chance—you'll both be convinced I did steal it and that I'm just taking the opportunity to give it back without any more unpleasantness. Neither of you will ever believe me." Tears rose to her eyes. "Oh, what shall I do?"

"Mrs. Parkes!" The old man's voice, loud and angry, calling from his room.

Mrs. Parkes went swiftly to the door and called, "I'm coming! Just one moment!" She turned back to Gina.

"Richard!" Gina said suddenly. "I'll phone Richard Knight! He'll tell me what to do!" Then she fell silent

K

as a fresh thought struck her, Richard's distaste at the notion of her being involved in accusations of theft. "No, I can't——"

Mrs. Parkes took a step towards her. "No, I shouldn't ring Doctor Knight if I were you." She shook her head. "It would be a mistake. Take my advice, go downstairs now and begin to look. I'll pacify the old man."

"I won't go," Gina said with sudden fierce resolution. "You can go down yourself and look for it. Or one of the servants can be sent for and told to search. If I go, if I find it, I'll never be able to clear myself." She clutched the back of a chair. "I refuse to go." Her face was pale and determined, her eyes dry of tears.

"Mrs. Parkes!" Mallinson's voice was louder now, with a hint of growing fury.

The nurse returned to the door. "I'm coming," she called back calmly. "He'll dismiss you," she said to Gina. "I may be able to persuade him to sleep on it, but if the money isn't returned by the morning, he'll dismiss you at once, without notice or a reference. Think about that. Doctor Knight wouldn't like that at all," she added significantly. "Mr. Mallinson is talking about sacking you now, this moment." She raised her voice in a last appeal. "I must go. Please do as I say, go down now and begin to search. I can square it with the old man if you return the money right away." She went briskly off, leaving the door open.

Gina threw herself down into a chair. A shudder ran through her, the muscles of her neck and shoulders quivered uncontrollably. It was some minutes before they began to relax.

When at last she felt in command of her limbs she stood up, closed the door with a firm, final little bang, switched on the radio, turning up the volume a little more loudly than before, returned to the easy chair and sat down, stretching herself out, propping her feet on a footstool. She

closed her eyes and made a strong effort to listen to the pro-
gramme.

Footsteps again in the corridor, the door opening without
the formality of a knock. Mrs. Parkes's voice saying tone-
lessly, "You've made up your mind, then? You're not going
down?"

Gina remained with her eyes shut, she gave the tiniest
shake of her head.

"Very well then, I'll go myself." The door closing again,
retreating footsteps. A voice from the radio spoke out firm
and clear, speaking of fog that had descended over the
northern half of England, of warning lights on the motor-
ways, the need for great care. Music began to play, soft,
insinuating, a sweet nostalgic waltz. The sound eddied about
the room, dipping and soaring. Time slipped by.

Mrs. Parkes came back. She stood in the doorway and
said something to Gina, clicked her tongue as the girl
made no response, came over to the chair, put out a hand
and shook her by the shoulder, none too gently. Gina
opened her eyes.

"I've looked everywhere," Mrs. Parkes said harshly. "No
sign of the money. I've told Mr. Mallinson. He demanded to
see you right away but I wouldn't allow it. He won't
sleep if he has any further agitation to-night."

"Tell him to take a tablet," Gina said suddenly.

"I did." Mrs. Parkes's voice held a hint of surprise. "But
he refused, said he'd be all right without one." She drew a
breath of irritation at the old man's stubbornness, the girl's
obstinacy, the waywardness of the entire universe. "I've persuaded him to let the whole thing stand over till the morning. I'll see if I can get Mr. David to speak to him to-
morrow, to put in a word for you." She sighed again. "But
I shouldn't count on it. I think you might as well start packing your bags."

Gina closed her eyes again. "Very well," Mrs. Parkes said,
moving her shoulders in frustration. "If that's how you feel.

No-one can help you, it seems." She moved away, paused by the door, speaking back to Gina. "There's still time, if you decide to come to your senses. You have till the morning."

The sound of her footsteps died away. The minutes moved past, one after the other. The music ceased and a voice recounted the news. Another voice made mention of the fog, growing worse now, threatening to deepen further before morning. Images moved behind Gina's closed eyes . . . Richard Knight looking up at her, saying 'I don't understand. You've been dismissed for theft?' His eyes, puzzled, withdrawn . . . A faceless woman in some secretarial agency miles away, shaking her head, telling Gina, 'I'm sorry, no reference, you see, impossible to place you . . .'

Gina shook her head, blinking away the dark images, opened her eyes, stood up, drew a deep breath and went on the strength of a fierce impulse out of the room into the corridor.

She stood for a moment listening. No-one about, the house bedded down for the long night. She looked along the corridor. A gleam of light under Mrs. Parkes's door, a bright strip showing from Mr. Mallinson's room. Both awake then, turning things over, pondering, deciding. She moved silently forward and knocked at the old man's door, entering at once on his answer.

"I hope I'm not disturbing you." Gina's voice was calm, controlled. He looked back at her, chill and hostile, looking away from her again, at the opposite wall.

She stood by the chest of drawers. "I came to say I didn't take the money, I know nothing about it."

He refused to look at her. "I'm trying to rest. All this is supposed to stand over now till the morning. It has been decided."

Her voice rose by a fraction. "I refuse to be treated as a criminal. You have no proof, you can't have any proof, I didn't do it and that's that." She turned her back on him as the tears started to her eyes.

"Nothing will be done till the morning." Mallinson spoke

as if with a great effort at control. "Mr. David will come in the morning, the matter will be gone into then."

"It isn't fair!" she cried. "It isn't just!"

"Justice will be done," he said. "You can be sure of that."

"You can't dismiss me!" Her voice became agitated. "I have nowhere to go! I won't be able to find another job!"

"I thought secretaries were in great demand." A hint of malice now. "You told me so yourself. Only yesterday. A couple of hundred a year extra, you thought you were worth that. When you didn't get it you felt entitled to help yourself." The control slipping now.

"It's monstrously unfair!" she cried. "I won't have it! I'll appeal to——" To whom could she appeal? She fell silent.

Mallinson lay back and closed his eyes. "I've had a long day," he said at last. "I think we had better all get some sleep now. You may see things differently in the morning."

He heard her take a restless step or two, approach the bed, pause, move away again. "This is doing your case no good." He was suddenly weary of the whole sordid business. She made no reply. He opened his eyes. She was standing over by the chest of drawers again, her head bent, her back to him, both hands extended on the polished surface. A look of finality about her stance, of something decided, something done.

"Good night," he said. "Be sure to close the door as you leave." She turned and gave him a look he couldn't quite read. She went out of the room, closing the door softly behind her.

In her comfortable bed next door, Mrs. Parkes turned over and came suddenly awake. The light was still on, she'd dozed off, forgetting to depress the switch. She yawned, glanced down at herself and discovered she was still wearing her quilted nylon jacket. She heaved herself up and shrugged it off, reached out and dropped it over the back of a chair, turned off the light and lay down again.

But sleep refused to return. The minutes slipped by and she grew more wakeful. Her mind began to worry at the problem of her son, never very far away from her thoughts.

A wave of wretchedness swept over her as she imagined him even now making his plans for emigration. Her eyes jerked open, staring into the darkness. I can't bear it, she thought . . . to see him leaning over the rail of a great ship, his family beside him, raising a hand in long farewell, and herself on the quayside, restraining her tears, trying to be brave.

She sighed, sat up and switched on the light. She picked up her handbag from the side table, snapped it open and took out the letter, unfolded it, drew it out and began to read it yet again, knowing it by now almost by heart. She sat staring ahead for a long time, pondering, calculating, looking into the grey future.

A sound from next door. She turned her head. Another sound, the old man turning restlessly in his bed. She put the letter back in her bag, stood up and pulled on her dressing-gown. She put out her hand and touched the bag, running her finger over the leather, her eyes veiled in thought. Then she went quietly into Mr. Mallinson's room.

The bedside light was still on. He was wide awake.

"I heard you moving about," she said softly. "Can I get you something? Some hot milk?" He shook his head. "One of your tablets?" Again he shook his head.

"I'll be all right, thanks, I'll get off to sleep soon."

She hesitated by the bed. "Are you sure? It won't do you any good to lie awake."

"I suppose she did do it?" he asked suddenly. "I don't see who else it could possibly have been. The boy was never anywhere near this side of the bed." He looked up at her, wanting her to agree.

"I thought we'd decided to leave all that till the morning," she said firmly. "You can talk it over with Mr. David. There's no point in going over it now. You must put it out of your mind if you want some sleep to-night. Won't you change your mind and have a hot drink?"

He shook his head stubbornly. "I detest hot milk. I don't want anything, I'll be all right. You get back to bed."

"Very well then, if you're sure." She fussed about for a minute or two longer, plumping his pillows, straightening things here and there, picking up a garment that had slid to the floor. He sighed and closed his eyes, willing her to go, to stop fiddling about, to clear off and let him get some peace.

"Shall I switch off your light?" she asked at last, ceasing her perambulations about the room.

He kept his eyes shut. "No, thank you. I'll switch it off myself. I won't forget."

When she had finally taken herself off he lay staring up at the ceiling, disturbed now, a little distressed. Could there be some other explanation? What if the girl were innocent after all? He strove to recall her tone, her manner. Desperation had showed through clearly enough. Was it the desperation of wronged innocence or confronted guilt? He couldn't decide and yet a little while earlier it had all seemed so clear, so certain.

He strove to remember every detail of the afternoon, aware that he would have to repeat it all to David in the morning. He had had the box in his hands, the boy had been standing over there, he had looked up and seen Gina, he hadn't heard her knock . . . he revolved it all in his mind, unable to reach a conclusion, deciding at last to do what he should have done a long time ago, put it all from him, turn over and go to sleep.

His gaze rested on the whisky decanter. He looked at it with sudden longing. A good stiff drink would lull him sweetly to sleep. He cast his mind back. He hadn't taken a tablet since—since when? Lunch-time? Teatime? He couldn't be absolutely certain. But I know I didn't take one to-night, he thought. He could remember Mrs. Parkes offering him one just now and again, earlier, when she'd been to see Gina. He'd refused them both—or had he accepted the earlier tablet? He wrinkled his brows. No, he was almost certain he'd refused them both. He smiled faintly. It would be all right then to slip out of bed and pour himself a good stiff peg.

He threw back the bedclothes and swung his feet to the floor. How silent the house was now at night! He picked up a glass from the table and carried it over to the decanter, feeling a thrust of pleasure at the thought of the warm glow of the whisky. He set the glass down on the table and got back into bed. He settled himself comfortably against the pillows and raised the glass, not bothering to add water.

A little while later an owl hooted from a branch just outside his window, but the old man didn't hear it. He had slipped far down into the dark abyss of sleep.

CHAPTER XII

IT HAD BEEN an excellent dinner, the food neither too rich nor undistinguished. And his speech had gone off very well. They'd laughed loudly at the jokes, listened to the serious part with little nods of agreement, applauding vigorously when he'd sat down again. He'd spoken for exactly ten minutes, long enough to develop his theme, short enough to hold boredom at bay. Yes, all in all, Dr. Burnett was satisfied with the progress of the evening, showing signs now of drawing to a close.

"Let me get you a brandy," someone said at his elbow. He looked up. One of the younger men, a rising consultant at a group of hospitals. Burnett smiled and shook his head.

"No thank you, I've had all I want. I've a long drive ahead of me. Can't go falling foul of the police." He smiled again. "Wouldn't look well in the papers."

"You're not driving back to Rockley to-night!" the other

man said with surprise. "Have you looked out at the weather in the last hour or two? There's a thick fog. You couldn't see a hundred yards ahead. Don't worry," he added, seeing the old man's look of disquiet, "they can put you up here, in the hotel. Plenty of room. Do you want me to speak to the manager for you?"

Burnett stood up. "I must get back," he said firmly. "If the fog's as bad as you say, I'd better make a start right away."

"You can't go now," the consultant said with a note of protest. "This affair'll go on for another hour or two yet. The night's still young."

"I must be back in Rockley for the morning." Burnett's voice was unyielding. He crossed over to the window of the smoking-room and drew aside one of the heavy curtains. He stood looking out at the white wreaths of mist. "It doesn't look too bad. If I take it slowly——"

"It may not be too bad just here," the consultant said, coming up behind him. "But I was talking to one of the waiters just now, he heard the late news. Said it was very dense in places, shows no sign of lifting to-night. I shouldn't risk it if I were you. I'm certainly not attempting it. I've got a room here. Let me speak to the manager."

"Very good of you." Burnett turned from the window. "But I've made up my mind. I'll start right away. I'll just find the President and make my farewells." He held out his hand. "Good to see you again. One likes to keep in touch with the younger men."

The consultant watched him go. He stood looking after him, shaking his head. An obstinate old boy, no reasoning with him once he'd made up his mind. Still, he'd probably be all right. A cautious man, he'd be a careful driver. And he'd have sense enough to admit defeat if the fog grew too bad, he'd find a motel, pull off the road for the rest of the night.

Why, it isn't too bad at all, Burnett thought as he came out of the mist into a clear stretch of road. He'd covered fifty miles or more in just over two hours. There had been only one or two really tricky patches where he'd had to lower the window and drive at a crawl with his head stuck out. And now the fog seemed to have disappeared. People exaggerated so, from an innate sense of drama probably. He smiled and pressed his foot down on the accelerator.

Twenty miles further on he rounded a sharp bend in the road and came without warning into a yellow bank of fog. He uttered an exclamation and brought his foot down on the brake, hearing at the same moment the sound of approaching wheels.

He felt the car begin to slide on the greasy road, he raised his foot from the brake, pulling hard on the wheel, touched the brake lightly again, on, off, counter-steering, one part of his mind hearing the sound of wheels grow louder, sharper.

There was no time—he brought both feet down in a last desperate attempt to avoid a collision, felt the car slip out of control, lurch sideways.

A loud, sickening roar exploding against his ear-drums, the shock of impact, a brilliant starburst of light, a blow striking him on the chest—and then there was nothing, only a long deep blackness, impenetrable chill, a drifting void, with sometimes, fleetingly, far out on the edge of it, a suggestion of voices, a hint of movement . . . and the sudden merciful descent again into the embracing arms of darkness.

Half-past six. The alarm shrilled its summons a couple of feet away from Tim Jefford's ear. He struggled up through the layers of sleep, stretched out a protesting arm and fumbled for the switch to press the damn' thing off.

Then realisation swept over him—he was taking the first train up to London, he had to get up, shave, put on the borrowed plumes. He heaved himself up out of the bedclothes, scratching his head, yawning, looking out at the new day with a mixture of interest and distaste.

He pulled back the foot of the mattress and drew out the

trousers carefully laid there before he went to sleep. Quite a good crease. Footsteps, accompanied by a faint rattling sound, whispered along the corridor. Ah! that would be the odd-job boy with the black coffee and toast. He took a coin from the little pile of silver on the bedside table, flung open the door and took the tray.

The lad nodded sleepily in acknowledgment of the tip. Half a crown this time. Things were looking up.

"Ten past seven, the bus into Hallborough," he said in a low voice. "Leaves from the end of the lane, you'll make it all right."

Half an hour later Tim let himself quietly out of the side door. The air was cool and damp but the fog had vanished, he was pleased to see. At least the train would run on time.

As the bus ground past the end of the long drive leading up to Whitegates he turned his head and stared through the trees at the distant outline of the house.

I wonder what happened last night after I left, he thought idly. I bet the old man found his roll of money stuffed away under a pillow or in the pocket of his dressing-gown. If he ever had a roll of money in his precious box in the first place. Old men, losing their grip on things, couldn't rely on them five minutes together.

Alarm stabbed at him for a moment. I hope he doesn't forget about me, he thought, sitting up suddenly. Be great if I got back with the fresh load of coins and he'd lost interest or forgotten all about me—or if the set-to last night had put him out of action for a couple of days.

He yawned widely without troubling to raise his hand. Wonder how Miss Gina Whatsit got on, he thought, settling himself comfortably back into his seat again, wonder if she managed to soothe the old man down . . . or if perhaps she did pinch the money after all . . . damn' silly thing to do though, couldn't hope to get away with it.

Seven-fifteen. Gina glanced at her little clock. She had

managed to fall asleep for a couple of hours, a disturbed un-refreshing sleep in which she wandered barefoot down an endless road in the echoing dark. She had woken up at five with her heart jumping and pounding, the bedclothes in a tangled heap. She had switched on the light, restored some order to the bed, found a book and tried to read, anything to occupy her mind till morning came.

And now morning had come. She swung her feet out of bed and reached for her dressing-gown. Her eyes felt gritty from lack of sleep. She thrust her feet into slippers and opened her bedroom door.

Along the corridor Mrs. Parkes was coming out of her room, already dressed in her uniform, neatly groomed for the new day. She turned her head and gave Gina an assessing glance, nodding a greeting at her. The girl looked pale, not at all well, dark smudges under her eyes.

Gina halted a couple of feet away from Mrs. Parkes, managed to say, 'Good morning,' and then fell silent, feeling the treacherous tears threaten to engulf her.

"Changed your mind yet?" Mrs. Parkes asked without any note of sympathy. "Save us all a lot of trouble if you have."

Gina shook her head miserably, still not speaking.

Mrs. Parkes raised her shoulders and let out a long breath. "Well then——" The gesture dismissed the girl and her follies. She turned to go along to Mr. Mallinson's room. Gina followed her, headed for the bathroom.

Mrs. Parkes came to a sudden halt. She put out a hand and touched Gina on the arm, jerking her head towards Mr. Mallinson's door, at the yellow line of light showing beneath it. She frowned, looked a little puzzled, a little anxious.

"He must have had his light on all night," she whispered.

"He may have woken up early, perhaps he couldn't get back to sleep," Gina whispered back.

Mrs. Parkes went swiftly to the door, rapped on the panel, and went in at once, leaving the door open. Gina stood hesitating outside, pulling the cord of her dressing-gown tightly about her waist.

No sound of voices from within the room. The slow seconds moved by. Mrs. Parkes came out of the room, closing the door behind her. She stood looking at Gina with a calm, thoughtful gaze. Gina looked back at her, her face even paler than before, her fingers twisting the silk girdle.

"You don't have to worry about the sack any more," Mrs. Parkes said in a cool, level voice. Gina's eyes blinked wide open, she took a step backwards, raised one hand.

"He's dead," Mrs. Parkes said in the same unemotional tone. "He's been dead some hours."

CHAPTER XIII

"OH—NO!" Gina gave a little cry, put her hands up to her face and burst into harsh sobs. Violent tremors shook her shoulders.

"I must ring Doctor Burnett," Mrs. Parkes said, making no attempt to soothe Gina, going past her with a quick firm tread, along the corridor, halting abruptly on the landing, wheeling round, returning to the door, opening it, taking the key from the other side, locking the door, pocketing the key, all without a word. She walked past Gina again in silence and went downstairs to the phone.

She dialled the number, heard the receiver lifted at the other end, the housekeeper's voice, polite, impersonal.

"Mrs. Parkes here, from Whitegates. Could I speak to Dr. Burnett, please? At once. It's urgent." A little break in her voice, the first crack in the professional poise. "I'm afraid Mr. Mallinson is dead. Some hours ago, I should think."

The housekeeper offered her sympathy as she had done countless times before. "I'll speak to Doctor Burnett right away. He isn't down yet, I don't suppose he got back till very late."

"Burnett," said the Sister. "A doctor apparently. An address near Hallborough, a village called Rockley. A country practitioner, I should think. I'll phone his home as soon as I get a moment, they must be anxious."

The young house physician drew the blankets up around Burnett's shoulders. He straightened himself. "No very great damage as far as I can see. No bones broken." He jerked his head towards the unconscious man. "Let me know as soon as he shows signs of coming round. We'll get him up to X-ray. Wonder what he was doing round here at that time of night. Driving in the fog." He shook his head. "You think he'd have more sense. At his age."

The Sister looked down at the papers in her hand. "Speaking at a dinner, apparently. There's a letter here ——"

"Better get on to the family. Tell them we'll let them know the result of the X-ray as soon as we can. No cause for alarm."

"Look!" The Sister took a step forward, raising her hand. "I think he's coming to."

Burnett opened his eyes and stared up at her with a dreamy, unfocused look.

"It's all right," the Sister said softly. "No need to worry."

Burnett shut his eyes, opened them again, made an attempt to raise himself. She put both hands on his shoulders and gently eased him down again.

"Don't try to move. You're quite all right. You had a little accident in your car. You were driving home in the fog."

Burnett drew a hand out from under the bedclothes and raised it in a despairing gesture.

"I must get back," he said. "At once. I'm all right." He struggled to rise again.

The house physician sat on the edge of the bed and took the patient's hand firmly in his own.

"You'll have to stay here for a day or two at least," he said gently. "You know that. "We'll have to do a couple of X-rays." His voice took on a briskly cheerful note. "Make sure there's no serious damage. Your patients can manage without you for a few days."

Burnett's eyes expressed alarm. "I've got to get back," he said again, his voice rising. "There's only young Knight—my partner—he's on his own——"

"He'll manage very well," the houseman said reassuringly. "I'm sure he's very competent. Now just lie back and rest. Sister is going to phone Rockley, you're not to worry about anything. Have you got a family? A wife?"

Burnett gave a long sigh and closed his eyes, accepting defeat. "No family," he said with infinite weariness. "No wife."

Richard Knight picked up the receiver from the hall table.

"Mrs. Parkes? Knight here. I'm afraid Doctor Burnett hasn't come back yet. The housekeeper has just been into his room and the bed hasn't been slept in. He must have decided to stay the night in the hotel. The fog, you know. Very sensible of him. I'm very sorry to hear about Mr. Mallinson. I hope you're not too upset. It was always on the cards of course."

"It was that upset last night," Mrs. Parkes said suddenly. "I blame myself. I should have known. I should have called you. I should have got you to give him something——"

"Now don't distress yourself," Knight said gently. "I'm sure you did everything you should. I'll be over in a few minutes. Get yourself a good strong cup of tea."

"You can take your time," Mrs. Parkes said. "There's nothing you can do for him now. He's been dead a long time."

Knight heard the first trace of hysteria rise in her voice.

"Try to keep calm," he said. "Don't start to blame yourself. I'm leaving now. You get along to the kitchen and get Cook to give you that cup of tea. Plenty of sugar. Do you hear?"

She had got herself under control again. "Very well, Doctor Knight," she said mechanically. "Plenty of sugar, I've got that."

He replaced the receiver. He glanced at the housekeeper hovering a yard or two away.

"I'm going over to Whitegates," he said. She went over to the hallstand and took down his overcoat. "I don't know when I'll be back."

The phone rang sharply. "Answer that, will you?" he said. "I can't stop now." He opened the front door and strode off towards the garage.

Pity about Mallinson, he thought, to go like that, all alone, not even Mrs. Parkes beside him at the end. A shaft of acute compassion pierced his professional armour. He imagined the old man opening his eyes in the empty darkness, gasping for breath, struggling to call out, to summon the nurse, falling back against the pillows.

All that wealth, all that success, the long striving years ending like that, none of his family near him, no-one to touch his hand, to give him a last word, a last embrace.

He gave a deep sigh, unlocking the garage door. One never got used to it, there was always this sharp sense of grief, of failure, however old the patient was, however expected the end.

Behind him the front door was flung open.

"Doctor Knight!" He turned his head. The housekeeper standing at the open door, her hand raised, calling him back. "Doctor Knight! Don't go! It's Doctor Burnett!"

Knight went back into the house at a run.

"He's had an accident," the housekeeper said rapidly. "It's the hospital. He's all right, he isn't badly hurt."

Knight snatched up the receiver. "Doctor Knight here,

I'm Doctor Burnett's partner." The look of sharp anxiety on his features began to relax as he listened to the Sister's calm voice. The housekeeper stood beside him with her hands clasped together.

"You'll let me know as soon as you have the result of the X-ray?" Knight said. "I can't really get up to see him, I can't leave the practice——" He thought rapidly. "If he's going to be in hospital more than a day or two, I'll try to make some arrangement, I'll try to get away."

"Will he be all right?" the housekeeper asked urgently when he had replaced the receiver. She began to cry quietly.

Knight put his arm round her shoulders. "He's all right," he said. "As far as they know." He gave her shoulders a little reassuring squeeze. "Don't upset yourself, he'll be back in no time at all, as right as rain." An accident, he thought, at his age. Even with no bones broken, there was the shock. He bit his lip. It might be weeks before Burnett was able to function properly again, months even . . . a thought struck at him. When Burnett discovered that his old friend Mallinson had died during his absence . . . the self-reproach on top of the shock of the accident—he might make up his mind to retire at last, to give up practice altogether . . . Knight shook away the encroaching thoughts.

"I must get over to Whitegates," he said with a sigh. "Mrs. Parkes will be waiting for me."

The housekeeper dabbed at her eyes and made a strong effort at control. "I'll have your breakfast ready as soon as you get back," she said. Habit reasserted itself. "You're going off without even a cup of coffee——"

"Don't worry about that." He threw open the front door. "I'll get some coffee at Whitegates. Take any messages while I'm gone. If the hospital ring again, if they want to speak to me, they can ring me at Whitegates."

Mrs. Parkes was standing in the drive a few yards away from the front door, looking anxiously out for him. She came up to the car as soon as he had slowed to a halt. She was shivering a little in the chill air.

"I was beginning to wonder where you'd got to."

He gave her a sharp glance. "Did you drink that tea? You look frozen. You shouldn't be out here without a coat."

"I'm all right," she said abruptly. "Was there any message from Doctor Burnett? Do you know when he'll be back?" She opened the front door. He pondered briefly—was it advisable just now to tell her of Burnett's accident? She looked as if she were only just holding off a collapse into helpless tears. But he'd have to tell her very shortly anyway. He put a hand under her elbow and propelled her gently into an easy chair. She looked up at him, surprised, frowning.

"Now don't distress yourself any further," he said. "Take a deep breath, relax, sit back."

She remained bolt upright. "What is it? Has something happened? Something else? You look as if——"

"It's not good news," he said evenly. "But it isn't too bad." He saw her hands stiffen. "I'm afraid Doctor Burnett had a little accident in his car." He held up a hand. "It's all right, nothing very serious, but it'll be a day or two before he'll be out of hospital. In the meantime——"

She stared up at him. He saw her pupils dilate.

"Doctor Burnett?" she said on a high note. "Mr. Mallinson will be very——" Then she put a hand up to her mouth. "Oh——" She shuddered, once, violently, then her hands grasped the arms of her chair. She closed her eyes for a moment.

Knight leaned forward. "Are you all right? Would you like something?"

She opened her eyes and gave him a little smile. "I'm quite all right, thank you." Her tone was stronger, steadier. "Just for a moment I forgot." She stood up and drew a deep breath, she squared her shoulders. "I'll take you up now, Doctor. Don't worry about me." And she did look more herself again, controlled, self-possessed, in command of the situation.

He walked beside her towards the stairs.

"It was that unpleasant scene last night," she said in an even tone, giving him a calm look. "I'm certain of that. I knew he was upset but he seemed to have settled down when I looked in on him last thing."

Knight frowned. "What scene was that?"

"He kept some money in a cash-box by his bed. He wanted to take some out last evening, there was a young man here, a coin-dealer, Mr. Mallinson wanted to buy a coin —and the money had gone." Her fingers toyed with the clasp of her belt. "He accused Miss Thorson of taking the money——"

"Gina!" Knight came to a sudden halt. "He accused Gina!"

Mrs. Parkes stood still. Her look held a touch of hostility. "Yes, Miss Thorson. It certainly appeared as if she had taken it. He was very upset but I persuaded him to let it all rest until this morning, to wait for Mr. David."

Knight put out a hand and gripped her arm.

"Gina denied it of course. She did, didn't she?"

She looked levelly back at him. "Oh yes, she denied it. But then she would, wouldn't she? He was threatening to dismiss her, without a reference."

Knight made an angry sound. Outside the house there was the sudden whir of a car approaching, halting sharply. He turned his head and looked down the stairs.

"That'll be Mr. David now," Mrs. Parkes said, withdrawing her arm from the doctor's grasp. "I phoned him. Or it might be Mr. Kenneth, I phoned him too, at the Swan." She stared down at the housemaid crossing the hall, dabbing at her eyes as she went.

"Of course Gina didn't take the money," Knight said in a low fierce voice. "It's a ridiculous notion. Any number of people could have taken it. Why pick on Gina?"

"I don't see any necessity to go into all that now," Mrs.

Parkes said in an unyielding tone. "I only mentioned it to let you know Mr. Mallinson's state of mind last night. I don't see why the matter should be raised now that Mr. Mallinson——" She broke off, looked down into the hall again, at the man following the housemaid. "It's Mr. Kenneth——" She looked undecided for an instant, not knowing whether to go down and speak to him or to continue up the stairs and unlock the bedroom door for the doctor.

"If you could wait down there for a moment, Mr. Kenneth," she called. "I'm just taking Doctor Knight up—I won't be long."

He raised his hand in acknowledgment, went and stood by the fireplace with his hands clasped behind his back, looking up at them. The housemaid said something to him, and he shook his head, not looking at her. She went back towards the kitchen quarters with her head lowered.

"I have the key here." Mrs. Parkes was moving up the stairs again. She slipped her hand into the pocket of her uniform. "I thought it best to lock the bedroom door."

Knight nodded briefly. "Yes, quite right." He was frowning, glancing along the corridor. A door opened a little and Gina's face appeared. She threw him a look compounded of appeal and apprehension. He opened his mouth to call out to her but the door closed again. Mrs. Parkes pursed her lips.

"Here we are." She inserted the key in the lock, opened the door quietly, as if the sound was capable of disturbing the occupant. She drew the sheet back from the old man's peaceful face with a steady hand.

"He must have gone in his sleep. There's no sign of any distress."

"You heard nothing in the night?" The doctor began his examination. "No movement?"

"I'd have come in at once if I had." Her manner was stiffly injured. "Surely you know that?"

"Yes, of course." He drew back Mallinson's eyelids. He stood up, frowned, picked up the drum of tablets from the bedside table, lifted the lid and glanced inside. "How many of these were there in the drum last night?" he asked in a voice that had grown much sharper.

"I don't know," Mrs. Parkes said.

"You don't know? Why don't you know?"

"We had a little accident with the tablets yesterday." She moved her head in disapproval of his tone. "Doctor Burnett spilled some—it wasn't his fault," she added quickly. "Mr. Mallinson was fiddling about with the drum and the doctor went to take it from him. He stepped on some of the tablets by mistake. I didn't count those that were left. I'm sorry, I suppose I should have done, I didn't think of it at the time. Doctor Burnett didn't suggest it." Her tone absolved herself from blame.

"Then you don't know whether or not Mr. Mallinson took any of the tablets after you left him for the night?"

She glanced at him with sudden anxiety. "You don't think —you mean, he might have taken—oh, I'm sure he wouldn't, he didn't have a tablet at all yesterday afternoon or evening, he said he didn't need one. Doctor Burnett said he didn't have to take a tablet unless he felt he needed it——" She twisted her fingers together. "He just died in his sleep, surely? He could have gone at any time—there's no suggestion——"

Knight frowned, looking down at the dead man. "I'm not altogether satisfied," he said. He bent down and raised the eyelids again.

"I wish Doctor Burnett was here," Mrs. Parkes said suddenly. "He wouldn't suggest——"

Knight stood up. "I'm suggesting nothing." He thrust his hands into his pockets and glanced about the room. His gaze came to rest on the whisky decanter. He took his hands from his pockets. "Whisky," he said abruptly. "Did Doctor Burnett allow him to drink whisky?"

She followed his gaze and Knight heard the little intake of her breath. "What's the matter?" he asked. "What's wrong?"

She was staring at the amber liquid. Barely half a tot

remained in the decanter. "He must have drunk some," she said. "There was more than that in it yesterday." She raised her eyes to the doctor. "He was allowed a glass provided he hadn't taken a tablet for some hours." She repeated Burnett's orders. "Mr. Mallinson understood it very well, he was very good about it, he didn't disobey orders like that, he knew it would be dangerous. Doctor Burnett explained it to him very carefully. I was here, I heard him."

Knight crossed over to the decanter, put out a hand to the stopper and then appeared to think better of his action.

"Have you some paper handkerchiefs?" he asked.

Mrs. Parkes looked at him with surprise. She turned and picked up a box of tissues from the table, handed them to the doctor. "Are these what you want?"

"Yes, thank you, they'll do fine." He drew a couple of tissues from the box, held one in each hand and delicately withdrew the stopper from the decanter. He bent his head and sniffed at the whisky. He laid the stopper on the polished wood, tilted the decanter and put a finger to the neck. He raised his fingers to his lips, tasted the liquid, tilted the decanter again, repeated his tasting.

"Is there something wrong with the whisky?" Mrs. Parkes asked anxiously. "It was Mr. Mallinson's special whisky, he wouldn't have any other brand."

Knight replaced the stopper with his tissue-wrapped fingers. "I'll have to get this analysed," he said. "I'll get it done right away." He looked ahead in thought.

"Analysed?" Mrs. Parkes's voice was sharply hostile. "Is that necessary?"

He gave her a brief glance. "I'd hardly suggest it otherwise." He looked down at the decanter. "I think it would be best to pour the whisky into a clean bottle, leave the decanter as it is." He turned his head. "Could you get me a bottle? See that it's absolutely clean. And dry."

"Oh yes, of course. Right away." She moved towards the door, then looked back, hesitant. "Will you be staying here? In the room?"

He nodded. "For the moment. I'll take the whisky and then I'll be leaving. I'll be back as soon as I can."

Recollection struck at her. "Mr. Kenneth's downstairs—and I expect Mr. David and his wife are here too by this time——"

"Tell them I'll see them in a few minutes. As soon as I've finished in here. And now, if I could have that bottle——"

"Yes, of course." She left the room and he heard her walking away down the corridor. He glanced rapidly round the room, his eyes searching the flat surfaces of furniture and shelves, looking for an envelope, a paper, but without success. He frowned and drew a deep breath, turned back to the decanter, grasped it lightly again with the aid of the tissues, repeated his tasting of the whisky, assessing the traces of bitterness behind the mellow surface flavour.

A low knock sounded at the door.

"Just a moment." He set the decanter carefully back in place and crossed to the door, opening it, finding himself looking down at Gina, her face pale and strained, her eyes red-rimmed. She stared up at him with frightened eyes, not speaking.

She wore no make-up. Her hair was drawn back from her face as if she had done no more than drag a comb through it. She wore a plain jumper and skirt. She looked very young, very defenceless, very unhappy.

"Gina!" He reached out and slipped an arm round her shoulders. "I can't talk to you now, but don't worry about anything, I'll see you later."

"Did Mrs. Parkes tell you?" she asked in a low, trembling voice. "About the money?" Tears glittered in her eyes. "I didn't take it!"

He stooped and kissed her lightly on the cheek. "No, of course you didn't. Don't worry, we'll get that sorted out. It isn't important now." He glanced along the corridor. "If I were you I'd go back to your room and lie down for a bit. You look as if you haven't had much sleep."

"Oh no, I couldn't do that!" she said. "There'll be things to do. I should be doing them now!" She looked up at him with anxiety. "There are all kinds of people I should be phoning, I should be letting them know about Mr. Mallinson——"

"I'll speak to David," he said. "He'll understand. He can do what phoning's necessary. His wife can help. And Kenneth." He gave her a bracing smile. "There are plenty of people to see to all that has to be done. You go and get some sleep, I'll explain, they'll understand."

"If you're sure it will be all right?"

He smiled at her. "Yes, of course I'm sure. Will you be able to sleep? Or shall I give you something?"

"No, I'll be all right. I can sleep now, I think."

"I'm on your side, remember," he said tenderly. "Just go and lie down, close your eyes and don't think about a thing. I'll look after you, I promise."

"Thank you." She tried to say something more but she couldn't, she gave him a half-smile and touched his hand. He stood watching her go back to her room, then he stepped back into Mallinson's room and closed the door.

Mrs. Parkes came back a few minutes later with the clean medicine bottle. "They're all here now," she said. "They wanted to come up and see him."

He took the bottle from her. "I'm afraid they won't be able to do that. Not until after I have had the result of the analysis. I'll speak to them." He threw her a sudden glance. "You didn't say anything, did you—about the whisky?" She shook her head. "That's right, no point in causing unnecessary alarm. I'll make some kind of explanation." He picked up the tissues and began the operation of transferring the whisky to the medicine bottle.

"I'll lock this door and take the key with me when I leave. I'll phone you as soon as I can, I'll let you know when I'll be coming back." He was silent until he had finished his task. He inserted the cork carefully into the neck of the bottle.

"I saw Miss Thorson, by the way," he said. "She looked very upset." Mrs. Parkes drew her lips into a thin line. "I told her to go and get some sleep. I don't think she ought to be bothered with any duties just now, there are plenty of people here to see to what has to be done."

"Very well," Mrs. Parkes said, not looking at him. "I'll see she's not disturbed." She stared at the wall, he saw that her fingers were pleating the skirt of her uniform dress. "The whisky——" she said in a light, strained tone, "you're not taking that to be analysed for fun." He made no reply. "If there's anything in it," she went on in the same voice, "then it must have been put there deliberately—and surely not by Mr. Mallinson himself." She paused again.

"Go on," Richard said. "Say what you have to say."

"If Mr. Mallinson decided—if he wanted——"

"If he thought of suicide, you mean," Knight said evenly. She raised her eyes and looked at him levelly. "Yes, that is what I mean. Then he would surely simply take a great many tablets and drink a glass of water——"

"If he wanted to be certain they would be lethal, then he'd drink them with whisky. He understood the effect of whisky in combination with the tablets. According to you, Doctor Burnett made that very plain to him."

"Well then," she said, "he'd have swallowed the tablets and drunk a glass of whisky with them. He wouldn't have gone to the trouble of dissolving something in the whisky. It would seem quite pointless."

Knight inclined his head. "Yes, I've thought of that," he conceded. "I imagine you've also thought of the logical deduction from that?"

She nodded. She was breathing rather heavily.

"Yes, someone else tampered with the whisky."

Knight gave her a long look. "In other words, Henry Mallinson was murdered."

She turned her head and looked at the window. She spoke carefully, choosing her words. "It would seem to be rather convenient for Gina Thorson that Mr. Mallinson is dead this morning. Now there won't be any investigation into the theft of the money."

Knight took a step forward as if he would raise his hand to strike her. Then he drew a deep breath. "There is no scrap of evidence that Miss Thorson stole the money. If the money was ever there to steal." His voice took on a sharper edge. "Have you considered your own position? In and out of the bedroom several times a day, without question. Who would have had a better opportunity to take the money than you?"

CHAPTER XIV

"Doctor Knight!" Mrs. Parkes was appalled. "How dare you suggest——"

"You don't care for the suggestion?" Knight asked. "I don't imagine Miss Thorson did either. I should watch what you say in future."

Mrs. Parkes bit her lip, made a strong effort at calm. "Perhaps I was a little hasty," she said reluctantly. "I'm sorry."

"We don't know that there was any money to steal," Knight said, moving to the door. "And we don't know that the whisky was tampered with. Mr. Mallinson may have died quite naturally in his sleep. It would be better if we wait for the facts to establish themselves before we begin to construct fancy theories."

"All the same," she said with a little thrust of malice, "you don't think Mr. Mallinson died quite naturally in his sleep, do you?"

He didn't answer her question. "Come along now, I'm going to lock the room and take the key." She followed him out into the corridor. He sighed. "You'd better come down with me while I speak to the relatives. I'll have to say something to them, but I don't want to spend any longer than I can possibly help. I'd appreciate it if you'd——"

"Leave them to me," she said. "I've had plenty of experience in these matters."

He was back in Whitegates in just over an hour. Mrs. Parkes came out to meet him as soon as he had stepped from his car. Her eyes looked a question at him. He nodded at her.

"A positive result," he said heavily. "The tablets had been added to the whisky—far more than a lethal dose. There'll have to be an autopsy, we'll have to know the contents of the stomach. Are the two sons still here? I must speak to them, I need their consent."

She gestured towards the house. "Yes, they're here. And Mrs. David." She led the way inside.

"I've made the arrangements already," he said. "The men will be here shortly." He put a hand on her arm, detaining her for a moment. "Remember what I said. Don't go round discussing this—with the servants or anyone else. And don't go round levelling wild accusations either. You may find some of them come home to roost."

She looked up at him gravely. "Are you threatening me, Doctor Knight?"

"I'm not threatening anyone, I'm waiting for the facts. If Mallinson's stomach shows the ingestion of a number of tablets together with whisky——"

"I wish Doctor Burnett was here," she said suddenly.

He finished his sentence. "Then it's a matter for the police. Not for speculation or action on our part. I'm afraid there's no question of waiting for Burnett. There was another message from the hospital, my housekeeper took it. They've had the results of the X-ray—no real damage. It's mainly a question of shock and his age. Cuts and bruises of course, but nothing worse, thank God. It'll be a few days before they let him out. Things will have to take their course here without him."

She nodded. "Yes, I suppose it can't be helped."

"Now, if you'd show me where the family are." He followed her across the hall.

The police-station in Rockley village consisted of a small detached house near the church where Police Constable Leach lived with his wife and children. The front room served as an office. It was warm, almost stuffy, this morning, from the heat of a large coal fire. Dr. Knight, Kenneth Mallinson and his brother David sat on upright chairs facing Leach who was esconced behind a flat-topped desk, making notes on a pad.

"I see." Leach raised his hand and scratched his head with the pen. "Result of the autopsy shows a large number of tablets taken together with whisky. Analysis of the remaining whisky shows a large number of tablets dissolved in the whisky." He breathed heavily, a little out of his depth. Never anything more exciting than a stolen bicycle or a straying dog in Rockley. "Mr. Mallinson left no letter, no serious indication of suicide." He raised his eyes and looked at the doctor. "Any possibility of accident?"

David Mallinson moved in his chair. "Accident? How could anyone remove the stopper from the decanter and drop in several tablets by accident?"

"I believe we can rule out accident," Knight said, ignoring David's interruption.

Leach rubbed his hand across his lip. "Which leaves us with murder," he said.

"We had to come to you in the first place," Knight said. "But I think you will agree it's really a matter for the Hallborough police. They have the men, the facilities——"

The constable nodded. "Yes, I was just about to say the same thing myself." His glance slid over the two sons. "I'll be glad to do anything I can to help of course, but it's not really my line of country." His tone held a hint of apology. He picked up the phone. "I'll speak to Hallborough now—if you'd care to wait in the other room for a moment. I daresay my wife will make you a cup of tea if you ask her. She's in the kitchen."

Detective-Inspector Ingram and Detective-Sergeant Yates sat side by side at the long mahogany table in the library at Whitegates. Detective-Constable Jennings sat at the end of the table, taking notes. The village constable, Leach, stood uncertainly by the fireplace, ready to make himself useful. A little in awe of the Hallborough men but pleased at the opportunity to learn from them, anxious to make a good impression, to earn a mark or two against the day when Authority might consider him for promotion.

Inspector Ingram gazed thoughtfully at the three members of the dead man's family ranged before him at the other side of the table. Kenneth and David Mallinson, the two sons, Carole Mallinson, David's wife. All three of them sitting stiffly upright, watching him in silence.

"We are treating this as a case of murder," he said in a clear unemotional tone. "Natural death, suicide and accident appear to be conclusively ruled out, for reasons which have already been made clear to you." His gaze travelled from face to face as he spoke, meeting the eyes of each in turn. Controlled faces, the expressions almost detached, giving nothing away . . . so far. Inspector Ingram was a patient man. He would continue to search their faces and the faces of every other person who appeared before him in the course of the next few days, waiting for the first crack in control, the first faint signs of unease, of agitation.

"A wealthy man, Henry Mallinson," he said. "The classic question—who stands to benefit from his death? I shall require a copy of the will." He raised his eyebrows at Kenneth, the elder son. "The name and address of the solicitor?"

Kenneth supplied the details. Ingram glanced at Constable Leach. "Did you get that?" Leach nodded. "Ring the solicitor, will you, right away. You can use one of the other phones." He turned his head, looking out of the tall window at a pair of police cars drawn up outside. "Send one of the drivers over to Hallborough to fetch a copy of the will. If the solicitor can bring it himself, so much the better, I'll want to talk to him. If he can't, if he's busy, ask him to come over here later in the day, get him to fix a time."

"Yes, sir." Constable Leach left the room at once, glad of the task, to be on his feet, moving purposefully off on a mission well within his powers, free of the somewhat oppressive atmosphere of the library.

"I daresay you know the contents of the will already." Ingram's eyes travelled from Kenneth to David. "And when it was made. Perhaps there's a copy here, in the house?"

"There's a copy of the old will here," David Mallinson said. "It's in the safe, in my father's study, as far as I know. He always kept it there."

"The old will?" Ingram said on a rising note.

"It's not of much consequence now." Kenneth Mallinson made a dismissive gesture with his hand. "The new will was signed yesterday morning."

David turned his head sharply and looked at his brother. No love lost there, Ingram noted, barely-veiled hostility in that glance.

"The new will wasn't signed," David said with firm assurance. "It was due to be signed in a day or two. The old will still stands."

Kenneth shook his head and the tiniest trace of a smile curved his lips. "You're wrong," he said in a light, casual tone. "I know for certain the new will was signed."

David looked at his wife sitting beside him. "My father mentioned the new will to you, didn't he? He told you it was going to be signed in two or three days."

"Yes, that's what he told me." She addressed the inspector. "I'm quite certain of that." He merely inclined his head in acknowledgment, holding his peace, letting them play it out, learning what he could from a tone, an expression.

"I saw the solicitor here, in the house, yesterday morning," Kenneth said in the same easy voice. "I spoke to him, he told me himself the new will had just been signed. He brought a couple of clerks over with him in the car from Hallborough, to use as witnesses. He couldn't use any of the servants here, they're all mentioned in the will."

Carole leaned forward, looking along the table at her brother-in-law. "But when I saw you—in the Swan—yesterday evening—we spoke of the new will then. You didn't say anything about its being already signed. I told you it was due to be witnessed in a couple of days and you didn't contradict me."

Kenneth moved one hand in a careless gesture. "I saw no reason to tell you. If that was what my father had told you, it was no business of mine to tell you otherwise." Carole levelled at him a look of open dislike, then she glanced at her husband. Ingram saw the exchange of looks between them, the eyes expressing sharp questioning, a hint of dismay, of incredulity.

A little tingling sensation rippled along the inspector's spine. We're getting at it now, he thought. Throw them a few more questions, watch them as they supply the answers. This was the moment above all others that he savoured, the first scent, the first movement in the undergrowth.

"Who benefited under the old will?" he asked quietly. "And who benefits under the new? Leaving aside all the minor bequests, to employees and so on."

"Under the old will," David said, "the bulk of the estate came to me." *Came*, the inspector registered, not *comes*, he is convinced now that the new will has been signed.

"I was not mentioned in the old will." Kenneth's voice was still light and easy. Ingram gave a little nod. A Hallborough man, he was aware of the rift in the Mallinson family, common gossip, and what little he didn't know had been readily supplied to him by Constable Leach earlier in the morning. "I understand—though of course I'm not absolutely certain," Kenneth went on, "that under the terms of the new will, the estate was to be divided between my brother and myself, though not equally, a sixty-forty division."

"With yourself taking the larger share? As the elder son?" Ingram asked gently.

Kenneth nodded. "But my father may have changed his mind, it's quite possible."

Ingram pondered the matter for a moment. Mallinson was known as a man of decision, not one to go chopping and changing his mind as the fancy took him. Still—an old man, an ill man, subject at the last perhaps to moods and whims.

The two sons were silent now, no longer looking at each other. Not much more to be gained just now from this line of questioning. Better let it go for the time being. They'd all know the terms of the new will soon enough, and both men were armoured now, prepared for surprise or disappointment, ready to school their voices and their expressions when those terms were disclosed.

He felt keenly alert, pleasantly stimulated. There's the motive, he thought, bright and clear. One of the two men sitting in front of him had carried out the murder, he was almost certain now in his mind. But which one? Kenneth, knowing the new will had been signed, anxious for some reason of his own to get his hands on the money without delay, fearful that the old man might change his mind once again, draw up yet a third will, not to Kenneth's advantage?

Or David, believing the old will still stood, dropping the tablets into his father's whisky before the new will could be witnessed, before his brother could snatch three-fifths of the estate from his grasp?

His eyes slid to Carole Mallinson, pretty and composed, her hands lightly clasped before her. A possibility that she had acted alone or with her husband, making sure in either case of a continuing life of ease and luxury.

Ingram drew a little contented breath. All the other possible suspects to be seen of course, all the other details to be waded through, but he saw them now as so much underbrush to be cleared away, tedious routine investigation, time-consuming, inescapable, but revealing in the end the true path clear and distinct.

A knock sounded at the library door. He came out of his thoughts, pleased at the interruption, holding perhaps the possibility of a fresh line of questioning.

"Come in!" he called. The door opened and the secretary entered. Thorson, wasn't it? He glanced at a list in front of him. Miss Gina Thorson. Pretty girl, though with a look of great strain. Understandable enough in the circumstances. Attached to her employer no doubt, out of a job now in all probability—or she would be when Mallinson's affairs had been cleared up. Still suffering from shock, only natural, waking up like that to find the old man dead.

"Yes?" He glanced enquiringly at her. She came up to the table.

"There's a solicitor on the phone for Mr. David."

"Henry Mallinson's solicitor?" the inspector asked.

She shook her head. "No. It's a solicitor representing Mrs. Stallard. He's just heard that Mr. Mallinson is dead——" her voice trembled slightly—"and he wants to know the position about Mrs. Stallard's compensation. He'd like to speak to Mr. David."

"Make a note of his name and phone number," David Mallinson said with a touch of irritation. "Tell him I'll get in touch with him later. In a couple of days. I really can't deal with it just now."

"I shall have something to say about the compensation too," Kenneth said lightly. David flashed him a glance that held both a hint of anger and the realisation that from now on it would be Kenneth who made the decisions in the firm. He sat back in his chair with a look on his face as of a man seeing a strange new landscape open out where he had expected the familiar sweep of well-known countryside.

Gina glanced at Inspector Ingram, waiting for him to confirm or contradict David's instructions.

"All right, give the solicitor that message," Ingram said

M

after a moment's rapid thought. He watched her go from the room.

"Now," he said briskly when the door had closed behind her. "Who is Mrs. Stallard? What is this compensation she may be entitled to? And why should Mallinson's death affect her claim?" He drew his brows together suddenly. "Stallard!" he said. "Is she the widow of Victor Stallard? Convicted of embezzlement some years ago? Committed suicide in his cell?"

"Yes, that's who she is." David looked weary of the matter already. "I've seen her two or three times in the last few days. I was trying to deal with the question of compensation, a lump sum and a pension."

"Stallard was cleared of course." Ingram ran over the details in his mind. He frowned suddenly. "Did she come here? To Whitegates? Did she see Henry Mallinson? What kind of a woman is she? Open to reason?"

"She didn't come to Whitegates," David said at once. "She wanted to, she was very insistent, but of course there was no question of allowing it. My father was in no condition to be troubled by that kind of business."

Ingram looked at him keenly. "You're quite certain she didn't see your father? Could she not have called at the house without your knowledge?"

David shook his head. "No, she didn't see him. My father would have told me—and Mrs. Parkes, the nurse, she would have mentioned it—or Gina Thorson. You can check of course, but I'm sure you'll find that she wasn't admitted to Whitegates."

I'll check all right, Ingram thought, making a mental note to despatch Sergeant Yates to see Mrs. Stallard later in the day.

"A difficult woman?" he asked.

"Yes, you could say that," David agreed. "I tried to get her to let a solicitor handle her claim." He smiled faintly. "I wasn't getting very far with her, she wouldn't discuss the actual figures for compensation, all she seemed to want

to do was confront my father, get him to eat humble pie,
I imagine. The whole thing could have been settled in half
an hour with a solicitor."

"Apparently she's seen reason at last then," Ingram said
slowly. "She has a solicitor now at all events." Anxious to
confront the old man, was she? Bent on revenge? I
wonder . . .

"She knew your father wasn't well, I take it?" he asked
David.

"Yes, I explained to her that was why she couldn't see
him."

If she'd got into the house somehow, without being
spotted, Ingram thought. If she'd had a sharp exchange with
the old man . . . would she have had the opportunity to
dope the whisky? She could have seen the drum of tablets
on the bedside table, seen the whisky decanter. It wouldn't
take much intelligence or much knowledge to realise that
the combination of tablets and whisky was probably a
dangerous one . . . Might she not have acted on the spur of
the moment, prompted by a fierce desire for revenge? Was
it possible for her to drop the tablets into the decanter without the old man seeing her? . . . He might have been
asleep of course, he might never have laid eyes on her at
all . . . She might have entered the room silently, stood looking down at him, have glanced about the room and seen the
tools of revenge before her, she might have been able to
take her time about it, act without the necessity for con-
cealment . . .

Ingram frowned. Only Mrs. Parkes's fingerprints on the
decanter and the prints of Kenneth Mallinson . . . Mrs.
Stallard might have worn gloves of course . . . very probably she had done so, a cold day, a woman in late middle
age, yes, she would probably have worn gloves.

He frowned again, not liking the intrusion of Mrs. Stallard into his clear vision of the case. If she had done it she
might very well get away with it, if no-one had seen her
enter or leave. But if she had come to Whitegates she had

used some method of transport, a car, a taxi, a bus . . . enquiry might turn up something there.

He glanced at his watch. Some time since food had passed his lips, he was beginning to feel the pangs of hunger. Carole Mallinson saw his glance.

"Would you like some lunch brought in?" she asked. "I can speak to Cook, it would be no trouble."

"Thank you, that would be very good of you. I'm sure we'd all appreciate it. And it will save us having to go back to Hallborough."

"I'll see to it. And if at any time you'd like coffee or sandwiches, just ask in the kitchen. It will be perfectly all right."

"You're very kind," he said formally. He was looking forward to lunch. They'd have good food in a house like this, better than lunching off dried-up sandwiches or a hurried snack in a Hallborough coffee-bar. He stood up.

"I'll have to see everyone singly after lunch, you realise that." He looked at Kenneth Mallinson. "If you could see that no-one leaves the vicinity of the house for the present. If anything arises, anything urgent, if someone has to keep an appointment, say, I'm sure it can be arranged. Just as long as we're told beforehand, as long as we know."

"I don't think anyone's going to make a bolt for it, if that's what you mean," Kenneth said. "It would scarcely be wise."

"That was not quite what I meant," Ingram said smoothly. "It's just that it makes our job a great deal easier if everyone's at hand if they're needed in the course of routine investigation." He opened the library door. "Causes far less inconvenience all round in the long run. I'm sure you see that. I'll send Constable Jennings along after lunch to let you know who we'd like to see first."

Kenneth inclined his head. Ingram waited till the three of them had left the room, then he closed the door and walked over to the fireplace. He yawned and stretched out his arms.

"Kenneth Mallinson for my money," he said softly. "What do you think, Yates?"

"It's a bit early to say," Sergeant Yates said cautiously. "That Mrs. Stallard, I wouldn't be surprised if she hadn't sneaked in and slipped a few tablets into the old man's whisky."

Ingram pulled his mouth down. "Possible," he said. "But not very likely. No, it's one of the two sons for me. And of the two I rather fancy Kenneth. Hadn't seen the old man for years, wouldn't seem as if he was poisoning his own father, more as if he was doing away with a stranger."

Yates considered the matter. "Ye-es, I see. Whereas David, working with his father all the time, living close by——"

"Exactly!" Ingram said with triumph. "A man'd have to be a bit of a monster to do away with his father in those circumstances. And David Mallinson doesn't strike me as a monster. Very well thought of in Hallborough—and in Rockley, Leach tells me. Kenneth on the other hand, bit of a dark horse." He moved his shoulders. "Stallard's widow. You can go over and see her later on. But I think she's just a red herring."

CHAPTER XV

TIM JEFFORD finished his lunch in the dining-car shortly before the train drew into Hallborough. Not at all a bad lunch, and the coffee had been quite drinkable. He grinned to himself, reflecting on how swiftly one's critical standards rose with the possession of a few pounds in one's pocket.

He was feeling reasonably satisfied with his morning's work. Four fine coins to show old Mallinson, with luck he'd buy two of them. A great pity he hadn't been able to purchase more from the dealer. If only Mallinson had given him that cheque for seventy-five guineas. He shrugged his shoulders. No point in wasting time on vain regrets. When he did get Mallinson's cheque—and the money Carole would undoubtedly hand over to-morrow in the station buffet— he could repeat his trip to London, buy a few more coins if the old man showed continuing interest. Strike while the iron's hot, he thought with cheerful confidence, I could keep this game up for another week yet.

The train slackened speed, drew into Hallborough. Tim stepped out on to the platform, almost with a feeling that he was coming home, looking round with a faint stirring of affection for the place where his luck had begun to turn.

He looked up at the station clock. Better take a taxi out to Whitegates, drive up in style. He was in good time for his appointment with the old man. He stepped into a waiting-room for a minute, to check his appearance in the mirror.

Quite a presentable reflection looked back at him now. He had had his hair cut during the morning, he'd invested a few pounds in a new pair of shoes, a crisp white shirt and half-a-dozen good handkerchiefs. He ran a comb through his hair, flicked a speck of dust from a lapel and went briskly out to find a taxi.

"Rockley," he told the driver. "Whitegates. Do you know the house?"

The man nodded, opening the rear door. "Yes, I know it."

Tim leaned back against the seat and closed his eyes.

"Pity about the old man," the driver said. "Very well respected in these parts, Mr. Mallinson."

"Yes." Tim said. They'd all know Mallinson round here of course, they'd all know of his illness.

"Tricky thing, the heart." The driver edged the car out on to the Rockley road. "Never know when it'll give out."

"Yes," Tim said again, not caring for this depressing thought, hoping fervently old Mallinson's heart wasn't going to give out before he'd bought a good many coins. He yawned audibly, putting an end to the conversation.

"Whitegates," the driver said some little time later. Tim opened his eyes, refreshed, ready to do himself justice at the interview. The taxi was turning in through the gates. He sat up and began to dig in his pockets for money.

"Hallo!" the driver said suddenly. "Police cars!" Tim's head came up with a jerk. Two black cars drawn up in front of the house. He was seized with a sudden wild impulse to fling open the taxi door, spring out and take to his heels.

"I thought it was natural causes," the driver said with an edge of excitement to his voice. "They wouldn't have the police for natural causes, would they? It couldn't have been suicide, could it?" He halted the car behind the other two.

"Suicide?" Tim asked, restraining a desire to lean forward and give the fellow a good shake. "Who are you talking about? Is someone dead here?"

The driver turned to stare at him. "I thought you knew, I mentioned it when you booked me. The old man, Henry Mallinson——"

"He isn't dead!" Tim cried in genuine regret. "Oh no!"

The driver nodded, pleased to have created a small sensation. "Died in the night. I heard it was heart." He jerked his head at the black cars. "Looks as if the police think otherwise."

Tim made a rapid survey of the situation. No point now in walking up to the front door and pressing the bell. No-one now in Whitegates who'd give a brass farthing for his precious coins.

"You'd better take me along to the Swan," he said. "My business was with the old man."

A uniformed driver opened the door of the car in front, stepped out and came back to the taxi, opening the rear door and addressing Tim.

"Did you want to see someone in the house? I don't know if you're aware of what's happened?"

"I've just heard." Tim jerked his head at his own driver. "I'll be going. It was Mr. Henry Mallinson I had an appointment with and if he's dead——"

The policeman drew back the door. "If you'd just step inside and have a word with the inspector," he said courteously.

Tim frowned. "I've nothing to say to the inspector. I don't know anything. I'm a stranger here."

"He wouldn't keep you long," the policeman said, fixing Tim with an inexorable gaze. "If you had an appointment with Mr. Mallinson, you never know, there might be some little detail." He gave a tiny smile. "Every little helps."

"Do you want me to wait?" the taxi driver asked. Tim saw there was no help for it.

"No thanks." He'd walk up to the Swan when he escaped from Whitegates, he couldn't go flinging his money around now. "How much?" He stepped out of the taxi and paid the man, reducing the tip he had originally intended by one half.

"Timothy Jefford," Inspector Ingram said a few minutes later, glancing at Constable Jennings to make sure he was taking notes. "Staying at the Swan in Rockley. Well now, Mr. Jefford, exactly what was the nature of your business with Mr. Mallinson?" He felt briskly energetic after the excellent lunch sent in from the kitchen. He looked to Tim like a plump and well-fed tiger, licking its lips, ready to pounce on any casual little passing animal, not out of hunger but from a simple desire for amusement and occupation.

Tim's mind began to function on two levels at the same time. Part of his attention was given to listening intently to the inspector's questions, assessing them rapidly for pitfalls and traps, supplying plausible answers as near as possible to the truth. Another, deeper, part of his brain was busy surveying the entire situation at Whitegates, picking up what scraps of information the inspector might accidentally let fall, running over the events of the previous evening, trying to work out exactly why the police were showing such a strong interest in the death of an old man known to have been ill, wondering if by any horrid chance their

keen noses had already picked up the scent of blackmail—
not to put too fine a point on it.

He settled himself back into his chair in an attempt to
appear at ease. He gave the inspector a disarming smile.

"I called here yesterday evening—by appointment—to
show Mr. Mallinson some rare coins. He was a collector,
you know. I'm a dealer in coins and small objets d'art. Only
in a small way at present. But I hope to expand." He uttered
a little deprecating laugh that sounded highly artificial to
his own ears.

"And you've just been up to London and back? Why was
that?"

"For some more coins that Mr. Mallinson wanted to see.
I can show you them if you like." He thrust his hand
obligingly into his pocket. "I have them here."

Ingram stretched out a hand. "Yes, I'd like to see them.
Just to check." He smiled expansively. "We like to check
every little detail, I expect you realise that." He examined
the coins with a show of interest. No watch, he thought,
and that suit was never intended for him, hangs from his
shoulders like a potato sack. Badly-manicured hands, marked
with traces of some ingrained coloured material, not at all
the hands one would expect from a dealer in costly and
beautiful objects.

He passed the coins back across the table, watching Jefford pick them up, looking at his stained fingers, the colour
embedded under the nails. Dye? Paint? He placed the tips
of his fingers together. Yes, paint, most likely. The fellow
looked a great deal more like a struggling artist than a respectable buyer and seller of antiques.

"Sold any pictures lately?" he asked suddenly. He saw
Jefford's eyes come up at that, the quick, startled look, the
pause for rapid thought.

Crikey, Tim thought, he knows about me. How? Surely
Carole hadn't opened her mouth? They hadn't been check-
ing on him already? Phoning the police station near his

Chelsea flat, having a man sent round to make enquiries?
A light sweat broke out on his forehead.

"One or two," he said with an airy wave of his hand.
"You know how it is, you have a good spell, and a bad
one."

Ingram nodded, knowing pretty well how it was.

"Did Mr. Mallinson buy any of your coins last night?"

Tim let himself relax a little, feeling himself on firmer
ground. Nothing to conceal about last night's interview
with Mallinson. He had a clear conscience as far as that
was concerned. Ingram saw the movement of his shoulders.
Jefford had no hand in Mallinson's death, instinct told
him. He's worried about something, but it isn't that. Could
be operating some kind of racket with his coins—fakes perhaps.

"Yes," Jefford said. "That is to say he wanted to buy a
coin. He kept it, I imagine it's upstairs in his room now.
He was going to pay me, in cash." All at once he remembered the business of the missing money. He drew a great
breath of relief, delighted to be able to throw a bone to the
tiger, to distract his attention from himself. "He had a cash-
box in his bedroom. He took it out to give me the money.
Seventy-five guineas." No harm in mentioning the figure,
let the inspector see he was dealing with a man of sub-
stance. He paused to give greater effect to his words. "But
the money wasn't there. It had been stolen."

The words produced an effect all right. Ingram sat up
suddenly in his chair, the little playful smile vanished from
his mouth.

"Stolen?" he said sharply. "You're sure of that?" He
glanced at Sergeant Yates sitting beside him. We heard
nothing about any theft, the look said as plainly as words.
How did we come to miss that?

Tim spread his hands wide. He was beginning to enjoy
himself.

"Well of course I don't actually know the money was
stolen. I mean I don't know there was anything in the cash-

box in the first place. I suggested at the time that Mr. Mallinson might have made a mistake. After all he was old and not very well, he might have forgotten things. But he certainly thought he'd been robbed. He made a terrific fuss about it, called in the nurse and the secretary. There was a fair old ding-dong. He said the secretary had taken the money."

"Miss Thorson?" Ingram said.

Tim nodded. "I could see I wasn't going to get any money just then, so I cleared out and left them to it. He'd already asked me to come round again to-day—now, that's why I'm here—to show him some more coins. I did ask him to give me a cheque but he was in such a tizzy about the theft, he didn't pay much attention to that, told me he'd settle up with me to-day, when he'd seen the other coins." He paused as a sudden thought struck him. "He didn't think *I* took the money, if that's in your mind, there was no question of that. I'd never even heard about his blessed cash-box till he leaned over and took it out of a cabinet. On the other side of the bed, that is."

Ingram turned to Sergeant Yates. "Get Mrs. Parkes and Miss Thorson," he said. "Don't say anything about the money, just bring them." Yates nodded and left the room.

"And now," Ingram said in a voice completely different from any he had already used to Tim, a colder, more incisive voice, the tiger no longer playing with its victim, ready for the kill. "Just why did you choose Mr. Mallinson to sell your coins to? Rockley is a long way from London. Had he heard of your eminence in the trade?" An openly sneering edge to the voice now. Tim moved his shoulders uncomfortably. His brain refused to throw up a plausible answer. "Had he sent for you? Expressed a desire to view your offerings? Had he asked his secretary to make an appointment with you?"

Tim stared down at the gleaming surface of the table, trying desperately to find an answer to the insistent questions.

"You had heard of Mr. Mallinson perhaps?" Ingram went on relentlessly. "You had some connection with Rockley? You had other business in the area and took the opportunity to make a little profit on the side, remembering that Mallinson was interested in rare coins?" Tim moved his head, looking down now at the parquet flooring, finding no inspiration there either.

"Come now," Ingram said icily. "You woke up one morning and decided to pay a visit to Rockley, a small village a good many miles from London, you decided to put up at the Swan. Exactly why did you decide that, Mr. Jefford?" A little pause that grew into a longer pause. Tim seemed to have become hypnotised by the parquet flooring, he found himself actually beginning to count the strips of wood.

"Just in case it's of any faint interest to you," Ingram said in a voice like a whiplash, "the reason the Hallborough police are troubling to enquire into everything that happened here in the course of the last few days is that Mr. Henry Mallinson was murdered."

Tim felt as if he had been struck a violent blow at the back of his neck. With immense difficulty he managed to restrain himself from staggering to his feet and making a wild run for the door. Danger! screamed every fibre of his being. The room seemed to swim before him. Ingram's face approached and receded.

"Why did you come to Rockley?" the voice said softly.

"There was a picture in the paper." The photograph rose before him, clear in every detail, it seemed to him now of immeasurable significance. "Carole's picture."

"Carole?" said the voice, even more softly.

"Carole Stewart." That was wrong, he shouldn't have said that, but for the life of him he couldn't remember why. "That is, she's not Carole Stewart now, she's called——" He put up a hand to his head, frowning, trying to think.

"Mallinson," the voice said gently. "Carole Mallinson."

"That's right." Tim sighed with relief.

"You knew her well at one time," the voice went on soothingly. "When she was Carole Stewart. You saw her picture in the paper, you realised she'd married a rich man, you thought you'd pay her a friendly visit. You looked up the Mallinsons, discovered Henry Mallinson collected coins. You bought one coin to give yourself a reason for being in Rockley, then you stepped on a train——"

"Not a train," Tim said. "I hitched a lift. On a lorry." The driver had ulcers, he ate mountains of fried food preceded by indigestion tablets. "I meant to take his name and address," he said, frowning at the memory of his own neglect. "I was going to send him a fiver. But I forgot."

Ingram let that go, not being able to make sense of it but feeling by instinct that it had little relevance.

"Why did you want to see Carole Stewart?" he asked. "Were you going to touch her for money?" He was searching his own brain rapidly, recalling the splash of the wedding a year or two back, the local paper full of the details of the dresses, the trousseau, the reception, but oddly reticent about the bride's background and antecedents. Something to conceal apparently, young Mrs. David Mallinson, not at all pleased to see a face rise up before her out of her past, ready to dip her hand into her pocket—a flash of light lit up his brain—or her father-in-law's cash-box—to pay for silence? He clasped his hands together tightly. Ready also perhaps to put her father-in-law to sleep for ever before Jefford had a chance to open his mouth, before the old will was superseded by the new? She hadn't known the new will had been signed. . . .

"How much did she give you?" he asked. But he had paused a fraction too long. As soon as the words left his mouth he saw it was too late. Jefford had already pulled himself together. His face had lost that sleepy, blurred look, the eyes were brighter, more aware, more disciplined.

"How much did who give me?" Jefford asked pleasantly. "I'm afraid I've rather lost track——"

Steady! he said to himself. Watch it! Say as little as

possible. He had a curious sensation as of a gap in the passage of time, some portion of it—seconds, minutes, even hours perhaps—having slipped past without his knowledge, a strangely dreamlike sensation not altogether unpleasant. But he sat up straighter, bracing himself, some watchful fragment of his brain perceiving the imminence of danger in that relaxed and dreamy state.

"Do you mean Mr. Mallinson?" he said. "He didn't give me anything for the coin, I thought I explained that. He'd been robbed, you see. The money was gone."

CHAPTER XVI

SERGEANT YATES came back into the room with Mrs. Parkes and Gina Thorson. Ingram stood up and gestured the ladies into seats. Tim Jefford didn't look up as the two women came in, he was sitting forward in his chair, staring down at his hands clasped on his knees.

Ingram smiled pleasantly at the women. "I won't be a minute. Make yourselves comfortable." They looked up at him with faintly apprehensive eyes. "Here a moment, Sergeant." He beckoned Yates out of the room, closed the door and said in a low rapid voice, "Take one of the cars and get up to the Swan. Timothy Jefford's room—the landlord won't make a fuss, he'll let you take a look round."

"What am I looking for?"

"Anything. Particularly anything that might be used in blackmail." Yates raised his brows. "Photographs," Ingram said. "Letters. Anything. You know, I've a pretty good notion he was putting the black on young Mrs. Mallinson."

"Mm," said Yates. "Interesting."

"See if he's got a wad of money tucked away anywhere. Under the mattress, in the soap-dish. Oh—another thing—before you get off to the Swan, phone Chelsea." He repeated Tim's address. "Anything known, any convictions, any information at all, never know what'll come in useful with a character like Jefford. Chelsea can ring back here, we'll be here the rest of the day and half the night as well, I shouldn't wonder."

"Right you are." Yates went off in search of a phone.

Ingram let himself back into the dining-room. Jefford flashed him a glance and the inspector looked back at him with bright blank eyes. Let him sit there and sweat for a bit, wouldn't do him any harm.

Mrs. Parkes was sitting stiffly upright with her hands folded in her lap. She looked neat and capable in her uniform . . . capable, Ingram pondered for a moment, picking up the copy of the new will the driver had brought back from Hallborough. He ran his eye over the typed sheets. Pretty substantial legacy for Mrs. Parkes . . . was she capable of helping her patient on his way, getting her fingers on that legacy without delay?

The old will had been destroyed but there had been a copy in Mallinson's safe. It lay now on the dining-room table. Ingram ran his finger down the pages, pausing when he came to the nurse's name. A much smaller sum under the old will . . . Wonder if she needed the money in a hurry, he mused, taking his time. Wouldn't do any harm to let the two women sit there for a minute or two longer. Keeping them in suspense often did wonders in loosening the tongue, setting the nerves on edge.

Mrs. Parkes . . . A widow? Or a cast-off husband somewhere, perhaps with a hand outstretched for money? A family, children? Grown-up now most likely, if they existed at all. Needing money for schemes and plans of their own perhaps? Asking Mum for money? . . . Might be something there. One or two questions he'd have to put to Mrs. Parkes.

But first the question of the cash-box and the theft—the alleged theft, he corrected himself—of Mallinson's little hoard of notes. He sat down and smiled reassuringly at the two women.

"One or two little questions," he said easily. The secretary looked pale and nervous, red rims to her eyes, as if she'd been crying. Dark circles underneath, hadn't slept too well, if she'd slept at all. "I'd like to hear what you both have to tell me about a cash-box that Mr. Mallinson kept in his room."

Mrs. Parkes gave a tiny smile at that. She looked just the merest bit more relaxed, better pleased. She was afraid I was going to ask about something else, he registered, something she believes now I've not spotted . . . What? But he had to let the question go for the moment, he had to give all his attention to the cash-box and the missing notes.

Mrs. Parkes showed no reluctance to talk, although Gina Thorson didn't so much as open her mouth.

"You'll have heard about it from Mr. Jefford," Mrs. Parkes said with a confident manner. "Mr. Mallinson was going to pay him for the coin, that was when he found the money was missing." She turned her head and slid a little malicious glance at the secretary. "He was quite certain Miss Thorson had taken the money, he wanted to dismiss her right away, but I persuaded him to let it stand over till the morning, to let Mr. David handle it. I didn't want anything done hastily," she added virtuously. "Not fair to Miss Thorson. I spoke to her about it. A girl on her own, I did what I could." She pursed her lips, admiring the generosity of her own impulses. "I told her to go downstairs and make a show of looking for the money. If she came upstairs with it she could always get Mr. Mallinson to think he'd picked it up himself and laid it down on a table or put it away in a drawer, absent-mindedly. Bring it back, I said, and there'll be no more questions asked, no-one will be able to *prove* anything. You won't be dismissed."

"And did she look for it?" Ingram asked.

"Not she. Paid no heed to me. Sat down and listened to the radio." There was a little pause. "And now Mr. Mallinson's dead," Mrs. Parkes said, the discipline of her tone slipping a little, allowing malice to show through a little more openly. "And she's not been dismissed. Still in my employ, the will says, he always put that in. She was still in his employ at the time of his death and so she gets the legacy. As well as the money she stole. A hundred pounds it was, all in notes. If Mr. Mallinson hadn't died in the night, she'd have been out of a job and out of a legacy. Think about that, Inspector."

Constable Jennings glanced up from his note-taking, he exchanged a look with the inspector. Vicious woman, said the look. Mrs. Parkes caught the interchange of eyes and drew a little breath. She re-arranged the expression on her face, her lips formed a smile.

"I tried to advise her," she said in a more kindly tone. "I treated her as if she'd been my own daughter."

"You have a daughter of your own?" Ingram asked casually.

She shook her head, "No, just a son. Only the one."

"Is he married?" Still a light, casual voice. "Any family?"

"Yes, he's married, two children."

"Do they live near here? Do you have much opportunity to see your grandchildren?" He smiled at her. A family man myself, the smile implied, I know how much grandchildren mean.

He saw the little look of unease in her eyes.

"Not very near. I don't see them all that often." Something there, Ingram thought, some centre of anxiety connected with the son . . . leave it for the moment, come back to it later, get the son's address, phone the local police, get them to send a man round, have a word or two with the son and his wife, see what he could dig up . . .

He turned his gaze to Miss Thorson. She had sat in silence listening to Mrs. Parkes's recital, almost as if it were nothing to do with her. Her eyes had a slightly unfocused look. Still in the grip of shock, he thought with a sudden thrust of compassion. Not much more than a girl, vulnerable-looking, still something of the defenceless child about the soft lines of the mouth and chin.

N

"You've heard what Mrs. Parkes has to say," he said gently. "Now, could we have your side of the story?"

She looked at him as if she had difficulty in making sense of what he said.

"I didn't take the money," she said in a barely audible tone. "If I did, it would still be in my room or hidden somewhere in the house. You can all look for it, you can search my room as much as you like, but you won't find it there because I didn't take it." She relapsed into silence, looking straight ahead.

We might find it in your room, Ingram thought wryly, even if you didn't take it. Have you thought of that? Someone else might have taken it and planted it in your room . . . to give you an apparent motive for murder perhaps, to avert the finger of suspicion from themselves and point it straight at you . . . Someone ruthless, someone who doesn't much care for you, someone who had a good enough reason to want Mallinson dead ahead of his natural time . . . His eyes strayed back to Mrs. Parkes, he looked at her thoughtfully, assessingly.

"Could I have your son's address?" he asked suddenly. He smiled at her. "Just for the record."

She frowned. "My son? I don't see what he's got to do with it. Why should you want his address?"

"Helps to keep things tidy," he said lightly. "We're awful sticklers for tidiness. Training, you know. We have it drummed into us. Where did you say he lived?"

"I didn't say." She wasn't looking at him now, she was biting her top lip, gazing fiercely down at a Persian rug.

"Well, would you say now?" he asked, still polite, still casual. She made no reply.

His voice took on an edge of steel. "Am I to understand you refuse to give the information?" The tiger poised to spring, Tim Jefford thought, I wish I was out of here, sitting safely perched in a lorry, heading back for the safety of the studio.

Mrs. Parkes raised her head and gave the inspector a

sharply hostile glance. "I didn't say I refused." She repeated the address in a flat voice.

Ingram flicked a glance at Constable Jennings. "I believe you said you had a phone call to make," he said, as if suddenly remembering, "You might just as well make it now." Jennings nodded, used to the inspector's devious little ways.

"Certainly, sir, I'm glad you reminded me." He stood up.

"We'll take a little break while we're at it," Ingram said cheerfully. "Put your head round the kitchen door and ask them if they'd be so kind as to let us have some tea. And a few sandwiches perhaps." Tim Jefford's face brightened for a moment. Ingram smiled. "You never know, there might be a bit of cake as well." He glanced at the two women. "I'm sure the ladies could do with some refreshment." Neither of them made any response to his pleasantries. Please yourselves, Ingram thought, nothing like investigation to make a man hungry, I want a bite of something even if you two have no appetite.

"I'll see what I can do, sir." Jennings left the room, making for the kitchen where he lingered for a minute or two longer than was strictly necessary, engaging in a little badinage with the good-looking housemaid, and then going to Miss Thorson's office and picking up the phone.

He drummed his fingers on the desk, waiting for the operator to connect him. He knew what to do all right. Get the local man to slip round to the farm, have a little chat with Mrs. Parkes's son and his missus, find out if possible just why Mrs. Parkes looked upset when her son was mentioned.

When he had finished his call he stood for a moment looking round the study. Very neat and tidy, everything in place. He glanced at the filing-cabinets with a sigh. They'd all have to be gone through, couldn't overlook anything— and he had a pretty good notion whose job it would be to go through them.

On the desk the phone rang suddenly. He picked up the

receiver. Might be Hallborough, wanting to speak to the inspector.

"Miss Thorson?" said a refined female voice.

"Miss Thorson is busy at the moment," Jennings said. "But I can take a message. Who is that speaking?"

The voice mentioned the name of a Hallborough shop. Jennings flicked through the card-index of his mind. Ladies' fashions, expensive place. Hardly Miss Thorson's style, way out of her reach, he would have thought.

"It's about the suède coat," the woman said. "Miss Thorson was in here shortly before we closed yesterday evening. She asked us to shorten the coat by two and a half inches."

"Yes," said Jennings encouragingly. "Is there any difficulty about it?"

"Well yes, I'm afraid there is. The fitter says it would interfere with the line of the pockets. She can shorten it by one and three-quarter inches and that's absolutely all. If Miss Thorson could just say if she's agreeable to that, then we can go ahead."

Jennings felt a stab of the keenest interest. A suède coat! At that place! Forty—fifty guineas? More perhaps! Shortly before closing yesterday evening . . . and the money had vanished from Mallinson's box sometime yesterday afternoon . . . if it was ever there in the first place, he remembered with a touch of disappointment. He brushed away the thought.

"The other things?" he said, playing his hunch. "There isn't any difficulty about those?"

"Oh no, there was no question of alteration to the other things, just the coat." So she'd splashed out on other stuff as well . . . Must have come to a tidy sum by the time she'd finished.

A hundred pounds perhaps? His lips curved into a smile.

"If you could ask Miss Thorson," the woman said with a trace of impatience.

"I'm afraid she can't speak to you just at the moment," Jennings said. "Things are a little disorganised here——"

"Yes, I heard about that," she said in a different tone, a trifle more human. "I'm sorry, though I suppose it was only to be expected. He was a good age."

"I'll give Miss Thorson the message, I'll ask her to ring you about the coat."

Jennings replaced the receiver and stood for a moment pondering whether to write down the information and hand it to the inspector or whether to deliver the message to Miss Thorson himself, openly, in front of the others. She must have pinched the money, gone straight into Hallborough and spent it—a damn' silly thing to do. How on earth had she hoped to get away with it? Sacked for certain if Mallinson had lived, sacked without a reference. And for what? For a suède coat and half a dozen other garments.

He shook his head at the folly of young women . . . and more than folly perhaps? Had she not only stolen the money but doped the old man's whisky too? Hoping he'd die before the theft was discovered? Making certain at the same time of her legacy?

He walked slowly back to the dining-room. A tricky customer, Gina Thorson. Didn't look a fool nor for that matter capable of murder. She looked like a girl in the grip of shock from the death of her employer, a defenceless girl, stunned into apathy by an unjust accusation of theft. If she was playing a part she was playing it pretty well.

Only a couple of yards separated him from the diningroom door. If he was going to write down the information he would have to stop and take the notebook from his pocket now, lean up against the wall and scribble it down. He visualised Ingram reading the slip of paper, digesting its implications, asking Mrs. Parkes and Jefford to leave the room for a few minutes. That would put the secretary on her guard, give her time to think, to invent a few answers to the questions she'd known were coming. The moment Ingram asked the other two to go and herself to remain, she'd know they were on to something.

But Ingram wasn't going to like it if Jennings stole his thunder. He liked to spring his little surprises himself, wasn't at all keen on sitting idly by while mere constables took the star part. Jennings thrust his hand into his pocket and then withdrew it, empty. If he delivered the message to Gina Thorson himself, she'd be taken aback, there'd be time for guilt, for agitation to show through the mask . . . and it wouldn't do the slightest harm afterwards, when the credits were being handed out, for Jennings's name to come up before the Chief for a word of praise. Promotion didn't always come in this game from a rigid obedience to the rules. He set his mouth into a firm line and opened the dining-room door.

Ingram barely glanced up as he entered. There was silence in the room. Jefford and the two women were sitting motionless, not looking at each other, staring ahead. The inspector's hands were full of papers. He had spent the last few minutes going over his notes, comparing the copies of the two wills, getting his thoughts into order, not bothering to speak to the three people opposite him, letting them stew in their own juice for a bit.

"Tea will be along in a couple of minutes, sir." Jennings took a few paces forward. "I made that phone call." He halted, choosing a position which gave him a good view of all their faces. Ingram nodded, expecting the constable to resume his seat at the end of the table. He bent his head again, studying his papers.

But Jennings remained where he was. Something about his manner, about the way he stood there, brought Ingram's head up again. He frowned slightly, his eyes looked a question at the constable.

"The phone rang while I was in the office," Jennings said and he saw the look in Ingram's eyes change instantly to one of alertness. "A message for Miss Thorson." The edge of significance in his voice flicked the inspector's eyes at once to Gina's face. They remained there, unblinking, keenly watchful, like a cat at a mousehole, Jennings thought suddenly.

At the mention of her name the girl's head turned a little. She looked as if she was just waking up from sleep. Jennings spoke again, before she had time to get her guard up, to re-arrange the expression on her face.

"One of the Hallborough shops. Miss Thorson called in late yesterday afternoon and bought a number of gar-ments." His voice was clear and level, as if he were giving evidence in court. "One of the articles was a suède coat. Miss Thorson asked for it to be shortened."

Dismay and panic now on the girl's face. She gave a little gasp that sounded quite clearly as Jennings paused for breath. Ingram's eyes never moved from Gina's face, he held the papers in front of him, a few inches above the table, not allowing himself to relax even sufficiently to put them down.

"Apparently it would spoil the set of the pockets if the coat is shortened by two-and-a-half inches." As if it was the length of a suède coat that held them all motionless, staring up at him. "But they can shorten it by one-and-three-quarter inches. That wouldn't interfere with the line."

A look of satisfaction, triumph almost, on Mrs. Parkes's face. She moved her head and glanced at Gina, drawing a little smiling breath. Tim Jefford's eyes narrowed in puzzled concern. He looked at the girl with sympathy. He would of course, Jennings thought, a pretty face, the mark of tears, that's all he sees. Jefford would like to jump up and knock me down, he'd like to rush over and put his arm round the girl, say 'Pay no attention, it's a load of nonsense, I don't believe you took the money, I'm sure you have a perfectly good explanation——' Ninety-nine men out of a hundred would always believe a pretty and tearful young woman to be innocent of any charge. If they caught her with a blood-stained knife in her hands, bending over a corpse, they'd still believe she had a perfectly good explanation.

"I said Miss Thorson was busy just now, that I'd give her the message. They want her to phone as soon as she can, to let them know about the coat."

Gina put a hand up to her forehead. Her face was very pale. She's going to faint, Tim Jefford thought. He felt a sudden surge of anger at the two policemen looking fixedly at the girl without a trace of compassion. My god! he thought, they think she did it! They think she murdered the old man! He drew in his breath and looked at her now with intense curiosity. Was it possible?

A slow surge of unbecoming red rose in her cheeks, flooding her forehead, beating right up against the hairline.

"How much did you spend on the clothes?" the inspector asked softly. "A hundred pounds?"

She clasped her hands together, the knuckles showed white and tense.

"Ninety-two guineas," she said with a kind of sobbing gasp. "I bought them on hire purchase." Her neck stiffened in a tremor. "A budget account, they called it, I had to sign some papers." Her voice stiffened. She seemed to regain control of herself with a supreme effort. The colour drained away from her face, leaving it pale but calmer now, more composed. "You can easily check." She relaxed her hands suddenly, she even gave the inspector a ghost of a smile. "If you phone the shop, they'll tell you." She sat up. She's going to make a fight of it, Tim thought with a stab of pleasure. "I had to pay a deposit. I went into the Hallborough post office, the main post office in the High Street. I drew ten pounds out. It's all they let you take out at once," she added, precisely, as if she were explaining something to a foreigner. "I paid ten pounds down, in cash. I can show you my post office book. And the shop will confirm what I say."

"Ninety-two guineas," Ingram said. "Rather a lot of

money to lay out all at once on clothes." His eyes strayed over her plain dark sweater and skirt, neat enough, becoming enough, but undeniably cheap, chain-store stuff. "Why should you want new clothes, expensive clothes, so many of them, all at once, in a great hurry? And at this particular moment?"

She doesn't have to tell you every damn' thing, Tim thought, fiercely resentful on the girl's behalf, acutely aware of the humiliation she must feel, having to dig up private reasons, exposing them for the general gaze.

There was a little pause that lengthened into silence.

"Why just now?" Ingram said again, less softly.

Gina bit her top lip. She flushed again, but a gentler, prettier flush. "If I could speak to you privately," she said.

Mrs. Parkes moved suddenly in her chair. "She's trying to hook Doctor Knight," she said loudly and aggressively. "Everyone knows that. He comes from a well-to-do family." She gave a tiny laugh devoid of mirth. "She was laying out a sprat to catch a mackerel."

Gina looked down at the parquet floor as if she were committing the pattern to memory.

Ingram looked at Mrs. Parkes with an impersonal gaze. Vicious creature, he thought with distaste, but unable to express the thought openly, even by so much as a change of expression, knowing that viciousness had its uses in this game. It was capable of provoking unexpected responses, disclosing unlooked-for information. But all the same he didn't enjoy being professionally allied to malice. One had to encourage it, make use of it, but one didn't have to reward it with a smile of approval.

"If you could produce your post-office book," he said courteously to Gina. "Constable Jennings will phone the shop. We can check all this right away."

She raised her eyes and nodded. The rattle of a tea-trolley echoed outside in the passage. Ingram stood up, glad to be able to stretch his muscles. He glanced at Jennings. "You can go along now, take Miss Thorson upstairs for the book and then make the call." The girl's story would be confirmed of course but that was no proof she hadn't stolen the money or slipped the tablets in the whisky, hoping death would intervene before the theft was discovered . . .

Gina followed Constable Jennings from the room. Relief in her step, in the carriage of her head. A parlour-maid wheeled in the tea-trolley and Mrs. Parkes busied herself in fussing about with cups and plates, wafer-thin slices of bread and butter, delicate sandwiches, insubstantial pastries.

Ingram sipped at his tea. Quite a clever little scheme—if the girl had indeed carried it out. Steal the money to buy the clothes, make a withdrawal from the post-office, open a budget account like an employee with only her salary cheque behind her, then, when the fuss had died down, find it convenient to walk into the shop and settle the debt—or simply pay it off month by month and use the hoard of notes for running expenses to balance her depleted bank account. All she had to do was find a safe hiding-place for the money, let it lie undisturbed till the police had withdrawn from Whitegates. He accepted a sandwich from Mrs. Parkes. I'll bring in two or three more men, he decided, I'll have them turn the house and grounds inside out.

CHAPTER XVII

TIM JEFFORD was making short work of the bread and butter. Not at all certain when he might eat again. Barely enough money left now to settle his bill at the Swan. He could flog the coins again as soon as he got back to London —but he might get less than he'd paid for them. Possibly only half of what he'd paid. A highly unpleasant thought, but he faced it with fortitude. He began an onslaught on the sandwiches.

"Shouldn't think you'll be wanting me here much longer, Inspector," he said with an air of cheerful confidence.

Ingram flashed him a look. "You can't push off just yet,
I'm afraid. Might want you, never know, some little detail
turns up that you can confirm or deny, not as if you're a local
man. Can't go chasing after you to London every time we
want to speak to you."

Haven't finished with you yet by a long chalk, his eyes
added. Might swing a charge of blackmail on you yet,
with luck . . . and in any case, I'm not absolutely certain
just what finger you had in this particular pie.

Tim read the look which spoke a great deal more loudly
than the words. He shrugged his shoulders lightly and
reached out for another sandwich.

The inspector's gaze rested on Mrs. Parkes who was
picking delicately at a pastry.

"Doctor Knight had never attended Mr. Mallinson before, I believe?"

She laid down her plate. "No, never. Mr. Mallinson didn't
trust young doctors. And in any case he and Doctor Burnett
were old friends. Doctor Knight wouldn't have been called
in now if it hadn't been for Doctor Burnett's accident."
She sighed, considering the strange ways of fate.

Knight's out of it then, Ingram thought. He's about the
only person connected with this case who is in the clear.
He had no opportunity of lacing the whisky, hadn't even
been inside the bedroom until after Mallinson was dead.
And it was Knight who'd spotted something was wrong
about the death in the first place . . . Wouldn't do any harm
to have another word or two with Knight, a sharp young
man, might have some interesting ideas about the case,
might come up with a lead.

It crossed his mind that if Burnett hadn't been involved
in an accident, the death would very probably have been
put down to natural causes. No post-mortem, no inquest.
Burnett would have written out the certificate and that
would have been that. An old man, Burnett, a lifelong friend
of Mallinson, not as quick on the uptake as Knight, donkey's
years younger . . . and if some suspicion had crossed Bur-

nett's mind, if the notion of suicide or accident had drawn his brows into a frown, he'd probably have said nothing, let it go. Not wanting to make a fuss, to unleash unpleasantness on the family.

Old doctors, country practitioners, Ingram had known many in his time. They didn't always go running to the nearest phone to ring the police when they scented something wrong about a death. More often than not they held their peace, shrugged their shoulders, signed the certificate and buried the suspicion along with the deceased. Working in small, close-knit communities, treating patients who were the children and grandchildren of patients . . . easy enough to criticise, but in their position he might very well have reached the same decision himself. And climbed into bed at night and slept with a clear conscience afterwards. Yes, he thought with a little shake of his head, many a country churchyard keeps its secrets. He held out his cup. "May I have some more tea?"

"Certainly, Inspector. And what about a little pastry?" Mrs. Parkes smiled graciously.

Ingram shook his head briefly, making no reply, waiting for his cup to be refilled. Not too smitten with Mrs. Parkes. Didn't allow himself to go so far as to take likes and dislikes to people involved in a case, particularly a case of murder. Didn't do, led to hasty conclusions and grave errors. But he did permit himself to formulate the notion that he wasn't crazy about Mrs. Parkes.

"I say!" A sudden excited cry from Jefford. "I've just remembered! There was a boy in Mallinson's room yesterday, before I called! Mallinson told me so himself. When he found the money was gone. I asked him if he couldn't have made a mistake, if he'd used it for something else and it had slipped his mind."

"Go on," Ingram said, sitting upright. "What did he say to that?"

"He said he'd had the cash-box out earlier in the day. It was his godson's birthday and he'd given him a present, some cash out of the box, I took that to be. And he was quite certain the stolen money had been in the cash-box when he opened it for his godson." He bent forward and picked up a cream-filled pastry, opened his mouth and took a huge, triumphant bite.

Ingram laid down his cup. He gave Mrs. Parkes a long, considering look.

"You made no mention of the boy," he said quietly. "Why not? Presumably he had just as much opportunity to steal the money as Miss Thorson—or yourself." Her mouth dropped open at that. A bright flush showed along her cheekbones, there was an angry glitter in her eyes. But her voice was level as she answered him.

"It never even occurred to me to mention young Norman Foster." The inspector jotted down the name. "Son of the gardener here, lives down at the cottage." She indicated the direction with a movement of her head.

The door opened and Constable Jennings came back with Gina Thorson.

"I checked with the shop, Inspector. They confirm Miss Thorson's story." The girl laid a post-office book on the table in front of Ingram. He opened it and glanced at the last entry without much interest, knowing it would agree with her story whether she was innocent or guilty.

"Have some tea," he said. "Both of you. Before it gets cold." Mrs. Parkes added hot water to the tea-pot, not looking at Gina. The girl took her cup and a pastry, she began to eat with a fair show of appetite. Getting her nerve back, Ingram thought, she's beginning to fancy she's in the clear.

"Norman Foster," he said suddenly to Gina. "He was in Mallinson's room yesterday. Did he see Mallinson actually take out the cash-box? Could he see how much there was in it?"

Gina looked at him steadily, then she shook her head. "No, I don't think he actually saw the box." She told him how she had walked into the room, of the little scene that had followed. "He had his back to Mr. Mallinson all the time." She smiled faintly. "Mr. Mallinson insisted he stood like that. He was secretive about the cash-box. An old man," she added, "they do get a bit odd about money sometimes. I didn't even know the cash-box existed until——" A little gesture of her hand finished the sentence for her.

Hasn't jumped at the chance to implicate the boy, Ingram noted. Innocence—or cunning? He didn't know. After all his experience he could still never be quite certain when someone was telling the truth or embroidering a lie. The ring of truth, he thought wryly. No-one in the force ever used that convenient phrase, possibly because they no longer had the comforting illusion of being able to recognise the phantom ring when they heard it.

"How much did Mallinson give the boy?" he asked. "Do you know?"

She shook her head. "I asked Norman if Mr. Mallinson had been generous." She drew her brows together, trying to recall his answer with exactness. "He said it was quite a handsome present, that was all."

"And he left the house at once?"

She set down her cup with a little rattle, remembering. "No, he didn't. I took him down to the kitchen for some tea, Mr. Mallinson told me to, and then Norman asked if he could stay in the library for a bit. He wanted to look at some reference books. He'd done that before, with Mr. Mallinson's permission. He's an apprentice at a garage and the library's full of technical books."

"Hm, ye-es." Ingram considered the new vista opening out before him.

"Mr. Mallinson was out of his bedroom for quite a time in the late afternoon." Constable Jennings ventured to prompt the inspector's memory.

Ingram nodded slowly. "The room would be empty during that time?" He glanced from Gina to Mrs. Parkes. "Anyone could have slipped in and taken the money? Anyone who knew it was there?" Neither woman offered any disagreement with the statement. "Norman Foster could have gone in . . ." Or half a dozen other people.

"Norman didn't see the cash-box," Mrs. Parkes said stubbornly.

Ingram didn't bother to reply, he merely glanced at her and away again. Unless the boy was a complete fool he'd have realised Mallinson had some kind of cash hoard by his bed. He didn't imagine the old man had made him turn his back for nothing, he didn't fancy the birthday present had materialised out of thin air.

The dining-room door opened and Sergeant Yates came quietly in, running his eyes swiftly over Jefford and the two women, attempting to assess the stage the investigation had reached from a look, an attitude, the expression of a face.

"Sorry I've been a bit longer than I expected," he said. He took a brown-paper packet from his pocket and laid it on the desk in front of the inspector. "I've been making a few enquiries round the village."

"The tea's cold, I'm afraid," Mrs. Parkes said. "I'll ring for some more."

Yates turned his head. "Don't bother on my account," he said pleasantly. "I had some tea at the Swan." He saw Jefford's eyes blink open at that with a look of open alarm. And well you might display alarm, my lad, Yates thought. Nice little bunch of letters thrust into the inner pocket of Jefford's ancient suitcase stowed away under his bed in the Swan. Not very likely though that young Mrs. Mallinson could be persuaded to bring a charge of blackmail against Jefford. She'd be down on her knees most likely, begging the police not to let her husband know about the letters.

Ingram slit open the brown-paper packet and took out the letters, still in their envelopes. He glanced across at Tim Jefford whose face wore now the alert, faintly panic-stricken look of a man trying desperately to work out a plausible explanation.

With deliberate slowness the inspector drew the first letter from its envelope. He read it right through, inclining his head once or twice, pursing his lips as he considered its contents. When he had finished the letter he refolded it carefully and returned it to the envelope. He gave Jefford an assessing glance. After a long moment Tim dropped his eyes like a disconcerted animal, unable to bear that penetrating gaze.

"H'm . . ." Ingram said. "Very interesting." He took out the second letter, ran his eyes rapidly over it, took out the third and barely glanced at that. Then he straightened the letters into a neat pile.

"You were anxious to get off, a little while ago," he said lightly to Jefford. "I'm afraid that won't be possible now. Better arrange to stay on at the Swan for a day or two." He flicked the pile of letters with a finger. "We must have a little discussion about these. Later on. There are other more pressing matters just now."

Tim sighed, nodding his head in despairing acknowledgment. How on earth was he going to pay for another couple of nights at the pub? That's the least of your worries, Tim, my boy, he thought with a disagreeable feeling in the pit of his stomach. If dear Carole chooses to open her mouth you'll find yourself doing a stretch in an establishment rather less comfortable than the Swan.

On the tea-trolley a single airy pastry lay on a plate. He sighed again, deeply, stretched out a hand and took the pastry, biting into it forcefully. One had to keep up one's strength for whatever might lie ahead, and he hadn't the faintest idea when or where he was likely to eat any dinner that evening, or if indeed he was going to eat at all.

The pastry was sweet and sticky, it oozed cream thickly against his tongue. The condemned man ate a hearty breakfast, he thought with a sudden stab of mirth. It took him all his time to suppress a wild desire to throw back his head and laugh aloud.

"I'd like a word with you, sir," Yates said deferentially

to the inspector. Ingram pushed back his chair and the two men stepped out into the passage.

"I spoke to Chelsea," Yates said. "They rang me back at the Swan. Nothing known against Jefford, but they sent a man round to his place to make enquiries. He's an artist of sorts, lives in a ramshackle studio. Doesn't appear to have twopence to his name. He certainly isn't an established dealer, he isn't anything as respectable as that. They had a word with one of the other tenants, a woman, some kind of writer, you know the type. She wasn't at all anxious to say anything against Jefford but it seems he isn't above cadging from her when he was out of funds—which is pretty nearly all the time. Quite attractive to the ladies apparently, our Mr. Jefford. I found those letters in his suitcase at the Swan. Interesting reading, I thought. Not the kind of letter Carole Mallinson would want her husband to see."

"Yes, we'll go into all that later," Ingram said. "What I want you to do now is go and see a lad, Norman Foster, son of the gardener here at Whitegates." He ran rapidly over the details of Norman's visit to the house. "I'm beginning to think he took the money. He could easily have slipped back upstairs to Mallinson's bedroom when he was supposed to be in the library. Put a bit of pressure on, he's young, only just turned eighteen apparently. If he did it you ought to be able to get him to talk."

"Eighteen," Yates said reflectively. "Perhaps we ought to see him with his parents."

Ingram considered the matter. "I think not," he said at last. "He'll shut up like a clam in front of them. He'll be at the garage now, you can see him there. Keep it discreet, don't want to go worrying his employers if the lad's innocent. If by any chance he didn't take the money, see if you can get him to admit at least that he saw it, if there was still a lot of money in the box. Help to narrow down the time of the theft at all events." He jerked his head at the door behind him. "I'll get back in there and get the two women to run over Mallinson's last hours." He let out a long breath, raised his arms and stretched his muscles, wearily resigned to the tedium awaiting him.

"Norman Foster?" The garage manager slid his eyes over the sergeant's face. "Yes, he's here." He nodded towards the workshop. "I'll take you through in a minute. May I ask what this is about?"

Yates moved his shoulders. "Just one or two questions I'd like to ask the boy. I won't keep him long." Foster could be innocent, no point in blackening his name with his employer.

The manager remained standing by his desk. "I thought it might be about the money." Yates flung him a sharp look. "Came in here yesterday, late afternoon it was, his half-day off as a matter of fact. Paid off what was owing on his bike." He glanced out of the window at the glittering machine parked over by the wall. "Paid every penny. More than ninety pounds."

Yates drew back a chair. "I think we'd better sit down," he said.

The manager resumed his own seat. His voice took on a confidential tone. "Not very surprised to see you as a matter of fact. The lad's looked as sick as a dog all day. I told him to clear off home half-way through the morning, but he wouldn't go. Said he'd be all right." He pulled open a drawer of his desk and took out some papers. "Here you are, it's all down here. Ninety-three pounds, seventeen shillings and sixpence. Paid in notes, fivers and tenners most of it. I knew there was something dodgy about it. I mean a lad on his wages, ninety-three pounds doesn't grow on trees."

"Let me see the papers." Yates stretched out a hand. "How did he look when he came in with the money? Nervous?"

"No, not really." The manager looked back at yesterday.

"A bit excited. Pleased with himself. I asked him where he'd got the money of course, only natural, he'd got behind with the instalments and here he was with the whole lot. I was worried about it." He spread his hands and gave a little laugh. "Told me to mind my own business, more or less. I took the money but I held on to those papers. They should have gone off to head office this morning but I had a notion someone might be along asking questions. So I kept the papers."

Yates stood up. "You did quite right." He gathered the sheets of paper together. "I'll take these if I may. Let you have them back later." The manager nodded. "I'll go along now and have a word with young Foster."

The manager pushed back his chair. "I'll come with you and point him out." He frowned. "If you could take him on one side—you can see him in here if you like, I'll clear out and leave you to it. I'd rather you didn't talk to him in front of the other men." A family man himself, sons of his own. Young Foster was a decent enough lad. Easy enough at his age to lose your head, over a bike, or a girl. "He's never been in any trouble before, I'm sure of that. I wouldn't like to think——" He sighed. "You know how it is, a young lad, his first bike, it's like the end of the world if they can't keep up the payments." He stopped suddenly. "The money—I still have it here, in the safe. I hung on to it, just in case."

"Better let me have it," Yates said. "I'll give you a receipt." The manager went over to the wall safe and took a bunch of keys from his pocket. "Perhaps you're right," Yates said. "I'll see the lad in here. If you could send someone to fetch him."

Norman was stripping down a carburettor when the summons came.

"What've you been up to?" one of the other mechanics said in a tone compounded of habitual cheerfulness and genuine anxiety. "The manager wants to see you in his office. Pronto. There's a copper with him, came in a police car. You haven't been and robbed a bank, have you?" He smiled, but his eyes were worried.

Norman made no reply. A wave of pure relief washed over him. He felt light-headed, as if he was about to faint. He stood up and wiped his hands on a rag.

"Do you know what it's about?" the mechanic asked.

Norman raised his shoulders and let them drop again, not answering. He knew what it was about all right.

The exhilaration of yesterday afternoon had drained away by supper-time. He had eaten nothing, causing his mother to wonder if he wasn't sickening for something. He'd gone to bed early, away from the searching eyes of his parents, but he hadn't been able to sleep.

And then in the morning, someone from Rockley pulling up at the garage for petrol, asking if they'd heard the news about old Mallinson, found dead in his bed, police up at Whitegates, talk of a post-mortem, of an inquest, foul play suspected . . .

He couldn't even look at his sandwiches at lunch-time, let alone eat them . . . Murder . . . the word kept flashing up at him. Why would anyone want to murder old Mallinson? To cover up a theft perhaps? Was that what the police would think? All day long he'd worked on the engines, waiting for the police to come. And now they were here. He was glad in a way. Anything was better than that sick feeling of waiting.

He flung down the rag and followed the mechanic to the manager's office. Just before he stepped over the threshold he turned his head and looked at his bike, a long loving look full of sadness, holding the calm finality of resignation, of a last farewell.

Three-quarters of an hour later Yates stood talking to Ingram in the corridor outside the dining-room at Whitegates. "I've left the lad outside in the car with the driver," he said. "He took the money all right, made no bones about it, couldn't wait to get it off his chest." He put up a hand to his pocket. "I've got it all here—and the papers." He ran rapidly through his recital. "But he doesn't know a thing about Mallinson's death, didn't even know the tablets existed. Hadn't seen the whisky decanter either, or if he had he hadn't noticed it."

"Could be a good liar," the inspector said, but without much conviction. Not the work of an eighteen-year-old working lad, Mallinson's death. Had to look at the possibility of course, but mainly in order to discount it, clear away the underbrush.

"Not much of a liar at all," Yates said, shaking his head. "Wouldn't stop talking once he'd started. He's no murderer, all he's really bothered about is that precious bike of his. He saw the money, he went back and took it and that's about the size of it. Wasn't very clever about it, either, not a hope in hell of getting away with it. Didn't stop to think." He shook his head again. "Not the type to plan a murder. No cunning. Not a bad kid, really."

"You'd better see the parents," Ingram said. "No need to take him into the station and charge him at the moment."

"Who's to bring the charge?" Yates asked. "With Mallinson dead? One of the sons? The executors?"

Ingram shrugged. "We can leave all that for the moment. The theft's a mere fleabite. Glad to have it out of the way of course, simplifies matters." He ran a hand over his forehead. "It's the other business that bothers me, Mallinson's murder. Too many people with access. But my money's still on Kenneth Mallinson. Strong motive. No love lost. Whether we can pin it on him or not—that's another matter."

"I rather fancy Mrs. Stallard," Yates said lightly. "The avenging angel. A lot more interesting."

"You'd better have a word with her after you've seen the Fosters," Ingram said. "Shouldn't think she had anything to do with it." He pulled down the corners of his mouth. "Sooner we get her out of the way, the better. She'll be at her hotel, I fancy." He glanced at his watch. "And don't be all day about it." He turned back to the dining-room.

"We know who took the money," he said as soon as he had sat down again at the table. "We know it was none of you." Gina Thorson closed her eyes for an instant and let out a little breath.

So she didn't pinch it, Tim Jefford thought. Nor Mrs. Parkes. He looked at the nurse with dislike. Vicious woman, wouldn't put it past her to have finished off the old man. What motive though? Didn't seem to have one. Mallinson was old, she'd have got her legacy before very long and she had a cushy job here in Whitegates, she'd have wanted it to last as long as possible. Killing her patient wouldn't have been a very sensible idea.

Mrs. Parkes looked at Gina. "She was going to be sacked," she said. "She'd have been out of a job, she'd have lost her legacy. And she wouldn't have wanted Doctor Knight to know she'd been sacked. Well-connected, Doctor Knight, he wouldn't want to marry a girl like——"

She was interrupted by a knock at the door.

"A phone call for Constable Jennings," the maid said. Ingram gave Jennings a little nod and the constable followed the maid from the room.

He took the call in the library, sitting down at the table as soon as he had replaced the receiver, writing down the information in his notebook for Ingram's eyes.

The police had been round to see Mrs. Parkes's son, had quite a little chat with him and his wife. Thinking of emigrating to Australia. Upset about it, Mrs. Parkes was. A couple of thousand pounds, enough to put down for a smallholding, and the son would have changed his mind, only too glad to stay in England.

Jennings wrote down the details with relish, not liking Mrs. Parkes very much, glad to be able to stop her in her tracks, going on about the girl like that. Jealous of youth and good looks, that was her trouble—or part of it. He stood up and went back to the dining-room, put the open notebook down in front of the inspector with a little look of satisfaction.

"I think you'll be interested in that, sir." He stood waiting by Ingram's chair with his eyes fixed on Mrs. Parkes, not wanting to miss her change of expression.

Ingram tapped his pen on the table. He raised his eyes to the nurse.

"Lucky for you Henry Mallinson died just now," he said evenly. Mrs. Parkes flushed. She sat up in her chair. "Means you don't have to wave good-bye to your family, to your grandchildren."

"I don't know what you mean." Mrs. Parkes put up a hand and touched her hair.

"I think you do," Ingram said, twirling the pen. "Quite a handsome legacy. Very handsome. Enough to set your son up in a little place of his own. Enough to keep him from emigrating." She bit her upper lip. "And your finger-prints were on the whisky decanter."

CHAPTER XVIII

MRS. PARKES's eyes blazed at the inspector. "Of course my prints were on the decanter. I dusted in Mr. Mallinson's room. But there'd be other finger-prints as well. Whoever put the tablets into the whisky. It wasn't me." She folded her arms and gave him an unwavering look.

Yes, there were other prints, Ingram acknowledged in his mind. Kenneth Mallinson's prints. He always came back to Kenneth Mallinson. He pushed back his chair and stood up. He looked at the two women.

"You can go, both of you, for the present." Gina Thorson opened her mouth in relief. "You're not to leave the house of course. I may want to talk to you later." He turned to Tim Jefford. "But not you, you can stay." He watched the door close behind the two women.

"I want a word with you, my lad," he said almost jovially. "This little matter of blackmail." Jefford looked back at him without hope. "Might as well come clean now. We've got the letters. No point in telling us a fancy story. Might get yourself mixed up in a murder charge. Just stick to the truth, the whole truth and nothing but." He gave him an encouraging smile. "The sooner you start, the sooner you'll be finished."

From long experience Tim could recognise a tight corner when he saw one. "All right," he said. "It was like this. I was sitting in my flat, looking at the evening paper . . ."

"Get Mrs. Mallinson," Ingram said to Constable Jennings several minutes later. Tim slewed himself unobtrusively round in his chair so that when Carole came in he was able to give her a little deprecating look, an apologetic movement of his shoulders. I'm sorry, his eyes said, I had to tell him all about it.

Carole returned his look calmly, he was pleased to see. Not easily shaken, young Mrs. Mallinson, she'd been in more than one tricky spot in her life, she could take emergency action without panic. Murder, Tim thought suddenly—was she capable of that?

"Sit down." Ingram's voice was polite but none too friendly. "The hundred pounds you gave Jefford, may I ask you where you got it?" Hardly relevant now, but he asked the question from habit, from never being quite certain what particular question held the key to the puzzle.

Her face remained as demurely pretty, her manner as composed as ever. "I sold a bracelet." She mentioned the name of a Hallborough jeweller. She touched on the difficulty of drawing money from the joint account without her husband's knowledge. "I was going to sell two or three other small pieces to-day. To pay Mr. Jefford the rest of what he wanted." She turned her head and gave Tim a level look. "I don't know if he mentioned that, Inspector. I was supposed to meet him in the station buffet at Hallborough."

Her lips curved in the suggestion of a smile. "I don't think I'll bother now."

Ingram frowned. "No, Jefford didn't mention that little fact." Tim spread his hands in a despairing gesture. I wonder how long you get for blackmail, he thought numbly, trying to visualise himself in a shapeless uniform, sewing mailbags. Or did they actually sew mailbags these days? Perhaps they'd let him have some paints, he might hold an exhibition when he came out . . . Scenes of prison life . . . not much of a market for them though, hardly the kind of thing you'd want to hang over your mantelpiece . . .

"Were you afraid Jefford would tell your father-in-law about your association . . . with him? Afraid Mr. Mallinson might strike you out of his will? That there might be difficulty with your husband?" The inspector's tone was impersonal, merely pursuing the facts. "Was that why you gave him money? So that he would hold his tongue?"

Tim felt a stab of injured innocence. I wouldn't actually have told the old boy, he thought. Or her husband. Surely they knew that? I was only trying it on, he said to himself in mild exasperation. I was on my beam ends and Carole had all that money. Anyone would have done the same . . . well, no, perhaps not everyone, he couldn't quite see Ingram stuffing letters into a suitcase and hitting the trail in search of a little easy money . . . But almost everyone . . . Jennings for instance, he wouldn't put it past Jennings . . .

"I don't think you quite understand, Inspector." Carole gave Ingram a charming smile, "Tim wasn't *demanding* money from me, he simply asked for it, as an old friend."

Crikey! Tim thought in astonished joy, she's not going to sell me down the river after all!

"Tim wouldn't have said anything I didn't want him to say," Carole went on. "And he's going to start dealing in coins, properly I mean. He sees there's money to be made at it." Good old Carole! Tim felt like cheering. Pity she had to go and tie herself up with a conventional stick-in-the-mud husband, they'd had some good times together in the old days . . .

The inspector gave them both a long look of distaste. "I take it then," he said to Carole, "you don't want to press charges?"

"Oh no!" She shook her head firmly. Tim let out a long breath of relief.

"You ought to. I'm sure you know that." I haven't swallowed a word of your nice little cock-and-bull story, Ingram's eyes added. But he had no real hope. She was hardly going to open her mouth and let her husband in on her little secrets.

"I don't quite see what charges could be brought," Carole said with an air of helpfulness. "Tim is an old friend. He asked me to let him have a little money, he'd fallen on hard times. I didn't want to bother my husband about such a trifle so I sold a bracelet. It wasn't a bracelet I was particularly fond of. And I intended to sell a few more trinkets I had no further use for. I can't really see anything illegal in that. And I still don't want my husband to be bothered in any way. He has other things to concern himself about just now." Oh Carole, my girl, Tim thought in an excess of affection and relief, I could spring up and kiss you! Better not though. Or not just at the moment anyway.

Ingram considered the matter. "It may not have to come out," he said at last, grudgingly. "Unless——"

"Unless what, Inspector?" She was a little more wary now.

"Unless it turns out that you or your husband or the two of you acting in conjunction, saw fit to drop the tablets in Henry Mallinson's whisky." An edge of steel in his voice now.

"You don't really believe that, Inspector," Carole said easily. She stretched out a hand. "May I have those letters, please? I'd like them back."

Ingram picked up the little bundle. "I'm afraid not.

Later on perhaps, if it turns out we have no use for them.
And then of course it would be Mr. Jefford we'd return
them to, they're his property."

She drew a little trembling breath. For the first time she
looked less composed. Let her digest that, Ingram thought
with a touch of malice. He glanced at his watch.

"That will be all for the present." Henry Mallinson's
solicitor was due at any moment. "But don't leave the house,
either of you. I may want you later on."

Tim got to his feet, elated at the prospect of temporary
freedom. He crossed to the door and flung it open, gesturing Carole through. He closed the door behind him and
smiled at her.

"Thank you," he said with genuine gratitude. "I really
was beginning to see the prison gates yawning before me."

She raised her shoulders. "You've nothing to thank me
for. It wasn't any consideration for you that prompted me.
Pure self-interest." Her eyes moved lightly over his face.
She seemed to bear him no grudge, she didn't really seem
to be thinking about him at all but of other more important matters.

'You didn't do it, I suppose?" Tim asked casually. "You
didn't poison the old man?"

She gave him a fractional smile. "What do you think,
Tim? Do you think I'm capable of murder?"

"Do you know," he said after a long moment, "I really
have no idea. I thought I knew you pretty well but
now——" Now he realised that he'd never known her at all.
She was like a stranger who resembled some girl he'd once
been passionately in love with. He felt a moment's sudden
and surprising sorrow at the notion.

Carole turned away from him. "Come along," she said like
a hostess to a diffident guest. "I'll find you a drink. I think
you need one." She flashed a smile at him over her shoulder.
"It's all right, I won't put anything lethal in it, I promise."

As they crossed the hall they saw a maid ushering in an
elderly man. "That's the solicitor," Carole said in a low

voice. "My father-in-law's solicitor." He glanced across at her, inclining his head in greeting, his face grave. "I'll just go over and have a word with him. You can wait for me here."

"I take it then," Ingram said to the solicitor a few minutes later, "that Mr. Mallinson, if he had lived, would not have invested any money in Kenneth's firm? Or made him a loan, however you like to put it?"

The solicitor spread his hands. "No, I couldn't state that categorically. My advice would have been not to invest or make any kind of loan, certainly. Kenneth's firm was just about as rocky as it is possible to be. But Henry Mallinson wasn't a man who always listened to advice. He seemed very anxious to heal the breach with his elder son. He might have been quite happy to advance the money without any real hope of getting it back. He was a very wealthy man. And there are other considerations apart from the financial ones." He pulled his lips down, deploring the existence of such unprofitable considerations, acknowledging the unfortunate necessity to take them occasionally into account.

"One other point," he added. "A little puzzling." Ingram leaned forward. "I was on the phone to my contact the day before yesterday." The solicitor moved his hand. "In the course of my enquiries about Kenneth Mallinson's business. There is a partner, you know, a junior partner. Apparently he'd been offered a job elsewhere, he'd been hanging on to see if Kenneth could raise a loan. My contact told me the partner has now accepted the offer of a job, that Kenneth Mallinson advised him to. He phoned from Rockley two days ago it seems, and told him to take the job."

"Any reason?" Ingram asked. "Did Kenneth Mallinson give his partner any reason? Did he say he'd decided to let the firm go bust? Or what?"

"My understanding is that Kenneth told his partner he was rejoining his father's firm," the solicitor said.

Ingram frowned. "Had there been any suggestion of that?

Had Henry Mallinson mentioned such a possibility to you?"

The solicitor shook his head. "No, he made no mention of such a course. He was quite satisfied with the way David managed things."

"I see . . ." Ingram drummed his fingers on the table. "And Kenneth made this call two days ago. Before his father died." He bit his lip.

"You don't imagine," the solicitor said with a level look, "that it was Kenneth who——"

"I imagine nothing," Ingram said heavily. But the expression on his face answered the solicitor's question. I knew it! Ingram was thinking with a touch of triumph. It all points to Kenneth! One or two red herrings still to be cleared out of the way . . . Mrs. Stallard for instance . . . Not that he took the idea of Mrs. Stallard very seriously.

In her small hotel-room in Hallborough Mrs. Stallard sat facing Sergeant Yates.

"Certainly I saw Henry Mallinson," she said, looking the sergeant straight in the eye. "I intended to see him and I saw him." Not bothering to deny it then, Yates thought. Innocence? Or cunning? Did she think someone had spotted her leaving Whitegates, that denial would be useless?

"And exactly when would that be?" He gave her an enquiring look. "How long did you stay? What happened while you were there?"

She returned his gaze calmly. Yates flicked a swift downward glance at her hands. The eyes and the voice easy enough to keep under control, but the hands often told a different story, people forgot their hands. But Mrs. Stallard's fingers were motionless, lightly clasped together on her black cloth lap. She looks like some sinister avenging angel in that get-up, Yates thought. You hardly ever saw a widow all in black these days. At the funeral perhaps, but not afterwards. Folk no longer thought it necessary to go round for months on end proclaiming their grief to an indifferent world.

An avenging angel . . . was that how Mrs. Stallard saw herself? Swooping down into Hallborough, into Rockley, into Whitegates, to exact revenge for the loss of her husband? A strong feeling for drama perhaps, that might lead a woman to deck herself out from head to foot in unrelieved black . . . and might not the same instinct have led her to the final scene of the last act, the dropping of poison into Mallinson's whisky while the old man lay asleep and defenceless?

"I heard it was his heart," Mrs. Stallard said. "Do you usually make these enquiries when an old sick man dies in his sleep?"

"Mine not to reason why," Yates said lightly. "I'm asked to make a few enquiries, I make them. If a person has nothing to hide, they answer them. Simple as that." He opened his notebook. "And now, Mrs. Stallard, perhaps you'd like to make a start on answering my questions."

Ten minutes later he closed his notebook and slipped it into his pocket. Mrs. Stallard hadn't seen any tablets—or so she said. Hadn't noticed the whisky decanter either. All she'd wanted to do was confront Mallinson with his responsibility for her husband's death, let him see widowed motherhood in the bleak flesh, not just a name scribbled out on a cheque, an entry in the pensions ledger.

And according to her that was all she'd done, no more and no less. If her tale was true Mallinson had said scarcely a word in reply, he'd just lain there and listened to her outburst. I don't blame him, Yates thought grimly, enough to bring on another attack, opening his eyes and seeing that pale face staring vengefully down at him.

He stood up. "I've got to be getting back," he said. "We may need to get in touch with you again."

He hadn't written her off, not by a long chalk. Only her word for what had taken place between herself and Mallinson. Though if she kept her head they might never be able to pin it on her if she had poisoned the old man. No-one had seen her enter the house, no-one had seen her leave, her finger-prints weren't on the decanter.

"You'll be staying on in Hallborough for a day or two, I imagine?" His gaze travelled round the neat room, came to rest on a small table by the bed, on a leather handbag and a pair of cotton gloves lying beside it. She'd have worn gloves for her visit of course, no need for her to take them off, she wouldn't have left any fingerprints.

"I'll be here till the day after to-morrow at least." She got to her feet without haste. Neat and silent in her movements, he noted, economical movements, nothing done without a purpose. "My solicitor will be in touch with the sons. I won't be leaving till things are settled." She followed him to the door. "I didn't murder Henry Mallinson," she said suddenly. "It's quite clear why you're asking so many questions." She laid a hand on the door-knob. "Someone dropped tablets into the whisky decanter." She opened the door. "I can't say I'm surprised. A man doesn't get to where Mallinson got without making enemies." She smiled faintly and Yates saw all at once that behind the face of obsession lay another face, that of an ordinary, decent, hard-working woman. "But it wasn't me," she said, still with that little smile. "I didn't murder him. It never even crossed my mind."

"Quite apart from what Mrs. Stallard actually told you about her visit here," Inspector Ingram said, "what did you make of the woman yourself? Instinct, hunch, call it what you like. Do you think she's the stuff murderers are made of? Able to carry out a crime like that on a sudden impulse, able to keep her nerve afterwards, stick to her story?"

Sergeant Yates put up a hand and scratched his chin, he stared reflectively down at the parquet floor. "I don't know," he said slowly. "I thought at first she could have done it—that obsessive type, great strength of purpose, and a feeling of moral righteousness, as if she'd be able to justify it to herself." He raised his eyes to the inspector. "No pangs of conscience to struggle with, you see. Absolutely certain in her own mind that she'd punished Mallinson for the death of her husband, judge, jury and executioner all in one." He sighed and shook his head. "And then, just at the end, I suddenly felt I'd got her all wrong, that she wasn't like that at all, just a woman who hadn't managed to come to terms yet with her loss, simply got things a little out of proportion for a while." He sighed again. "I'm sorry, I'm afraid I'm not being very helpful. All I can say is that we can't altogether discount her."

"Ah well——" Ingram raised his shoulders. One always hoped for that sudden sharp scent, the unmistakable tingle along the spine, the inner voice that cried out clear and distinct, 'This is it! The trail! The one right path!' Trained as he was to consider the evidence and only the evidence, the long years of experience had taught him never to underestimate the value of a reasonless, inexplicable hunch. There had been a case after the war, detectives carrying out routine investigations in a private hotel after one of the residents had disappeared. Nothing remotely suspicious about any of the other guests, every question satisfactorily answered, the disappearance about to be written off as just another never-to-be-explained case of someone vanishing without a word from an apparently settled existence—impulse, whim, secret and compelling reasons, not the concern of the police, however much the action inconvenienced or disconcerted friends and relatives. The detectives were leaving the hotel, were walking through the dining-room on their way to the exit. The guests sat eating the evening meal, raising their heads to glance at the little party making their discreet way between the tables. And then one of the party, a policewoman, had heard that inner voice loud and insistent. She had paused for an instant, halted by that silent command, and looked back at a table she had just passed, at a man lifting a spoon to his lips.

'That's him!' she'd said in an urgent whisper as soon

as the party was outside the dining-room. 'That man! Over there. It's murder. And he did it." And she'd been right.

Ingram drummed his fingers on the table. There didn't seem to be any blinding flashes of inspiration about the Mallinson case, but there was always the evidence. He ran a hand across his forehead.

"We'd better have some coffee brought in." He glanced at his watch. "I think we've got a pretty clear picture now of everything that happened—or as clear a picture as we're likely to get. We'll run over the notes, see what we can make of it."

Constable Jennings pushed his chair back "I'll see about the coffee, sir." He paused half-way to the door. "There is just one thing. It might not have been a moment of impulse on Mrs. Stallard's part." He hesitated.

Ingram frowned. "She couldn't have known about the tablets. Or the whisky, come to that."

"Yes, I know that, sir." Jennings made a deprecatory movement with his hand. "But it occurred to me that she might have intended to do away with Henry Mallinson by some other method." He cleared his throat. "For all we know she might have had a gun in her handbag. Or a knife." He smiled suddenly. "Or she might have thought of putting a pillow over his face. Then she could have spotted the whisky and the tablets, realised they'd make a pretty deadly combination, and abandoned her first idea."

"It's a thought, anyway," Ingram said pleasantly. Didn't do to squash subordinates, however unsubtle their bright ideas, there was always the chance they'd come up with something really useful one day.

"I'll go and ask for the coffee then." A rather deflated air about Jennings as he crossed to the door.

"You don't feel we're in a position yet to make an arrest?" Yates raised his eyebrows at the inspector. As far as he was concerned, the case was in a total muddle.

"We'll know that better when we've been over the notes." Ingram straightened the sheaf of papers in front of him.

P

Everything points to Kenneth Mallinson, he told himself again. No question of hunches now, just plain solid evidence. Motive, opportunity, emotional set-up, everything. He blew out his cheeks, puffing away the notion of Mrs. Stallard, a red herring if ever he saw one.

Several cups of coffee and half a packet of cigarettes later he tilted his chair back and surveyed the other two.

"No doubt about it in my mind. Kenneth Mallinson it is."

Yates bit his lower lip. "All of them had opportunity enough. And anyone would know the tablets and whisky together could be fatal. Common enough knowledge, you've only got to read the newspapers. Half a dozen different motives for doing away with the old man. And the fingerprints on the decanter don't amount to all that much. You'd have to be pretty dim nowadays not to know about fingerprints. Gloves—or a handkerchief, even a bit of paper—anything to cover the fingers while you're touching the decanter."

He spread his hands wide. Going over the notes might have served to clarify the inspector's mind but it had merely contrived to widen the range of possibilities for the sergeant. This was the stage of an investigation he always hated, the moment when you had to stand back, survey the entire pattern as far as you could see it, and then jab a confident finger at a single thread running through the design. It took superb assurance to cry out, 'That's it! That's the vital thread!' Assurance, nerve, concentration. And Yates was tired from the long day, tired and more than a little confused. Ingram stood up and began to pace about the room with his hands thrust into his pockets and his head jutting forward. His brows were drawn into a fierce frown. He looked as fresh and alert as when he had begun the day.

"Kenneth Mallinson didn't have sense enough to remember about fingerprints. He left his on the decanter. What innocent reason could he have for touching the decanter? His father never offered that whisky to anyone else, everyone's agreed on that. His own special brand, one of his little meannesses. Kenneth knew his father's ways, he'd never have put the old man's back up by helping himself to a tot from that particular decanter. Especially not when he was trying to soften the old man up for a pretty hefty loan." He jerked a hand from his pocket and stabbed at the air.

"He deliberately concealed from his brother and sister-in-law the fact that the new will had been signed, although the matter was discussed between the three of them over dinner at Tall Trees." His voice took on a triumphant note. He paused in his pacing and rapped the table with his knuckles. "And he rang his junior partner and told him he was going back into the family firm. You can't get away from that! Told the partner to clear off and take the job he'd been offered. There'd been no mention of Kenneth going back into the family business. But he knew the terms of the new will, he knew he'd have a controlling interest when the old man died. And he intended to see that the old man did die. Very soon." He glared at Yates, demanding an answer.

The sergeant expelled a long breath. Put like that, he thought despairingly, it sounds open and shut. But he'd seen cases before that had developed a disconcerting trick of creaking themselves open again after the lid had been slammed shut.

"There you are, you see!" Ingram said with pleasure. "You can't fault it." And Yates couldn't. He sees it clear and distinct, he thought wearily, he could be right, it could have happened like that. He ran a hand over his face, pressing away the tiredness, the tension.

"I suppose you're right," he said heavily.

"Of course I'm right!" Ingram glanced at Jennings, whose opinion hadn't been solicited and wasn't going to be solicited. "We'll have Kenneth Mallinson in again now, we'll see what explanation he can offer. If he can offer any explanation."

And this was the part of the investigation Jennings detested most, the moment when you opened the door of a

room, ran your eye over the waiting ring of wary faces, let
your gaze rest for an instant on one particular face—no getting away from that, you had to look at the face, at the eyes,
you couldn't turn your head away while you said, 'If you'd
like to come along, sir, the inspector wants another word
with you.' The immediate slackening of taut muscles in
every pair of shoulders but one, the audible release of other
breaths. And the trapped look in that one pair of eyes, the
involuntary movement of the hands, the jerk of the head.
Never a man for blood sports, Jennings, never a man to
relish the gun or the snare, the moment always sickened
him, turned his stomach.

He reached the room where the family sat waiting, paused
with his head lowered, drew a deep breath, braced himself,
raised his hand and knocked.

CHAPTER XIX

"I CAN EXPLAIN that," Kenneth Mallinson said with an air
of brittle lightness. He had refused to sit down, he stood
facing Inspector Ingram across the dining-table, taking
up a defensive stance behind the upright chair Jennings
had pulled out for him. He clutched the curved back of the
chair with both hands so that the knuckles stood out round
and white. "Go on, then," Ingram said encouragingly, "Explain. I'm listening. Plenty of time, no need to rush it."

Kenneth turned his head and looked round the room, at
Jennings standing a few feet away from the inspector, a
look of casual alertness on his solid features, at Yates sitting
at the foot of the table with a pen poised over his notebook, carefully not meeting Kenneth's eyes, not wanting to
see that trapped look.

Kenneth's gaze came to rest on the huge gilt-framed mirror over the fireplace.

"It was a very good offer—the one my partner had. It

was a question of making my mind up at once. He wasn't likely to get another offer so good." He addressed the words to his own image in the glittering glass. His attention wandered for a moment from what he was saying, caught by the sight of that pale face staring back at him, the lips moving like a fish in a bowl. Panic written sharp and distinct on those features at once familiar and disturbingly unknown, the face of a man imprisoned on the front page of a newspaper, caught in the flash of a photographer's bulb, the wanted man, held for questioning.

Appalled by the guilt on that mouthing reflection he fell silent, withdrew one hand from the chair and put it up to his face. Over the fireplace he saw the mirrored fingers shielding that look from the eyes of justice. At once he dropped his hand and felt the wood of the chair, firm and oddly reassuring in his grasp. With a strong effort he forced his eyes away from the glass, compelled himself to look straight into the inspector's face.

"I had to be fair to my own partner, you see." That was better, he heard the sensible note in his voice, firmer now, under control, he liked that air of appeal, one man-of-the-world to another. "So I decided to let my own firm go bust, make it up with my father and come back into the family business." To his immense relief he found that he could manage a smile. "It's my rightful place, you see, where I belong."

There was a small silence. Ingram looked back at him, still with that easy, expectant gaze. Without speaking, without any change of expression he pushed back his chair and got to his feet with slow, deliberate movements.

"I'd like you to come down to the station." He began to gather his papers together. "To Hallborough, that is. We can take a proper statement there." Implying that in some way the station would be more comfortable, more appropriate than the dining-room at Whitegates, there would be better facilities, a more professional air about the proceedings.

"I could make a statement here," Kenneth said without

hope. He heard himself give a high, tinny laugh. "I'm quite ready to make it now."

"I think not," Ingram said easily, courteously. "The station is more usual . . ." He glanced at Jennings. "Tell the rest of them to hold themselves ready for further questioning, then meet us outside at the car. The other men can stay." A couple of uniformed men from Hallborough to be left on watch in case anyone tried to make a bolt.

Jennings left the room. Ingram and the sergeant stood waiting for Kenneth to move. He wanted to say, 'Am I being arrested? Am I being charged with the murder of my father?' But instinct, deeper than reason, warned him to hold his tongue, as if not framing the words would somehow prevent the notion from entering the inspector's mind.

It's a mere formality, he told himself with a desperate effort at reassurance, they always take statements at the station, it's more business-like. Assisting the police with their enquiries, they call it. He saw the words marching in columns across the front pages . . . A man spent last night at the Hallborough police station, assisting the police with their enquiries . . . How did one assist in enquiries, locked away behind a cell door? He saw the cell with its bleak narrow bed, the grating high in the wall.

"If you're ready," Ingram said politely. Across the back of Kenneth's neck and shoulders the muscles tensed into tight bunches, he felt an uncontrollable shudder begin to ripple through his body.

"Yes, I'm ready." He took a step forward, turned his head and saw that other man behind the shining glass start into motion, the hands clasped in front of him, the shoulders drooping, like a condemned man on the way to the gallows.

"Was the lemon meringue pie to your liking, Doctor Knight?" The housekeeper saw with pleasure that he had eaten more than half of it—and that after a good helping of roast chicken—for all he'd come in half an hour ago with

his face set into lines of weariness, telling her he could
only manage a cup of soup, he was too tired to eat.

"Oh—yes, thank you. Very good indeed." He smiled at
her. "I feel a new man."

"Nothing like a good meal when you're feeling done up,"
she said. "Never does to skimp on food, simply asking for
trouble." She shook her head. "And we've enough trouble
at the moment, goodness only knows. What with that nasty
business up at Whitegates and all." She set about clearing
the table with her usual briskness, sliding a little sideways
glance at the young doctor to see if he was going to be com-
municative. "Poor Miss Thorson must be ever so upset."

Richard Knight said nothing, he frowned down at the
tablecloth. Very sweet on Miss Thorson, was Doctor
Knight, the housekeeper knew how it was, she'd been young
herself once and not above a bit of dalliance. And she'd
heard quite a number of rumours when she'd slipped up to
the village shops in the late afternoon. Wild rumours, most
of them, not to be seriously countenanced by a sensible
woman, snatches of gossip filtering from the tradesman's
entrance at Whitegates out to the Rockley stores, losing
nothing in the retelling among the little knots of headscarved
housewives pursing their virtuous lips over the canned soups
and the packets of cornflakes.

"I'll bring the coffee in in a moment." She took a little
brass-headed brush from the sideboard and swept the
crumbs from the tablecloth into a miniature tray. "Miss
Thorson will be out of a place now—unless Mr. David
finds her a place in the business."

One particularly unpleasant rumour had reached her
ears, Miss Thorson accused of theft from the old man, a
substantial sum by all accounts. There was nothing in it, she
was sure of that, but it was wicked the way folk talked,
taking away a person's character behind their back. She
longed to mention the rumour to Doctor Knight, just to let
him know what was being said, just so he could take steps
to silence the gossips. But it was hardly a thing you could

put into words, not in cold blood. She sighed in frustration, clattering the crumb-tray on to the trolley.

Richard Knight raised his head. "I'll be going up to Whitegates as soon as I've had my coffee." He gave her a faint smile. "I'll tell you all the news when I get back. I won't be very long, not more than an hour or so." Long enough to find out what was going on, to slip an arm round Gina in some quiet room, tell her not to worry, he'd look after her.

The housekeeper wheeled the laden trolley to the door. "I won't be easy in my mind till Doctor Burnett comes home, and that's a fact." She paused on the threshold and looked back at Richard. "Miles away up there in a strange hospital and not a soul to visit him." She drew a deep breath. "At his age, too. Doesn't bear thinking about."

Out in the hall the phone pealed loudly. "I'll get it," she said, abandoning the trolley. A couple of minutes later she came back into the room at a run, calling out as she came. "Oh, Doctor Knight! It's the hospital—about Doctor Burnett! He's disappeared!"

Richard sprang to his feet, knocking his chair to the floor. He ran into the hall.

"They want to know if he's here!" the housekeeper cried behind him. Tears smarted under her eyelids. She snatched a handkerchief from her apron pocket and dabbed fiercely at her cheeks. She clasped her hands together and stood waiting a few feet away from Doctor Knight, listening to his rapid questions, making what she could of them. At last he replaced the receiver and turned to face her with his brows drawn together.

"Where is he?" she cried. "What's happened to him?" She dug into her pocket again for the handkerchief.

"I don't know." His eyes looked strained and anxious. "The nurse went into his room half an hour ago—he'd been having a sleep, he was getting on very well—and his bed was empty. She thought he'd gone to one of the bathrooms, she wasn't worried at first. When he didn't come back she went to look for him but he wasn't any-where in the hospital. Then she thought of his clothes, she went back to his room and found his night-clothes stuffed into the locker. His own clothes were gone. He must have got dressed and left the hospital, slipped out as soon as he was left alone for his sleep."

"How long ago was that?" she asked sharply. "Do you think he's coming back here?"

"I don't know. He's been gone a good three hours or more, I should think. He may have been confused, suffering from concussion, he may not have known where he was or where he was going."

"Do you mean he's delirious?" She began to cry again. "Wandering about, not knowing where he is—or even who he is?"

"It's possible." He bit his lip in rapid thought. "He may turn up here of course, safe and sound——"

"But how?" she asked. "His car—that was damaged, it'll be in a garage somewhere now, surely, waiting to be re-paired."

"He could have got on a train—or even hired a car." He frowned. "I wonder . . . could he have gone back up north?"

"You mean to where he used to live before? He could have woken up and forgotten about Rockley, thought he was still practising up north, he might have gone there?"

"Yes, he could have." He looked down at the phone, de-bating whether or not to ring the police. "I think we'll leave it for the present," he said at last. "Give him till to-night. If he doesn't turn up here by then, we'll have to do some-thing about it." He glanced at his watch. "Look, I'll go up to Whitegates right away, I won't wait for coffee." Gina would be looking out for him, he'd promised to call in. "If the hospital rings again, if there's any news at all, phone me at Whitegates. I won't be long." A sudden thought struck at him. "I suppose he couldn't be heading for Whitegates?"

She was puzzled. "You mean—he was worried about Mr.

Mallinson's death, he got confused and thought he ought to be there?" She put up a hand to her head. "No, that couldn't be it, he doesn't know Mr. Mallinson is dead, surely?" She tried to think. "They found Mr. Mallinson this morning and by that time Doctor Burnett was already in hospital. He couldn't know about Mr. Mallinson, could he? There was no-one to tell him."

"No, he doesn't know, of course he doesn't," Knight said. "I got muddled there for a moment. I didn't say anything to the hospital, there wouldn't have been any point, and no-one else knows exactly which hospital he was taken to."

"So he wouldn't be thinking of going to Whitegates," the housekeeper said. "He wouldn't have any reason to."

Richard took his coat from the hall stand. "I'll be as quick as I can. And don't start worrying, it won't do anyone any good."

She opened the front door. "I think I'll just slip upstairs and switch on the electric blanket in Doctor Burnett's bed." She gave a faint smile. "You never know, he might turn up here before long."

She had washed up the dinner things and set the kitchen to rights when she heard the car swish up the drive. She glanced at the clock. Doctor Knight hadn't been much above half an hour at Whitegates. Either he had found Miss Thorson all right again, no longer in need of much comfort —or else he had torn himself away in his anxiety about Doctor Burnett. She took off her apron and went into the hall.

The front door opened and someone came in as she switched on the light.

"Hallo there!" Doctor Burnett said. "I'm back." She stood staring at him with her mouth hanging slackly open. Then she pulled herself together and ran forward with a little cry.

"Are you all right?"

He gave her a brief nod, turned and said out into the driveway, "Come inside, we can settle up in here."

A man stepped into the hall, holding a peaked cap in his hands. Dr. Burnett took his wallet out. "Here you are, thank you very much."

"Thank you, sir." The driver touched his forehead in a sketchy salute and took himself off. The housekeeper closed the door behind him. She was still trembling.

"We were worried to death about you, Doctor Burnett. Are you sure you're all right?" She helped him off with his overcoat, threw open the door of the sitting-room and urged him into an easy chair by the fire. "What shall I get you? Some coffee? Or soup? I could easily get you something more substantial if you feel you could manage it."

Burnett held up a hand. "Don't fuss, there's a good woman. I'm perfectly all right." And he did look a good deal better than she had dared to hope, a little pale and tired but in command of himself. He smiled. "I'm a trifle stiff, I'll admit, I didn't escape without a few bruises, but it's nothing to worry about. What I'd like is a good stiff peg of whisky, then I'll get off upstairs and have a sleep for an hour or two, I'll have something to eat later. Where's Knight?"

She was already pouring the whisky from a decanter on a side table. "He's up at Whitegates. He won't be very long, he just slipped up to see how Miss Thorson was bearing up——" She broke off abruptly and stood looking down at him, holding out the glass. Of course, Doctor Burnett knew nothing about the death of his old friend. She bit her lip. What a fool she'd been, letting the words slip out like that. Far better to have let the news wait till he was stronger, more rested. One shock on top of another, wouldn't do him any good.

He took the glass and sipped at the whisky. "Ah, that's better!" He shot her a keen glance. "Is Miss Thorson in some kind of trouble?" She turned her head away, looking down at the carpet. "Well——" She could think of nothing whatever to say. "In a way——" Inspiration failed her.

Burnett took a longer drink of the whisky. "Something

wrong at Whitegates?" He set down the glass with a little
clatter. "Mr. Mallinson—is he worse? Has he had another
attack?" His voice took on a note of irritation. "Tell, me,
woman! I'm not likely to go off in a swoon!"

She twined her fingers together. "I didn't mean to let it
out like that, it would have been better to wait till you'd
had a good night's sleep." He was frowning fiercely at her
now. "I'm afraid Mr. Mallinson is dead." He drew a sudden
sharp breath and put up a hand to his eyes. "I'm sorry,"
she said lamely. "It must be a dreadful shock to you."

"When was it?" he asked in a low voice, still with one
hand over his face. "How did it happen?"

"They found him early this morning—Mrs. Parkes and
Miss Thorson. He must have died in the night."

"Heart?" he said in a muffled voice. "He had another attack?"

I could say yes, she thought wildly, and then he could be
told the truth to-morrow, when he's stronger. I could warn
Doctor Knight to say nothing about murder to-night. She
opened her mouth to frame the lie. But she had already
paused for too long. Burnett had taken his hand away from
his face and was looking at her now with sharp alertness.
She knew he would at once detect the falsehood from her
look, her manner.

"I'm afraid this is going to be another shock," she said
at last. "Doctor Knight wasn't altogether satisfied with the
circumstances. He called in the police."

"Police . . . " He picked up his glass and drained it. "Do
they think it was . . . suicide?" He said the word with
difficulty, not meeting her gaze.

She saw the passage of deep and bitter emotion across
his face. She could guess at what he must be feeling—his
old friend, alone, deserted, in pain, weary of the effort, the
struggle, himself miles away, powerless to offer the help
that would have saved him.

She wanted to take his hand, to cry out, 'It wasn't like

that!' But what she had to tell him was no comfort, the truth was even more painful than what he had mistaken for the truth. But there was no help for it.

"No, not suicide," she said slowly, trying to give him time to adjust. "He must have helped himself to some whisky from his decanter. Some of his tablets had been dissolved in the whisky." She was watching him intently, fearing a suddenly increased pallor, a change in breathing. She saw him lower his shoulders as if deliberately relaxing himself, attempting to take the blow as calmly as possible. "They think it wasn't an accident, and they don't think Mr. Mallinson put the tablets into the whisky himself." Colour unchanged, breathing all right. "They think someone put the tablets into the decanter deliberately. They think he was murdered." The word dropped into silence. She heard the coals shift on the fire. Burnett closed his eyes and leaned back in his chair. He looked very old and very tired.

"I'll ring Doctor Knight," she said rapidly. "He'll be over here right away." She took a couple of steps towards the door.

"No, don't do that. Get me another drink." She turned, hesitated, looked back at him. His eyes were still closed, one hand was raised to halt her.

"I'm quite all right," he said. "No need to bring Knight back just yet. I'll ring him myself in a few minutes. Just get me that drink."

She filled the glass again. He sat up and drank half of it at a single gulp. He gave her a sharp look and she was un-utterably relieved to see him more himself again. He set the glass down.

"Do they suspect anyone in particular?" He made a sudden sharp movement with his head. "They haven't made an arrest, have they?"

"No—or they hadn't when I last heard. Doctor Knight may know something more by now. I was in the village this afternoon and there were all kinds of rumours. You know how it is, a lot of gossip, servants and tradespeople talking.

They seem to suspect everyone from Miss Thorson to young Foster."

"Foster?" he said in deep puzzlement.

She gave a little smile. "The gardener's boy. As if a lad like that—but these small places, they get hold of something and get to work on it, nothing's too wild for them to credit." She struck her hands together. "I've just remembered, I must phone the hospital. They rang earlier, they were very upset when they found you'd vanished. Doctor Knight promised to let them know as soon as we had any news of you."

"Oh yes," he said without interest. "The hospital. Yes, you'd better ring them right away. Tell them I'll be in touch with them later, tell them I'm perfectly all right, no need to fuss. Then you can go and get me something to eat, something light, eggs perhaps, while I ring Knight."

"There's no reason at all why you shouldn't go up to your room and go to sleep." Richard Knight tilted his head back and looked at Gina sitting beside him on the sofa in a small sitting-room at Whitegates. "I can't really see Ingram doing any more questioning here to-night." Now that he's got Kenneth Mallinson down at the station, he added in his mind. Had Kenneth really done it? An unknown quantity to Richard, he'd never met the man till a few days ago. I suppose it's possible, he thought, men have been known to murder their fathers for gain. Someone had certainly murdered the old man and it seemed as if Kenneth stood to gain more than any of the others. He kissed Gina lightly on the cheek.

"Will you be able to sleep?"

"Oh yes, I'm sure I will. I'm very tired. I feel a good deal better now," she added hastily, "but I'm still rather tired."

He patted her hand. "If by any wild chance the inspector does want to ask any more questions to-night, someone can always go up and call you."

She hesitated. "I think I'd like something to eat first."
She'd scarcely eaten all day and now all at once she felt a
sharp pang of hunger. "I'll go and ask Cook to make me
something light." She glanced up at him with appeal. "Stay
with me while I eat it." She smiled. "You can have something too."

He shook his head. "No thanks, it's not long since I ate
an enormous dinner. But I'll have some coffee while you
eat."

There was a brisk knock at the door. A maid put her
head into the room. "Oh—Doctor Knight—there's a phone
call for you. It's Doctor Burnett!" Surprise and lively interest in her tone—they'd all heard about Burnett's accident.

"Burnett?" Richard was startled. "Where's he speaking
from?"

The maid threw the door wide. "He's at home, here in
Rockley."

"Oh, good!" A wave of relief washed over him. "I'll come
right away." He spoke over his shoulder to Gina. "You go
and speak to Cook." He paused on the threshold. "I'll come
back and see you when I've talked to Burnett. But I'm
afraid I won't be able to stay, I'll have to get back at once."

"Oh! All right," she said in disappointment and acceptance. She didn't want Richard to go, not just yet, she felt
safe while he was with her, shielded from the looks, the
unspoken thoughts behind all those other eyes. "Couldn't
you just——" But he was already gone.

"You gave us a good fright," Richard said into the phone
with affectionate severity. "We had a vision of you wandering about with concussion——"

"I'm perfectly all right." Burnett sounded impatient of
fuss, himself again, Richard was relieved to hear. "And
the housekeeper's been on to the hospital, so there's no need
to worry about that. She told me about Henry Mallinson."

The devil she did, Richard thought. Couldn't she have
held her tongue till the morning?

"I'm sorry," he said. "It must have been a bad shock for

you." How much had she told him? About himself calling in the police? All at once he knew with blinding certainty that Burnett wouldn't have summoned the police, whatever uneasiness, whatever suspicions he might have felt, he would have let his old friend go to the grave in peace and dignity. But I'm not Burnett, he thought, Mallinson was no old friend of mine, I did what common sense and justice demanded. He certainly wasn't going to put himself in any defensive, apologetic position with his senior partner.

"I'm ringing to ask if there's any news," Burnett said. "I'm just off to bed now for a good sleep, but I wanted to know first if the police have made any real progress." So he knew all about it. Richard silently cursed the housekeeper and her wagging tongue. "I gather there are a lot of wild rumours flying about the village." The silly woman must have talked non-stop from the moment Burnett staggered in through the front door. "So I want to know the facts."

Ah well, there was no help for it. Richard sighed. "I'll come back at once. I'll just find Gina and say good night, then I'll be over. I'll tell you all about it then."

"No, don't do that." Burnett sounded fiercely impatient now. "No need for that at all. You can stay and comfort your Miss Thorson. I'll see you in the morning. All I want to know now is what the position is, if they've made any progress, if they suspect anyone in particular. I don't want to sit up half the night talking, I want to get off to bed. Dammit, man, you can answer a straightforward question, can't you?"

Richard sighed again. "Yes, of course I can." Burnett could be very irritating. Directness was one thing but rudeness was another . . . He gave the news without any further attempt at softening it, he'd done his best—and with small thanks.

"They've taken Kenneth Mallinson to Hallborough police station for further questioning—and, I gather, to make a statement."

"Kenneth!" Burnett's voice was appalled. "Surely they don't imagine——"

"He had ample motive apparently," Richard said abruptly, weary all at once of the whole depressing business, of the long, fatiguing day. "Motive and opportunity. The new will—the position of his own business——" But Burnett would know all about those matters of course, he'd have talked them over with Henry Mallinson. "I had to call the police," he added and was at once seized with anger at himself for defending his action after all. "I couldn't close my eyes to murder."

"Has anyone suggested that you should have done?" Burnett replied with sharp hostility. Why are we talking to each other like this? Richard asked himself with a little shock of astonishment. As if we are quarrelling? Why on earth should Mallinson's death cause us to quarrel? We've always got on reasonably well before.

"No, of course not," he said with an attempt at mildness. "Look, I'll tell you all about it in the morning. It's too bad that you had it sprung on you to-night. I'm sorry. You must go and get a good sleep."

"And don't hurry back," Burnett said, unmollified. "Stay and pursue your courtship." A little click as Burnett replaced the receiver. The phone buzzed uselessly in Richard's ear. He slammed it back on its rest and stood drumming his fingers on the table with irritation. Light footsteps sounded in the corridor outside. He drew a deep breath, squared his shoulders, made a strong effort to dismiss unrest from his mind and crossed to the door.

Gina was standing just outside, smiling hesitantly up at him.

"Are you going now? Is Doctor Burnett all right?"

He forced himself to smile at her, he summoned up an air of gaiety. "No, I'm not going, not just yet." She gave him a wide smile of pleasure. He put an arm around her shoulders. "I'm going to have that coffee with you after all. Burnett's perfectly all right apparently. He's going off to

Q

bed, he doesn't want to see me to-night. There's no need
for me to hurry back—not unless I get a call from a patient
of course."

She moved her shoulders in relief. "I'm so glad. Come on,
we'll go back to the kitchen and tell Cook we'll want a lot
more coffee."

"Black coffee," Burnett said firmly. "And plenty of it.
Right away, please." He glanced at the housekeeper hovering uncertainly by the door. "I have one or two important
things to see to, a couple of letters to write before I go to
bed. I'll have the coffee in my study."

The housekeeper made no attempt to carry out the order.
"But I thought you were going to bed right away." Anxiety
for him lent her boldness. "I'm sure Doctor Knight wouldn't
like it if he knew you were going to start bothering about
work at this moment. Is he coming back?"

He glared at her. "I'm old enough to do as I please without consulting young Knight." Or you, he added savagely
to himself. "Go on, woman, get that coffee. And stop fussing round me. Knight will be back later on. I don't need
either of you nurse-maiding me. I wasn't mortally wounded
in the crash, you know, I got off very lightly." If only that
crash had never happened, if only there had been no fog,
if only he'd backed out of the engagement at the last
moment—if only—if only—but it was too late now for if
onlys——

"You'll never be able to sleep after black coffee," the
housekeeper said with astonishing stubbornness, still rigidly
unmoving.

Burnett closed his eyes and spoke between his teeth. "Am
I to make it for myself then?"

She had to acknowledge defeat. She bent her head and
felt the tears spring to her eyes. "No, of course not, I'll get
it right away."

At last, Burnett thought, angered at the way everyone
was conspiring to thwart him just now. He flung open the

door of his study, aware all at once of weakness, of appalling fatigue, of just how much the accident had taken out of him—the accident, and old age and shock. He crossed to his desk, sat down before it, opened a drawer and took out paper and envelopes. Then he propped his elbows on the desk and dropped his head for a long minute into his cupped hands, banishing weariness with a mighty effort of will, summoning up strength and resolution.

CHAPTER XX

IT WAS WARM and cosy in the small sitting-room. Gina leaned back against the downy satin cushions with her eyes closed, feeling Richard's arm firm and comforting around her shoulders.

"I didn't want you to be ashamed of me when you took me home," she said. "I wanted to be a credit to you." Amazing how simple it had been after all to tell him about the clothes. She felt more at ease with him at this moment than she had ever done. In love, yes, she'd been in love with him almost from the first day she'd seen him, but always until now there had been that disconcerting nervousness, that feeling of her own inadequacy, the fear that she would never be able to measure up to what would be expected of her as the wife of a rising young doctor.

Richard took her hand and played with the fingers. "You worry too much about trifles," he said lightly. "It's a foolish habit, it takes a lot of the pleasure out of life." But he didn't altogether blame her for getting into a state about her wardrobe, about her visit to his parents. It could be a trifle overpowering for a vulnerable girl like Gina to find herself plunged into the midst of strangers, assessing her with shrewd and worldly eyes. "You'll be a great success, they'll all love you." He tilted her face up and kissed her. "As I do."

And she was prepared now to believe they might . . .

The thought of her new clothes lay like a reassuring bulwark at the back of her mind. It's going to be all right, she told herself with relief and delight, everything's going to be all right . . . after all . . .

A light, double knock at the door. Gina jerked herself out of Richard's embrace. Fear struck at her again. "It isn't——" Not the police come back again, surely? Not wanting to question her again, to make her sit facing them over the gleaming table, boring into her with their sharply intelligent eyes?

But it was only the maid. "It's Doctor Burnett again," she said apologetically to Richard, not liking to disturb young love, having a soft spot in her heart for romance. "He's on the phone, he'd like to speak to you."

Richard frowned. Surely Burnett should have been fast asleep in his bed by now? He got to his feet. Was he feeling ill? Or unable to sleep perhaps, going over the distressing news in his mind?

Gina followed him to the phone, standing a couple of yards away, listening without subterfuge, obscurely afraid of what might be said.

"What is it?" Richard asked. "Are you all right? Do you want me to come over after all?"

"I've written some letters," Burnett said, his voice firm and clear. "You'll find them on the desk in my study."

"Letters?" Knight was deeply puzzled. "I thought you were going to bed."

"I rang to say good-bye," Burnett said. "I felt I owed you that." A cold tide of unease rose in Richard's brain.

"Good-bye?" he echoed and the word formed itself in letters of fire inside his head. "Wait there, I'll be over in a few minutes."

"I killed Henry Mallinson," Burnett went on as if Richard hadn't spoken. "It's all in the letters. I couldn't let Kenneth take the blame."

"Hold on!" Richard cried. If only he could keep Burnett at the other end of the phone. "It's the accident—you're

suffering from shock, you don't know what you're saying."
He covered the mouthpiece with his hand, jerked his head
at Gina and called in a low, fiercely urgent voice. "Get
someone round to Burnett at once—the police or David
Mallinson. I'll keep him talking. Run!"

He saw her eyes blink open, she turned and ran from the
room. He was faintly aware of the sound of her racing
feet as he snatched his hand away from the mouthpiece.

"If it hadn't been for the fog," Burnett was saying in a
calmly explanatory tone, "I'd have been there to sign the
certificate, there would have been no bother with the
police at all. Natural causes, no questions asked. Of course
I didn't know he'd drink the whisky on that particular
night, he might not have touched it for days." Part of
Richard's mind caught the slam of a door, voices calling
out, feet pounding outside on the gravel, a car thrust into
motion.

"Why should you want to harm Henry Mallinson?" he
asked. How long for the car to reach the house? Four
minutes? Five? If he could just manage to keep Burnett
talking . . . "I can't believe you know what you're saying.
It's the shock——"

"Don't imagine I don't know what you're up to," Burnett
said with a hint of amusement. "In your position I would
be doing exactly the same. Putting your hand over the
mouthpiece and calling for help. But I'm afraid help won't
get here in time."

"In time for what?" Richard's brain was working with
lightning speed, part of it engaged in holding Burnett's
attention, part of it visualising the car swooping along the
road, the driver grinding it to a halt, hurling himself up
the steps, through the front door, grappling with Burnett—
and some other section of his mind seeing the doctor standing in Mallinson's room, idly chatting, distracting his patient's attention from the fingers dropping the tablets into
the neck of the decanter . . . He did it! cried that rapidly
churning section of his brain. That's the way it was!

"In time to stop me swallowing a dose of cyanide," Burnett said, still with that odd touch of amusement. "I've left you everything. I made a new will some little while back, when Mallinson was first taken ill. I knew my chance would come, you see, I wanted everything to be in order. I wish you every happiness," he added with formality. "You and your Gina." For the first time his voice sounded uncertain, it trembled slightly. "Live long and be happy, both of you. Good-bye, Richard."

"Wait!" Richard cried in agony. "Hold on!" But the line was dead. He slammed the receiver down and turned to see faces staring in at him from the doorway. Carole Mallinson, her face pale, her eyes wide—Mrs. Parkes, one hand up to her mouth—a couple of servants—and Gina pushing her way through to him.

"David Mallinson and one of the constables," she cried. "They've taken a car, they've gone. What is it? I didn't know what to tell them, just that they had to get over there, to Doctor Burnett——"

"I'm afraid they won't be in time," he said, not knowing what to do, what action he could possibly take. "I'm afraid he'll be dead before they get there."

Carole Mallinson gave a stifled cry. Mrs. Parkes clutched at Richard's arm. "Dead? Doctor Burnett? Why——?"

He shook himself free. "I must go." Nothing he could do but he must get into his car and drive off. "Stay here," he called to Gina, seeing that she was about to follow him. "There's nothing you can do." He pushed his way through them and went to the front door at a run, knowing that his haste was useless, merely a reflex action prompted by his whirling brain, preferring any action to none.

He flung himself into his car and ground it into motion, roaring off down the drive, out through the gates, into the road. Why? Why? his brain screamed at him. Why, at the end of a long life, should Burnett drop the tablets into the decanter of his old friend, his patient? What ancient resentment, what rancour or grudge had driven him on?

He was in the lane now. Only a few hundred yards separated him from the front door. Had Burnett done it at all? Was he suffering from delayed shock, confused, grief-stricken, filled with guilt and anger at himself, that he'd left his boyhood friend to die alone?

The house was in sight now. Richard could see the open door, lights streaming out into the driveway. Did Burnett believe Kenneth had killed his father? Had the news of Kenneth's arrest urged him to this mad, quixotic gesture, prompted him to shoulder the blame himself, make amends to his old friend by absolving his son from patricide, allow Henry Mallinson to lie in his grave without the final shame of having been despatched there by the hand of his eldest-born?

Burnett had neither wife nor child, he was on the edge of retirement, he might have dreaded an empty and lonely old age, he might have felt he was sacrificing nothing worth having. Swamped by shock, depression, guilt and grief to-gether, he might have been glad at one single stroke to pay a debt to the past and obliterate the future.

He brought the car to an abrupt halt, banged open the door and ran into the house. Voices upstairs, the sound of movements overhead. He was half-way up the flight when someone came out of Burnett's room, into the corridor—a young uniformed policeman. He came on, down the stairs, talking to Richard as he came.

"Too late, I'm afraid. Cyanide." He shook his head. "I'm just going to ring Inspector Ingram in Hallborough." Richard stood aside to let him pass. "Don't touch anything," the constable called back at him. "You can go on up, but I'm afraid there isn't anything you can do."

He could hear the low sound of the housekeeper's sobs as he stepped across the threshold. She was standing over by the curtained window with her back to him, her hands raised to her face.

"Oh—Knight—you'd better have a look at him." David Mallinson stood at the foot of the bed. He gestured with his hand at Burnett lying fully dressed on the white bed-spread. "We found him like this when we got here a few minutes ago." David looked pale and shaken. "I think I'll sit down if you don't mind." He lowered himself on to an upright chair and sat with his head bent, regaining composure.

Richard went through the useless formalities, feeling for the pulse, slipping a hand under the jacket, sniffing at the lips. Burnett's eyes were closed. He looked relaxed and peaceful, as if he had lain down at the end of a busy day to snatch a rest before dinner. His right hand was flung out on the covers, the fingers still clasping a heavy silver photograph frame.

Mindful of the constable's instructions, Richard didn't touch the frame. He bent down and looked at it closely. Two figures, clearly visible in the overhead light. He could remember having seen the photograph on one of the rare occasions when he had had occasion to step inside Burnett's bedroom, but he had never done more than glance at it without interest. Now he studied it, searching for a clue, an explanation.

A young man—Burnett surely years and years ago? His arm lovingly round the waist of a smiling girl. No-one Richard had ever met, no-one he knew . . . or did he? He frowned down at the radiant face, recognition beginning to wake in his brain . . . something about the mouth . . . Kenneth Mallinson's mouth . . . and the eyes . . . David's eyes . . . He saw all at once the portrait in its ornate gilt frame hanging over the fireplace in the hall at Whitegates . . . the same face . . . was it possible? Before the years had traced sorrow and unhappiness about the laughing mouth, the lovely eyes? Behind him he heard David's voice, clear and expressionless.

"My mother," David said. Richard straightened himself and half-turned, not meeting David's eyes, not wishing to read their expression. "Burnett was engaged to her," David said. "He worshipped the ground she walked on, they were

going to be married." A tiny silence before he continued . . .
"And then he introduced her to his old friend . . . my
father . . ."

Richard could think of nothing to say. Fragments of half-
remembered information jostled together in his mind . . .
Burnett had left Rockley, had gone away up north to practise, he'd stayed away till—he drew a sudden breath—till
just after Margaret Mallinson's death. Had he sworn revenge then, knowing the bitter story of her marriage? Had
he taken on Henry Mallinson as his patient, brooding, waiting for the day when he could exact retribution for her years
of suffering, for his own solitary life?

He glanced at the housekeeper, more in command of herself now. She met his gaze.

"I didn't know," she said, spreading her hands wide. "I
was in my sitting-room at the back. The first thing I knew
was——" she gestured at David Mallinson, jerked her head
towards the corridor, towards the constable downstairs—
"when they came bursting into the house." She drew a long
shuddering breath, remembering the uproar, the calling
voices, the running feet, doors snatched open. "If only I'd
known——"

Richard went round the foot of the bed and put a hand
under her elbow. "We might as well go downstairs. The
police will be coming over from Hallborough soon. I'm
afraid there'll be questions, statements——"

She sighed. "I'll make some coffee." Glad of the homely
activity.

David pushed back his chair and left the room without
glancing at Burnett. Richard Knight paused in the doorway
and looked back at the bed. He had found Burnett an aloof
man, not the easiest man to work with. Now, suddenly, he
felt a rush of affection and compassion, wishing uselessly
that he'd got to know him better, that he'd talked to him
more, realising—now that the realisation could help no-
one—that he'd never really known his partner at all.

The constable came out of Burnett's study. "He left some

letters," he said to Richard. "One to Inspector Ingram, one to the coroner, and one addressed to you." He held up a hand as Richard took a step towards the study. "Better not open it yet, sir, it's as well to leave it till the inspector arrives. I spoke to him, he's coming over at once." He flicked a glance at David Mallinson. "He's bringing Mr. Kenneth with him. And a couple of men, a photographer and a detective."

"This lets Kenneth out of course." David seemed to take in the fact for the first time. Impossible to tell from his tone whether he was glad or sorry. "I suppose I'll have to wait here?"

The constable nodded. "Yes, sir, if you wouldn't mind. The inspector will want to speak to you."

"I'll make that coffee." The housekeeper vanished towards the kitchen. Richard threw open the door of the sitting-room.

"We might as well wait in here. There's a fire. It's a little more cheerful."

They came to Rockley from all the surrounding villages for Dr. Burnett's funeral. A thin mist over the churchyard, a fine rain dripping from the trees. They came in cars and buses, on bicycles and on foot. Dr. Burnett had brought some of them into the world, long ago, when he was a young doctor, when he still looked out on life with optimistic eyes, expecting happiness.

"Curiosity, half of them," Sergeant Yates said in a low voice.

"Affection, too." Ingram was in a peaceful, relaxed mood, as always when he drew the last line under a case. "And a kind of loyalty." He bent his head as the men began to drop spadefuls of damp earth into the grave. "She turned up, I see." He gave a little nod to where Mrs. Stallard stood apart from the crowd of villagers, looking for once suitably dressed in her deep black.

The Whitegates folk were there in force, the family a few

yards away from the clergyman, the servants a little farther off, Mrs. Parkes occupying an indeterminate position half-way between the two groups. A delicate decision, that, Ingram thought—whether or not to turn out for the funeral of the man who had sent the head of the family on a brief time before him. He glanced at that other grave, still with its tributes of flowers, and back at Kenneth Mallinson standing with his head bowed. Kenneth at all events had reason to be grateful to Burnett. Yes, he decided, they did the right thing, coming to witness the committal.

In his capacity as chief mourner Dr. Knight stood behind the vicar, Gina beside him, her pink-and-white skin, her shining fair hair thrown into sharp relief by her dark clothes.

The vicar closed his prayer-book, turned and spoke a few words to Richard Knight. Movement among the ranks, the groups began to break up.

"Come back to Tall Trees," David Mallinson said to his brother. Whitegates was scarcely a cheerful place to return to after a funeral, not at present anyway, too full of ghosts, of memories.

"Yes, do come," Carole said. "I'll give you some tea."

Something good came out of it all, Ingram thought, watching the three of them moving away together, some diminishing of bitterness, some weakening of old hostilities, ancient jealousies.

"What do you propose to do about young Norman Foster?" David asked when tea was almost over. So that's how it's to be, Carole thought, he's accepted the position, the younger brother deferring to the elder, the subordinate consulting the head of the firm. She gave a faint smile of relief, of pleasure.

Kenneth pushed away his plate. "I see no reason to prosecute." He looked enquiringly at David. "What do you think?" It's going to be all right, David thought, feeling the taut muscles of his shoulders relax, I can work with him after all, we can manage to run in double harness.

"Norman's only a lad," he said. "Hardly more than a child." He gave a little smile. "You remember what it's like at that age—easy to make a stupid mistake, to lose one's head." It wasn't only Norman they were both visualising as he spoke, there were other shadowy presences there in the elegant room, the two of them years ago when they were young. He wanted to say something about forgiving, forgetting, but the words were too difficult to utter.

"There are the parents," Carole said hesitantly. "A very respectable family. It would break their hearts if the boy were taken to court."

"We're not compelled to prosecute," Kenneth said. "We can have a word with Ingram, he'll see reason." He drew his brows together in thought. "The bike can be sold and the money returned to the estate. The boy can make up the rest from his wages, week by week." He spread his hands. "He can't be let off scot-free, he ought to be taught a lesson."

David nodded. "Yes, that should meet the case. The lad should be given his chance. People grow up, they mature." His eyes met Kenneth's fair and square. "They see the error of their ways in the end. With luck. Before it's too late."

Kenneth leaned back in his chair like a man suddenly more at ease. "That's settled then." And all three of them were aware that he referred to something of far greater moment than the obsessive love of a boy for his first motorcycle.

"Mrs. Stallard? What do you propose to do about her?" David asked. "You saw her at the funeral? She must have come back specially for it. I must say I was rather surprised, she left the Hallborough hotel some time ago."

"She's ready to agree terms now." Kenneth pulled down the corners of his mouth. "She's nothing to gain by persisting in being obstinate. The lump sum and the pension—even her solicitor feels we're being pretty generous, he made no secret of it." He smiled. "I think he'll be glad to see the back of her. Not very enlivening company, Mrs. Stallard." He stood up. "I'd better be getting along to Whitegates."

"Stay to dinner," Carole urged. "You won't want to——"
Eat it in that great room all by yourself . . . she didn't finish
the sentence.

Kenneth shook his head. "No thanks, not this evening.
There are things to be seen to. Mrs. Parkes is leaving, I
must have a word with her before she goes." He smiled down
at her. "Ask me again, though."

"I'll walk up to the house with you," David said. "I'd
like to speak to Mrs. Parkes myself. She was a good nurse."

Carole stood on the step, watching them go. They looked
right together, two brothers walking side by side. Kenneth
turned to wave as they rounded the bend in the drive. Then
she heard a little movement in the shrubbery. She frowned
and took a step forward. The branches parted and Tim
Jefford came out, grinning at her. He put up a finger to his
lips.

"It's all right—don't call out!" he said softly. "I just
want to see you for a moment." He thrust his hand into his
pocket. "I've something to return to you." He took out a
brown-paper packet.

She shivered slightly in the cool air. "You'd better come
inside—but only for a moment." He followed her into the
house.

"I brought you these, the famous letters." He thrust
them into her hand. "Ingram gave them back to me this
afternoon. I saw him in Hallborough, before the funeral."

She turned the packet over in her hands. "I didn't see you
at the funeral."

"I was there all right, wedged in among the farmers and
their plump ladies. I saw you. I walked over here afterwards,
I've been hanging about outside, wondering how I was going
to get a chance to see you."

"There was no need to see me. You could have burnt these
yourself."

He pulled a wry face. "I thought you'd prefer to burn
them, then you'd know they were gone for good. I thought
of going round to the back and getting the maid to ask you

to come to the door." He laughed. "I was going to tell her to say it was a casual labourer asking for work in the garden."

She threw him a sharp look. "Are things that bad?"

"No, as a matter of fact they're pretty good at the moment. And they look like getting better. I sold my coins at a decent profit. I found out the names of a few collectors and called to see them. I'm thinking of going into the business seriously, I've got quite interested in it." His tone was light and cheerful. "And Ingram's going to see I get back the coin Henry Mallinson had from me—I never got paid for that. Not a bad stick, Ingram—for a copper. He read me a lecture on blackmail," he added ruefully, giving her an apologetic grin. "I'm sorry about that, Carole, I wanted to tell you so, in person. I'll pay you back the money I had from you, every penny of it. I can give you twenty pounds now." He took out an old wallet. She was amused to see that he actually looked embarrassed.

She smiled. "There's no need for that. You can keep the money. I don't bear you any grudge, things must have been pretty grim for you."

"No, I must pay my debts." He began to count out the notes.

She leaned forward and closed the wallet. "I absolutely refuse. If you give it to me I shall drop it into the fire."

He laughed. "That would never do." He raised his shoulders. "Thanks, Carole. I'm glad there's no ill-will." He couldn't disguise the relief in his tone—there was precious little more than twenty pounds in the wallet. He bent down and kissed her lightly on the cheek. "Good-bye, my dear. You won't be seeing me again."

"Good luck," she said, smiling up at him. "Try not to get into any more mischief." He let himself quietly out of the house, a slice of her past, of the old days, her foolish youth, vanishing for ever. She went over to the hearth, knelt down and thrust the unopened packet into the flaming coals, not wanting to read the letters again, to be reminded of the way things used to be. She seized the poker and stabbed at the packet until it was reduced to ashes, astonished to discover that her eyes were full of tears.

"I think that's everything." Mrs. Parkes looked searchingly about her room, scanning the bare surfaces. She was dressed in outdoor clothes with an uncompromising felt hat jammed on her head. Her cases were already stacked in the front hall. She picked up her gloves and handbag.

"If I do find anything after you've gone," Gina Thorson said, "I can always send it on." Gina was remaining in the house until her marriage, Kenneth Mallinson was taking her on as his secretary. She was to divide her time between working for him in the Hallborough office and helping to clear up Henry Mallinson's affairs at Whitegates.

"Thank you." Mrs. Parkes moved towards the bedroom door. "You have my address, haven't you?" She was going to stay with her son for the present, until she found another private post.

"Funny how things turn out." She stepped into the corridor. There was no question now of emigrating. Her son had already started to look for a suitable smallholding, he could borrow the money from the bank until her legacy was paid out. She flashed a look at Gina. "I hope you'll be happy, my dear." Now that she was leaving she'd begun to feel quite fond of the girl. "Write to me, let me know when the wedding's to be." She smiled. "I'll send you a nice present."

One of the Whitegates cars was to take Mrs. Parkes to the station. Gina stood by the rear door, exchanging small-talk while the cases were stowed away in the boot. There was a sound of wheels along the drive and Richard's car swept into view.

"There's Doctor Knight now." Mrs. Parkes was pleased. "I'd like to say good-bye to him."

He came over and leaned inside the car, holding out his hand.

"I hope you have a pleasant journey. And that you find

your family well. Drop us a line, let us know how you get on."

"I wish I'd been able to get along better with her." Gina sighed, waving as the car disappeared. "I never really felt at ease with her—not until the last few days. Now I realise she was just a rather lonely woman, she can't have had an easy life."

Richard slipped an arm round her waist and propelled her gently towards the house. "She'll be all right, she'll enjoy spoiling her grandchildren. It wasn't your fault that you didn't get on, she was envious of you. Of your youth and beauty," he added lightly.

They crossed the hall. "I can't stay long," he said, halting in the middle of the room. "I've dozens of things to see to." Burnett's papers to be cleared up, a locum to be advertised for, the practice to be steered through the difficult days ahead. And the housekeeper, still in the grip of grief and shock, needing a delicate touch, wary handling. He sighed. "I can spare half an hour, then I must get back."

Gina looked up at the portrait above the fireplace. "A beautiful face," she said softly. "Beautiful but not happy. . . . All that money . . . and no happiness . . ." She thought of Burnett, crossing the hall on his visits to the house, raising his eyes each time and looking up at that half-averted face. "Odd what men will do in the name of love." She felt a shiver run through her at the thought of Burnett lying now fifteen yards away from Margaret Mallinson under the silent earth. She gave Richard an appealing glance.

"We'll be happy, won't we?" Her fingers pressed his arm.

He put up a hand and touched her bright hair. "We'll be happy, my love, I promise you." And his arm round her shoulders gave her strength and courage to reach out and grasp that happiness, to trust in it, to take the first steps forward out of the past into the days to come.